NIGHTFALL BAY

NIGHTFALL BAY

by

Carolyn J. Rose

Many thanks to Ginni and Cindy and, of course, to Mike.

CHAPTER 1

January
Rain

"It's time. She wants you with her."

Her grandfather's words rang in Rain Paxton's mind as she gunned her car east from Vancouver toward the Columbia Gorge. When the sun rose, her grandmother Meadow would pass from this world. And the gift would pass to Rain.

If she was worthy of it.

If she accepted it.

If, when the moment came, she had a choice.

She hadn't been surprised when the phone rang deep in the January night. Sleep hadn't come easily, and fire and water had overrun her dreams.

And, as Morgan said in his first curt sentence, it was time.

As always, he hadn't waited for a response. Her grandfather stated fact or opinion and moved on, following his own course and assuming she would follow hers. Knowing, if he was inclined to use his long sight, what her course would be.

The highway narrowed to two lanes. Her headlights bored a tunnel through wind-whipped fog and rain. Soon Meadow would leave her body, tumble down what she called a well of twilight, and make her way to Nightfall Bay for the final time.

Despite her wool coat and a blast of hot air on her feet, Rain shivered. Before long she might also journey to the crossing place. Then, as Meadow had done for years, she would search among souls waiting beside a vast dark ocean. She would hunt for those missing or murdered, listen to their frightening accounts, and return to solve mysteries and end the fearful imaginings of friends and relatives. Finding answers—and sometimes justice—freed waiting souls and let them cross.

Rain shivered again.

Each journey to Nightfall Bay took a toll.

This time, her grandmother would remain with those who waited, lingering until Morgan joined her.

Rain's headlights caught the familiar red mailbox and she signaled for a left turn. The slick dirt driveway rose steadily, slicing through pasture long abandoned, widening at the farmhouse and garage, then continuing to the barn at the foot of the orchard. Rain parked beside Morgan's ancient blue truck, slapped a broad-brimmed leather hat over long brown hair, and dashed to the entrance to the mudroom. She wiped her feet, hung her hat and jacket on wooden pegs, and went into the kitchen.

Morgan turned from the counter beside the stove and handed her a mug. "Get that inside you. I'll tell her you're here."

Rain drank the strong coffee laced with heavy cream, crossed the living room, and entered her grandparents' bedroom.

Her grandmother's body was shriveled, her veins thick and dark beneath papery skin. Her breathing barely lifted the rainbow quilt drawn to her chin. But when she grasped Rain's hand, her grip was still strong.

"I have much to tell you. And we have less than an hour." Meadow patted the edge of the bed. "Sit here, close by."

Rain glanced at her grandfather. Morgan nodded once, his weathered face as impassive as the rock walls of the gorge. He might have been sitting anywhere—perhaps in a boat on the river, waiting for a tug on the line—instead of hunched in the low rocker in the corner of the bedroom he'd shared with Meadow for more than half a century. But Rain knew he saw everything, felt everything. As her grandmother often said, Morgan was still water, he ran deep.

"I know it's weighing on your mind because it weighed on mine before my day came. If you don't accept the gift, the world will keep turning. Some won't have answers, but that's always been the way. Always will be." Meadow released Rain's fingers and tapped her wrist. "Think of all the questions *you* don't have answers for."

Most of those questions concerned her mother. Where was Holly Paxton? Was she dead or alive? And if she was alive, did she know Rain had forgiven her?

She decided, once again, that she wouldn't search for her mother. Sometimes knowing caused more pain than not.

"If you accept," Meadow murmured, "take on only what you *can* do, not what you think you *should* do."

She glanced up, toward the second floor of the farmhouse and the slope-ceilinged room under the eaves where she launched her journeys. The meaning of her words was clear— Rain shouldn't do what Meadow had done after her daughter wandered into a wilderness of pills and promises of forgetfulness. Holly hadn't refused the gift outright; she had made herself unworthy of it. With no one to pass the torch to, Meadow had gone on. Perhaps to atone for Holly, she continued long past the point where she was able to regain all the strength she lost on each journey.

3

Blinking, Rain tried to thrust aside vague and fleeting memories of the woman who abandoned her 24 years ago. She recalled the pungent aroma of her mother's cigarettes, the cold granite steps of a church, a one-eared Teddy Bear, and a letter scrawled in pencil on a paper bag, a letter that presented her to her grandparents like a gift wrapped in a moth-eaten blanket. They had the letter still, locked in a fireproof safe in the cellar with other documents, including the one giving Rain a name, something her mother hadn't bothered with. It was a family tradition to draw names from nature, and Meadow had picked hers because it signified a washing away of her past.

"When the day comes . . ." Meadow clawed at the fraying edge of the quilt she'd made as a girl and spread on their bed when she married Morgan. "When the day comes, there will be a dog."

"Motley?" Rain gazed at the massive mutt resting his muzzle on the far edge of the bed. Brown and gray and black, he was the latest in a line of companion canines—three that she remembered. Each seemed to know his duties the moment he arrived at the old farmhouse. Each trotted up the road on the morning after his predecessor departed. Each was large, strong, no longer a puppy.

Like the others, Motley had instantly obeyed Meadow's hand signals or the direction of her gaze. Morning and evening he trotted along the perimeter of the property. He slept beside the front door at night, and he growled but seldom barked— except to urge Meadow to return from a journey.

"Not Motley," Morgan answered. "When his work is done, Motley will leave to find her and the others. And, after a time, I'll join them."

Meadow turned her gaze to her husband, her eyes bright with love. "From the moment you took my hand in yours, I never had a doubt you'd be with me for the whole journey, Old Hoss."

Rain remembered laughing at this nickname the first time she heard her grandmother use it, remembered insisting her grandfather was a man, not a horse. "I'm both," he'd told her. "My name is the same as a breed of horse. And I'm what some call the willing horse."

"He means he's a hard worker," her grandmother had clarified. "Sometimes too hard. He doesn't know when it's best to leave a small task undone to use for seed."

When she lived on her own after college, and especially after she began to work as a freelance editor for novelists, Rain understood what that meant. Completing a simple task launched her into the day. She thought of a task intentionally left undone as a cup of starter fed with fresh flour and water and set aside for the next batch of sourdough bread. Checking a task off her list early in the day raised her spirits the way yeast raised a loaf.

"But don't be hurrying to leave here, Old Hoss." Meadow pointed a trembling finger at her husband. "Time is not the same at Nightfall Bay. I'll be there only a blink and a wink. You have much to do for the child."

Almost 29 and still "the child."

Rain stroked her grandmother's fine, thin hair, hair as brittle as new ice. "I don't want either of you to go," she said in a voice that faltered and broke. "But I don't want you to stay because of me. I can take care of myself."

"You can feed and clothe yourself," Morgan said, his tone matter-of-fact. "Change a tire on your car and work that fancy phone. But there's more you'll need to know before long. Things they didn't teach in college."

What skills did they feel she lacked? How long would it take to learn? How would she use them and in what particular circumstances? Had Morgan looked at the years ahead?

"Blame me." Her grandmother squeezed her hand. "I begged him to see if you would be all right, or whether I should try to hang on."

She coughed, a dry, stuttering sigh of air escaping from her lips. Barely enough to loft a tiny feather.

Rain swallowed tears. "Well, you know what? You'll just have to hang on." She stood and adopted the posture she'd often taken as a child—chin tipped upward, fists on her hips. "You can't go. It's inconvenient for me. I won't stand for it."

Motley raised his upper lip in a silent snarl, stopping when Meadow managed a faint chuckle. "You were such a feisty child, a little bolt of lightning. And I wish I *could* stay—to help you master the gift. But Morgan tells me you'll come through it. He's never been wrong."

What, exactly, was ahead that she'd have to come through?

Rain didn't glance at her grandfather. His expression would give nothing away. He would tell her in his own time.

Or not.

Probably not.

"If you're too prepared," he often said, "you can close your mind, and your eyes, to other paths, to ways through or around."

But he'd peered into the future. He knew she'd be all right.

She felt both safe and sacrificed. Relieved and infuriated. Not for the first time she wondered what it would have been like to be raised by people who were "normal." Granted, she couldn't have been loved more, but sharing what-we-did-this-weekend stories with friends in high school would have involved far more fact than fiction. Telling friends your grandmother's spirit traveled to a place where she talked with the dead was a sure way to make yourself an outcast. Not to mention guaranteeing you'd spend hours with counselors.

Rain sat once more, and her grandmother reached for her hand. "You can refuse, you know."

How?

The gift, Meadow had told her years before, would arrive in its own time and its own way—and not until she was ready to receive it. If she decided the burden would be too great, how could she refuse it? Like her mother had? Sleeping with strangers, begging for crumpled dollar bills to buy drugs and a few hours of oblivion?

And what would happen to those in need if she refused it? Rain was the last of this family. Were there others somewhere with gifts of their own? Others who could help those searching for answers and closure?

"You're steel at the core," Meadow said. "I feel you're not afraid of the obligation."

"My mother was."

"My fault. I failed to shield her. She saw too soon the bottomless reservoir of pain and loss in the world, and the cost of visiting Nightfall Bay. She didn't believe I was glad to pay the price."

Rain stroked her grandmother's hair once more. She'd said they had less than an hour. How much time remained? "What does it feel like?"

"It's a sliding, tumbling fall down a well and through water, wind, and hail. And then you're on a long curving beach. The sand will be gray, and the sun won't give off much light, but it will be enough for you to find your way among the ones waiting there."

"You once said there were thousands of . . ." Rain paused. What should she call them? Were they still human? "Are they ghosts? Shades? Shadows?"

7

"They're the essence of the people they were," Meadow said. "They're lost and confused. They feel forgotten and abandoned. And many are horribly wounded, but—"

"They won't hurt you," Morgan said. "Although some might frighten you."

"But only because of what was done to them," Meadow whispered. "Or because the years haven't damped down their anger."

Rain nodded and heard the rocker creak and Morgan's feet shuffle on the wide pine planks. Was it time? So soon?

Morgan sat on the edge of the bed opposite Rain, smoothing the quilt, then scratching Motley's ears with his right hand and offering his left to his wife. Meadow took Rain's hand, put it in Morgan's, and enclosed them in both of hers. "Wish me well, my darlings. Then let me go."

Motley whined and nosed her arm.

"Hush." Meadow blew him a kiss. "You'll be with me soon. We'll run in the sand with Merle and Mustard and all the others."

Rain choked back a sob. Nightfall Bay didn't seem like a place for romping with a pack of dogs. But her grandmother had said time was different there. Perhaps, if you were no longer alive, colors and sounds were different as well.

Meadow squeezed their hands, gazed past them toward the wide window, and smiled, her eyes alight.

Rain turned to see sunlight gilding the frosty branches of a clump of hemlock trees beyond the orchard.

When she turned to her grandmother again, the spark had died in Meadow's eyes.

CHAPTER 2

January
Pierce

Head thrust forward, Pierce ran the trail he'd cut through his forested property west of Portland, battering a curtain of sleet, battering a wall of memories. The wall was thick and high. Trying to ram through it was, most likely, an act of futility. After all, in the more than two years since Ariel disappeared, he hadn't found a way over or under or around.

Often he felt overwhelmed by small tasks he'd once performed almost unconsciously—showering, dressing, eating. Her absence occupied so much of his mind that sometimes he feared his brain, like a computer, might freeze up.

As for the larger jobs he'd taken on after his father died shortly after she vanished—reviewing spreadsheets, chairing management meetings, acquiring and divesting—well, after a few weeks he'd handed those over to paid experts with drive and ambition he never had. By now his father must be spinning in his grave fast enough to generate power. Perhaps enough power to light up the San Francisco headquarters of the conglomerate of businesses he'd bought and sold and traded like baseball cards or antiques.

Pierce laughed and punched sleet. If rage was fuel, the old man would spin for years to come. For a century. Or more.

Pierson Jennings, never a patient or temperate man, had cornered the market on fury when his first-born son died less than a week after birth. The second-born smaller twin survived. When four years passed, it became clear Diane Donovan Jennings would never produce another heir. There was no question of divorce. Diane Donovan Jennings wouldn't go quietly—or cheaply. So Gareth was renamed Pierson Jennings Jr.

Along with the name of his dead brother, he'd been saddled with the family expectations.

And there were many. Enrollment in the right schools where he would achieve the right grades and receive the right degrees. Memberships in the right clubs. Marriage to the right woman, preferably the daughter of a business partner or, barring that, the daughter of a worthy and wealthy rival.

He'd tried.

Always wishing his brother hadn't died, wishing he could be Gareth, the second son, Pierce had gone along with most of the plan. Getting the grades—that part was easy because his mind was quick to see connections and make comparisons, and because recalling facts and figures was no more difficult than breathing. Getting into important clubs was also not difficult. His family name was enough for invitations, and his self-designation as a follower helped. Followers were always welcomed by those who would be leaders. By the time they realized he wouldn't follow far, or for long, his mission of membership had been accomplished.

And so he got through college. Nodding. Going through the motions. Cutting nicks into his arm to atone for being the one who lived. Running to exhaustion when cutting failed to relieve the stress of conflict.

And there was *always* conflict.

As his father frequently said, Pierce wasn't the son he'd wanted. Pierce wasn't committed to what counted—business, success, wealth. Pierce wasn't attracted to the scent of deals to be brokered, conquests to be made.

And, as his mother often said, Pierce didn't contribute to enlarging the family's social circle and political connections. "You could at least pretend to enjoy yourself," she'd carp when he failed—again—to act the part of a charming and witty escort for yet another event characterized by enormous diamonds, expensive gowns, and ersatz smiles.

He'd met Ariel at one of those events—a fundraiser for a candidate no one liked but everyone supported to ensure business as usual. She lacked the diamonds but had perfected the smile. In a black-and-white caterer's uniform, she'd circulated through the crowd, offering flutes of sparkling wine.

"You're an impostor," she'd whispered.

Her statement unmasked Pierce.

It also claimed him.

After that night, he stopped caring what either of his parents thought about anything.

Edgy, wild, and passionate, Ariel was a world apart from the smoothed-down and tucked-in beauties Pierce often squired to parties and weddings. She found the scars on his left arm exciting. She touched each one with the tip of her tongue before she took him to bed.

She flaunted convention and sometimes the law.

She tantalized and scandalized.

She delivered him from all he found dull or distasteful.

And she damned him to desire.

After three weeks, without a word to his parents, he married her.

Plans for an empire-building alliance thwarted, the ferocity of his father's anger was the stuff of saga. Social status tainted by his choice, the chill of his mother's disapproval seemed to halt the advance of summer. In public, however, they maintained the pretense that Pierce's happiness was paramount. They told friends that Ariel was a lovely girl.

At first, Pierce thought Ariel wasn't aware of their simmering anger. But soon he knew she fed it, even thrived on it. She reveled in creating discord, disrupting dinner parties by baiting women, flirting with men, and offering outrageous opinions.

He didn't object when his father "requested" that he move to Portland and take responsibility for managing a software company. In fact, although he wouldn't have admitted it, Pierce felt relief.

Looking back, he saw how predictable his relationship with Ariel was, how sordidly similar to so many other unhealthy liaisons. He and Ariel had been oil and water. No, they were more like vinegar and baking soda. The reaction was strong and immediate. A rush. A fizz.

Over in moments.

"A story told a thousand times." Pierce struck at hailstones with a one-two punch, his feet sliding as the trail curved around a giant sequoia and angled along a stream. He thought of Macbeth's famous soliloquy comparing life to a tale told by an idiot, a tale signifying nothing.

"And I was the idiot," he roared.

He picked up his pace, feet pounding the trail to the beat of the repeated word. "Idiot. Idiot. Idiot."

When discussions became arguments, Pierce blamed Ariel's mercurial nature and the drugs that removed what few inhibitions she had. Ariel wasn't an addict. She was an experimenter. Or so he told himself. She enjoyed mixing and matching and sharing with friends she made easily. And why not? Thanks to his money, she could buy a key to any candy store and treat them all.

Every time he considered turning off the cash spigot, he considered the price—anger, recrimination, and retribution. So he took the line of least resistance and transferred a large chunk of money to her personal account each month. $10,000. Often, if she pleaded or demanded, even more.

He suspected—and later hoped—she siphoned funds off to a walking-away stash. If it hadn't been for the anticipated barrage of I-told-you-so comments from his parents, he would have paid her to walk.

And then he came home to find overturned chairs, smashed lamps, and spatters of her blood on the bedroom walls.

The horror of that discovery, and the on-going anguish of not knowing what happened or where she might be, had rebooted his brain. Discord, broken promises, suspicions, and betrayals were shuffled into separate mental folders and closed. The loop of memories that ran in his mind was drawn from a series of pretty moments collected during their first weeks together.

He knew enough now to understand there was little spontaneous about those moments. Weaving fresh experiences with feigned passion, Ariel had crafted them to hook him.

But, counterfeit as the memories were, they balanced the horror of what might have happened to her in the sea-foam-colored room with a panoramic view of the Willamette River. And what might have happened to her afterward.

His phone vibrated against his chest, throwing off his rhythm. Never mind the hour, or the circumstances, he took every call, always hoping Ariel had survived. This call, however, came from Malcolm Wallace, the CEO he'd hired to run his father's empire. Sheltering beside a Douglas fir and jogging in place, he poked his phone to life. "Mal? Everything okay?"

"Better than okay. Check this." Wallace reeled off a string of numbers.

Pierce listened instead to the thud of his feet and the wind in the branches, grunting with approval now and then. He suspected Mal Wallace knew he had no interest in what he'd come to think of as an enormous game of financial chance. But Mal had interest enough for both of them. And he had no objections to the way Pierce insisted he run the businesses—treating employees well, adhering to the strictest environmental standards, and funneling chunks of profit to charity.

All of that would make the old man spin like a wind turbine in a typhoon. His voracious appetite for bottom-line profit had been legendary.

Pierce, however, had no taste for gorging at the expense of others.

Even following restrictions and rules, there was plenty of money to be made.

And plenty already in the bank. Or, rather, in an extensive portfolio of investments. Even Diane Donovan Jennings, with her penchant for shopping and adventures with men not much older than Pierce, barely made a dent in the yearly profits.

Wallace summed up the numbers and issued a glowing projection for the coming month, then disengaged. "Won't hold you up any longer." He managed to say that as if he believed Pierce packed each day with vital activities.

"Thanks. Got a lot on my plate today."

And, in fact, he had—a meeting of the multi-state task force he'd funded. Funded on condition he would be part of it.

Getting it off the ground had involved a series of actions he'd once sworn to avoid. But his need to learn what had become of Ariel far outweighed personal morality and ethics. So, after months spent hounding police detectives, hiring private investigators, and chasing down leads on his own, he'd borrowed a few pages from the old man's book.

"If political puppets allow you to pull their strings, then you're a fool if you don't," his father had been fond of saying.

So Pierce pulled.

He'd reminded governors of campaign contributions, jobs created, and tax incentives offered by other states.

"Money talks" was another of the old man's sayings.

So Pierce put up enough cash to shout.

He'd slapped an offer on the table to fund facilities, staff, travel, and overtime for detectives working cases of interest to the task force. He'd included a hefty budget for forensic experts, equipment, lab work, and supplies. He'd built in a huge slush fund for incidentals and miscellaneous items.

And, in only a few weeks, he had what he wanted—a task force he hoped might find answers to the fate of Ariel.

And the others.

Two hours later he sat at the long glass-topped table in the conference room of a suite on the top floor of an office building near the Portland airport. He had never presumed the position of task-force coordinator and the place at the head of the table would be his. In fact, he'd offered the seat to a retired detective who had once publicly accused him of killing Ariel.

Marlin Simmons, he knew, still harbored suspicions about Pierce and his possible involvement in his wife's disappearance. In fact, Pierce surmised he'd accepted the position in order to keep a close eye on the man who signed his paychecks.

And that was okay. Pierce might have done the same if their positions were reversed. Keeping your enemy close was sound policy.

15

A terrier of a man, his body short and wiry, Simmons had retired after a stroke 18 months ago. He'd emerged from the experience with a foot that dragged, lips that drooped on the left, and knowledge that time was fleeting. He managed the task force by barking at the heels of researcher Claire Dawson and the "dogs" still in harness—detectives from Washington, Oregon, Idaho, California, and Nevada. Their annoyance had abated slightly as he proved himself by collecting and compiling information, and by improving communication. Simmons, after all, was a man as consumed by the search for answers as Pierce.

And that search cast a wide net.

Because Ariel was one of many believed to have fallen prey to a killer Claire Dawson described as the consummate door-to-door salesman. They called him the Peddler. He sold death. And he seemed set on becoming a colossus among his kind.

CHAPTER 3

January
Rain

Meadow's lifeless hands dropped to the quilt.

Morgan kept a tight grip on Rain's fingers as if to assure her he had no thought of leaving.

Although she told herself death was the inevitable final act of life, and this act belonged to Meadow, Rain felt a selfish emptiness. Through streaming tears she stared into the depths of a hole in her life. She knew she could never fill it, would never want to.

Morgan squeezed her hand and she felt a stab of guilt. His grief must be so much more profound. He'd had more than twice as many years with Meadow. She remembered a college friend saying healing from a breakup took half as long as the length of the relationship. Dying was its own horrible brand of breaking up. She'd need a dozen years to heal. Her grandfather would require at least a quarter of a century.

But he'd be with Meadow again long before that.

Turning her head, she gazed at the sunlight on the hemlock branches, wondering what else Meadow had seen. Had someone come to meet her? Perhaps her loyal dogs. Perhaps

17

her mother or grandmother, women Rain knew only from sepia-toned photographs.

She turned to Morgan to ask, but his narrowed eyes and pressed lips told her he was deep inside his mind. If he heard her at all, he wouldn't respond.

After a moment he released her hand, rose, and shut the door to the bedroom. Then he turned off the lamps, closed the heat vents, and opened the east window wide, drawing in the sharp scent of evergreens and the whisking sound of wind through branches. He kissed Meadow's lips and stretched out, gathering her close against his chest and humming a tune Rain couldn't identify.

Shivering, and feeling lost and unnecessary, Rain retreated to the kitchen to cry, pounding her fists on a pine table scrubbed so often the wood glowed nearly white. She craved comfort and human contact. She wanted her grandfather to hold her, rock her.

But that wasn't his way. Never had been. Wouldn't be now.

Sucking back sobs, she lit a burner on the ancient stove and made a fresh pot of coffee. "Give him space," she told herself. "He'll get cold. And hungry. He'll want breakfast."

But when she returned to the bedroom an hour later with a cup of coffee, he hadn't moved. Neither had Motley. The big dog's muzzle lay against Meadow's arm and his eyes were focused on the woman he'd served. Neither seemed to know Rain was there. Neither responded when she spoke their names.

Rain watched until the coffee in the cup no longer steamed, then brought a down comforter from the blanket chest to cover her grandfather. She found heavy wool blankets to screen Motley from a frigid breeze that made the gauzy white curtains billow. When neither protested, she located a heating pad in a bathroom cabinet, turned the dial all the way up, and pressed it against her grandfather's back. It would do no one any good if he got hypothermia and died while carrying out what she assumed was a ritual.

Hour after hour, he and Motley kept their vigil. Morgan brushed aside whispered offers of coffee, tea, and soup. Motley wouldn't wet his tongue in the bowl of water Rain brought. Wrapped in quilts, she curled in the rocker and kept watch with them, shivering, sipping cocoa, and struggling to stay awake. Twice Morgan signaled with a slant of his gaze and a flick of his fingers that she should leave if she wanted, but she shook her head.

When night fell, the breeze died, and Morgan whispered, "Light the candles."

Rain found matches in the kitchen and lit half a dozen beeswax candles arranged on the bureau and nightstands. The sweet fragrance twined through the air on invisible ribbons of warmth. The glow softened the planes of Morgan's face and made Meadow appear young again. She'd been not much more than 20 when she accepted the gift and made her first journey to Nightfall Bay. Had she been afraid? Had she ever—even once—considered refusing the gift?

The candles guttered with a soft spitting sound that brought Rain awake with a start. She glanced at the clock and saw the night was nearly gone. Motley's eyes were mere slits, but Rain didn't doubt he was awake and alert. The lids of Morgan's red-rimmed eyes drooped, but his gaze remained fixed on Meadow.

One by one, the candle flames died. The curtains swayed in a fitful breeze, and black night gave way to blue dawn. When the sun gilded the hemlock branches as it had at the moment of Meadow's death, Motley raised his muzzle and howled. The sound seemed ripped from his throat. Raw, primal, it made Rain's teeth ache.

Morgan tossed aside the comforter and stood, joints popping as he flexed his shoulders and bent his knees in a slow shuffle to the door. Swinging it wide, he turned to Motley. "Are you ready to find her?"

Motley barked, nosed aside the screen of blankets tucked around him, shook, and trotted to the door.

Cocooned in quilts, Rain followed into the warmth of the living room and watched Morgan open the front door.

Motley barked again, looked toward the bedroom, then trotted across the threshold and the wide porch. The trot became a lope as he crossed the side lawn, and quickened to a run. Rain took Morgan's arm and helped him down the steps and to the driveway where they tracked Motley's progress.

He raced past the garage, past the barn, and into the orchard. Rain caught glimpses of him as he shot up the slope. He cleared the sagging barbed wire fence in a long leap, his body stretching out like taffy. And then he disappeared into a stand of Douglas fir.

Morgan sighed and led the way inside.

Rain shifted from foot to foot, wondering what to say, what to do, wondering what came next. How would Motley get to Nightfall Bay? Would he run himself to death? Or would he find the well of twilight Meadow described, the tunnel through time and space and death?

Again, she wondered about the dogs that appeared over the years. Where did they come from? And where would they go on to after Meadow and Morgan joined them at Nightfall Bay?

"Breakfast. Bacon. Eggs. Toast. Coffee." Morgan headed for the kitchen. "Then I have calls to make. And there's a task laid out for you in the woodshop."

The woodshop, a long room at the rear of the garage, was her grandfather's domain. Rain had passed hundreds of hours watching him build tables and bookcases and cabinets while

20

inhaling the scent of sawdust, and listening to the whine of saws, the whirr and bite of drills, the rasp of sandpaper, the slick whisper of brushes spreading paint or varnish. A pencil tucked behind his ear, a measuring tape clipped to his belt, Morgan talked to each board, apologizing for any pain it suffered, explaining what its new purpose would be. Every move seemed choreographed and certain. When she was old enough, Morgan taught her how to plan a project, measure and cut, care for tools, develop patience, and hold her temper when the result didn't match her vision.

The last skills were the toughest. Patience, she thought, would come with age, but that temper thing . . .

Whenever she lost it as a teenager, Rain passed the blame to the unknown man who contributed sperm for Holly's egg. Morgan would shake his head. "Own it," he'd say. "It's yours. Now and for the rest of your life."

Rain started a pot of coffee, took a frying pan from a hook above the stove, and lit a burner before she spoke. "I don't know what you have in mind, but I hope it doesn't require a lot of concentration. I'm pretty played out."

Morgan sat and rubbed his eyes with the heels of his hands. "It's only a little painting."

"That I can manage." Rain got bacon and eggs, milk, cheese, and green onions from the refrigerator, and dug a loaf of rye bread from the freezer.

"Flowers and trees. Maybe birds."

"Birds that will look like porcupines or wheelbarrows. As you well know, I'm not much of an artist."

"It's what Meadow wanted." Morgan stood and ferried mugs, plates, butter, and jam to the table. "She said we'd need a good laugh and this would be one sure way to get it."

"Well, if that's the plan, I'm happy to be of service." Holding strips of bacon at arm's length, Rain laid them in the hot pan where they sizzled and spit. "What is it I'm painting?"

"Her casket."

Rain dropped an egg. It broke on the granite countertop. She grabbed for a paper towel, setting the roll spinning on its dowel, towel unwinding and piling in the draining rack while raw egg oozed toward the loaf of bread.

Morgan smiled and rescued the bread. "Appears I don't have to wait 'til you start painting to get a chuckle."

Knowing her artwork would go into the ground, Rain relaxed, mixed colors from dribs and drabs of paint saved in glass jars, and produced a pair of swallows that seemed more like birds than boomerangs. They soared above a field of flowers hemmed in by green-gray forest. Morgan smiled when he entered the woodshop early in the afternoon and examined her work.

"You're supposed to laugh."

"And you're supposed to get less paint on yourself than on the casket." His smile broadened, then faded. "Doctor's coming soon to write out the certificate. Ben and some of the others are getting the word out. We'll lay her to rest tomorrow morning. Up on the hill."

Up on the hill meant the tiny cemetery east of the stand of fir trees where Motley had disappeared. The cemetery was small, once merely a family plot, now managed as a non-profit corporation according to Washington law. A few long-time neighbors served on the board.

"Hole's already dug," Morgan said. "Right where she wanted it."

Rain wasn't surprised Meadow had marked the spot where her body would be buried. She'd often quoted the old saying about everything having a place.

"We'll plant a lilac beside her. One of those deep purple ones."

"They were her favorites."

"We bought it last week."

Of course they had.

Rain carried her brushes to a sink in the corner and put them in a jar to soak.

"Spindly little thing. Won't bloom this year. But we'll give it a shot of fertilizer and hope for next."

Morgan tapped the casket. "I'll have mine ready when you need it, but I'll want something different on it. Horses, maybe."

"Horses it is." Rain blinked away tears. "But don't let me hear you complain if they look like hippos or camels."

Morgan managed a chesty chuckle. "Hard for a man to complain when he's six feet under."

CHAPTER 4

January
Pierce

Pierce followed Marlin Simmons down the steps from the private jet and across the tarmac to an aging car spewing exhaust into the frigid air. Three hours earlier they'd received a phone call with sparse details—a shallow grave at the far edge of an orchard and a woman's body rolled in a tarp.

If the Peddler remained true to form, he wouldn't have left a bit of evidence to reveal who he was. Or where he'd kept this victim until he killed and buried her.

Pierce felt a numbness that had nothing to do with the wind sluicing down the Wenatchee Mountains and slashing at the exposed skin of his hands and face. If the woman in the grave was Ariel, he'd have a piece of his personal puzzle. He'd know she was dead. He'd know how she died. He might, after a time, be able to turn a page in his life.

If this wasn't Ariel, if she might still be alive, the page would remain unturned. He would continue to stare at the images imprinted upon it—the smashed cellphone near the front door of their condo, the single shoe in the hallway, the blood spatters on the bedroom wall. She'd been hurt. She'd fought. She'd tried to escape.

Investigators had spent weeks combing through the call history on her phone and questioning what Marlin had described as "the collection of lowlifes and opportunists" she'd spoken with in the months before she disappeared. The efforts led to a number of arrests for miscellaneous crimes, but no information about Ariel's fate.

If the dead woman wasn't Ariel, was she another of the Peddler's victims? If so, which one?

Tuning out as Simmons barked orders to the gray-haired off-duty deputy recruited to drive them, Pierce reviewed the list of missing women whose remains hadn't been discovered. Eight. Including Ariel. None had lived in this area. The closest was an interior decorator from Spokane. She'd been taken only six weeks earlier. The Peddler kept his victims alive for at least six months, so unless she'd cheated him and died before he was ready to kill her, she wouldn't be the woman in this grave.

Deferring to Simmons, Pierce slid into the rear seat and buckled up. Distances didn't seem to deter this killer. The four women whose badly decomposed bodies were found last year in a dump site in Anacortes had come from Sacramento, Reno, Medford, and Boise. Would they find more than one grave in this orchard? Would they find a woman who wasn't on their list of women believed to have been taken by the Peddler?

Simmons and Claire Dawson had built that list after weeks of combing reports of disappearances around the region. There was only one case in the Wenatchee area, but they hadn't included it. "They like the son for it," Marlin had insisted. "They just can't prove it yet. Besides, she wasn't our guy's type."

His type.

The Peddler's type wasn't easy prey. She wasn't a prostitute, a woman who drank to excess, hitched rides, camped on the streets, or lived in a sketchy neighborhood.

His type was someone like Ariel—young but not too young, slender, pretty, healthy, married or in a relationship, and living in a place that seemed safe and secure.

The Peddler was no spur-of-the-moment killer. He thrived on challenge and knew, despite the risks, that the odds were in his favor. He planned and prepared. He knew when his victims would be alone, he got in, and he got out with his prey.

Pierce had read the profile. But aside from approximate age, probable race, and possible background, his image of the killer remained fuzzy, unfocused. He thought he had to be strong. And perhaps handsome, or at least harmless looking. Charming, perhaps. A smooth talker.

And the Peddler was lucky.

Twice a husband had returned home earlier than usual. Twice the blood spatters had been fresh, wet.

He'd been lucky, too, at the dump site discovered a few months ago on a hillside in Anacortes. The narrow asphalt road made a sharp turn above the site and ended a few hundred feet farther along. The neighbors—three sets of them—all had dogs. But as one neighbor said, "We got coyotes and feral cats on the prowl every night. Unless the dogs set up a world-class ruckus or yelp like they're up against more than they can handle, we roll over and go back to sleep."

Still, the Peddler had returned to the site four times with four mutilated bodies, all scrubbed with strong soap and bleach, all wrapped in the kind of tarps available at most hardware and home improvement stores. Four times he ran the risk that someone might peer out a window by chance, or come home at the moment he hauled a body from the trunk of a car or bed of a truck or van. Four times he risked being seen before he rolled the bodies into a tangle of blackberry canes.

But no one had seen him.

And no one discovered the grisly cache until a surveyor cut his way through the snarl of undergrowth to size up the hillside for a developer with expansive dreams.

Another neighbor who'd gone head-to-head with the developer at a planning meeting had mixed feelings about the find. "I'm sorry as hell about those women, but at the same time I feel lightning will strike me because, thanks to them, the developer had his plans put on hold. Gave us time to get organized and file appeals. He wants to put eight houses on that hillside! That's six too many."

The deputy braked and made a hard left onto a dirt road, the car fishtailing, pebbles pinging against the undercarriage. Simmons cursed under his breath and clutched the door handle. Pierce treated himself to a faint smile as they barreled between rows of bare trees. Apples, probably. What kind, he had no idea. He knew apples by colors—red, gold, green—not by varieties or whether they were best for pies or sauce or eating.

"These trees will be firewood soon," the deputy said. "Or mulch. Farmer's going with grapes."

Pierce nodded. One thing he did know about apples was that demand for Northwest crops wasn't what it used to be. Neither were prices. This farmer wouldn't be the first to gamble on wine grapes.

"Never understood this wine thing," Simmons said. His voice, channeled through the drooping side of his mouth, made a liquid sibilant sound. "Just to be polite, I'll raise a glass of the grape for a special occasion, but I'd rather have whiskey."

The deputy grunted agreement.

Pierce choked down a laugh at the idea of Simmons being polite, and considered whether the wine comment was a dig at his lifestyle. Correction, *former* lifestyle. Unless Mal leaned on him to put in an appearance at a corporate event, he avoided cocktail parties, opening-night events, or testimonial dinners. These days he drank beer. And he usually drank alone.

The road curved around a white two-story farmhouse set on a rise of ground. Wreaths with silver bows hung on the porch pillars and two wicker deer, one with a red nose, stood beside the walk. Had the family put off the task of taking down the holiday decorations? Or had someone decided they added a note of cheer to the browns and grays of the January landscape?

Last fall, in an effort to brighten his mental landscape, Pierce had strung colored lights along the eaves, on the rhododendrons flanking the porch, and throughout the house. He'd turned them on perhaps three times, including once when he hit a switch by accident. The tiny lights made a nice glow in the winter fog and against the pine paneling in his den, but he hadn't noticed a significant lift in his spirits.

Perhaps the experience needed to be shared and enhanced with holiday meals, toasts, and gifts. But he'd done none of that. His home sat in the center of a 50-acre chunk of forest and fields. In the past year, his only visitors had been a plumber, a cable repairman, and two women asking if he'd like to attend their church.

Despite occasional grim moments of wondering if this was the way it would play out for all the years to come, he liked the isolation. And silence. The condo he'd shared with Ariel had been large, but he'd found himself growing restless, pacing the rooms, annoyed by every sound from units below and beside theirs.

After she disappeared, he got out—first to a hotel and then to what he described to Claire as the outskirts of the sticks. The old man would have hated it. That, of course, made Pierce like it even more.

But he didn't sell the condo. Wouldn't consider that until he knew Ariel's fate.

Sometimes he was certain he saw her. Once he swore she drove by two lanes over on the freeway. Another time he was sure he'd spotted her turning a corner ahead of him as he left a bookstore. He'd given chase, only to find no trace of her.

Imagination.

Probably.

But perhaps . . .

Ariel had been taken more than two years ago, only a few months after Reba Culp had disappeared from Sacramento. Experts estimated Reba had been killed and dumped in Anacortes about 18 months before her body was discovered. That meant she'd been alive for half a year after she was taken. And it was the same for the others—at least six months after they were taken, they were killed and dumped.

The math told him Ariel was dead.

Unless she'd escaped.

It was possible the trauma of her ordeal might have affected her memory, even wiped out much of it. But she'd decorated the condo where they'd lived for two and a half years. Pierce felt—or perhaps simply *wanted* to feel—that she'd be able to find her way to it. If she couldn't recall the combination to the lock on the door, the management team had her photograph and instructions to let her in.

He'd stocked the refrigerator with her favorite wines and cheeses and chocolates. He'd arranged for fresh flowers to be delivered twice a week and placed in the vase in the entryway. And he'd left a note welcoming her home.

But he hadn't left directions to his house or a key to his door.

He wanted Ariel to be alive.

He wanted to arrange for help and support if she returned.

29

But he didn't want to be her husband.

Telling himself she was drug addicted and mentally unbalanced, he'd forgiven much of her erratic behavior—or at least made a good-faith attempt to forgive. But, for self-preservation, he wouldn't forget her lies or infidelities. And he certainly wouldn't forget the night she ended an argument by handing him a steak knife and telling him to cut his arm deep enough to "end his narrow little existence."

If it had been narrow then, it was no wider than a thread now. His whole focus was on finding the Peddler, finding answers.

The deputy spun the car through another turn and past a weathered barn, then gunned the engine as the road straightened and ran through a gate and down the middle of another orchard. These trees were smaller, scrawnier, some with trunks split from age or disease.

"This guy has cast iron balls," Simmons said. "Driving right past the house to dump a body."

"There's another road." The deputy pointed to several long, low buildings ahead and to the right. "To the packing sheds and migrant worker housing."

"What?" Simmons crumpled the notebook page on which he'd jotted directions. "Why the hell did you take us on the scenic route?"

The deputy shrugged. "I came the way you said."

"And you didn't think to—"

"It's fine." Pierce cut Simmons off and nodded toward a cluster of cars. "We're here now. And from what they told you on the phone, this isn't a fresh burial. A few minutes won't matter."

Simmons shot him a glare that said he was wrong, no more than a rank amateur, and should keep his mouth shut. Pierce took it on the chin, keeping his expression neutral. Simmons was as crusty as dry bread, but Pierce was convinced he was the best man for the job. He was impatient and driven, but at the same time meticulous and cautious. He was quick to form theories, but he didn't allow any single hypothesis to dictate direction. He set ideas aside while he juggled others, perhaps working them in later. And he never hesitated to let a defective idea drop—even if it was *his* idea.

The deputy braked, slewing the car in beside a dark sedan. Simmons swore once again, swung his door wide, and slammed it hard. He hustled through spitting rain to a group of uniformed men and women. They'd gathered along a length of yellow nylon rope strung from a series of posts driven in the ground at the edge of a wasteland of toppled trees and pulled stumps.

"What's his problem?" the deputy asked.

"FBI." Pierce climbed out of the back seat, raising the collar of his black wool coat. "He claims they don't work and play well with others."

The deputy snorted.

Despite all Pierce's attempts to persuade them otherwise, the feds had declined to appoint a representative to the task force. The stated reason was that this project duplicated and diluted the effort to catch the killer. Privately, Pierce had been told they considered it "an amateur operation."

"Marlin says their behavior is a cliché," he told the deputy. "And he should know. So is his."

The deputy snorted again, and shut down the engine.

Pierce picked his way around stumps waiting to be jerked from the ground by a red tractor with flaking paint and a rusted bucket. Halting every dozen steps, he used the camera on his phone to record the scene.

Simmons was toe-to-toe with a man in a dark blue suit, a man as calm as Simmons was choleric. The man had reason to be serene. And smug. It was his crime scene, and he was in control. Arguing wouldn't get Simmons any closer to the grave. And it certainly wouldn't result in Pierce getting past the rope and getting a chance to determine if this was Ariel.

But, as he'd learned from Claire, often there were other ways.

Pierce edged along the rope, taking in the tent erected over the grave. Getting details about the burial and autopsy would involve some powerful persuasion, the calling in of favors, the greasing of skids, and perhaps a series of end runs. Simmons was far too up-front for any of that, but watching the old man wheel and deal had given Pierce an education in influence, inducements, manipulation, exploitation, and flat-out bribery. Not that he thought he'd have to employ much of that. In the past few months he'd discovered that many of those in various law enforcement hierarchies who had been put in their place by a federal agent often had no qualms about off-the-record chats with Claire.

Surprisingly, Simmons helped prime that particular conversational pump with public conflicts like this one.

"How many women have to die before you see it's smarter for us all to work together," Simmons raged.

The agent's eyes barely flickered. He turned away, walked to his car, and closed himself inside.

Simmons stomped in a tight circle, his face approaching the color of ripe eggplant.

"Talk about not working and playing well."

Pierce turned to see a grin on the deputy's face.

"Yeah, Simmons doesn't hold it in."

"Neither do the gossips." The deputy hooked a thumb toward a knot of men and women on the dirt road that led to the highway. "They say the farmer's boys found the grave yesterday."

"Yesterday?"

"Playing soldiers. That's their No Man's Land." He thrust his chin toward uprooted stumps and heaps of branches.

"Yesterday?" Pierce asked again.

"Right. Came across the mound of soft earth in the long grass between the orchard and the ditch along the road, dug around, pulled aside the tarp, and tossed their cookies. Didn't mention it to their parents until this morning."

He shrugged and added, "Kids." As if that explained everything. "They're at the middle school."

Telling their friends all about it.

Pierce almost felt sorry for the FBI agent. Forget trying to contain this story.

"School lets out in half an hour," the deputy said. "Want to collect that heart attack on legs and head over there?"

"I thought you'd never ask."

Pierce fingered the bills in the money clip in his left front pocket. With promises of ice cream or burgers or movie tickets for the kids who found her, they might learn if the woman in the grave was Ariel.

It wasn't.

The boys' strongest impression was the smell and the way the woman's skin "kinda slid around" on her arm. But they agreed she had long red hair. Real long, "like way down way past her boobs." And not a wig. "It didn't come off like a wig woulda."

Ariel's hair had been blond and styled in the shortest of pixie cuts. Even with two and a half years of growth, it wouldn't be as long as the boys said.

Besides, the long red hair matched that of a woman snatched from Redding, an accountant named Mona Bernstein.

"This is one time I'm glad I'm not wearing a badge and in charge of an official investigation," Simmons said as the jet lifted off and aimed for the setting sun. "I'd rather drop a concrete block on my foot than have to tell a family it's time to give up hope."

Pierce wondered what it would feel like to know Ariel was dead, to give up hope that she might return. Pure relief? Stabbing pain? Or a mix of both?

He sometimes thought of hope as the light at the end of the tunnel, a light he walked toward, but might never reach. If he stopped hoping, would the light blink out? Would the tunnel collapse? Or could he turn around and walk the other way?

Toward what?

Setting the questions aside, he transferred photos from his phone to his laptop, then brought up an aerial view of the farm.

Simmons leaned across the space between seats and tapped the screen. "Think he picked that spot by chance?"

"No." Pierce traced the road from the highway to the dump site. "I think he'd been there before. I think he knew no one would be around this time of year when the trees are dormant—not at night, anyway."

Simmons wiped the drooping side of his mouth with the knuckle of his index finger. "So he buried her after the harvest and packing, but before the farmer started to tear up the orchard."

"Seems to me he didn't know about plans to turn the land over to wine grapes."

"Or he would have gone to Plan B."

Pierce traced the road again. "That might mean he's not from this area."

"Might," Simmons agreed. "Or might not."

CHAPTER 5

February
Rain

Rain stared at the array of weapons her grandfather had laid out on the kitchen table. A rifle. A shotgun. A revolver. A broad knife with a wicked blade. A canister of pepper spray.

The sight of the guns didn't rattle her. When she was in her teens, Morgan taught her to shoot a rifle and instructed her to be on watch for rabid animals. In the course of a summer, she'd killed two sick raccoons with a single shot each. The next summer, when a rattlesnake disputed her right to enter the garage, she ended negotiations with the shotgun. Their nearest neighbor, Ben Cameron, had scoffed at the idea of a rattler so far west in the Columbia Gorge and insisted she was mistaken. The following day he discovered one laying claim to the space beneath his toolshed.

As a college graduation present, Morgan had given her a revolver, paid for professional instruction, insisted she get a concealed-carry permit, and further insisted she take the gun along on hiking and camping trips. "Not everyone goes to the woods for solitude or to contemplate the beauty of nature," he'd said. "Some have a darker purpose."

Twice she discovered he was right.

35

She'd never had to fire her weapon. And she'd never worried him with details of the encounters.

What rattled her now were these questions: What was she expected to do with the guns? And the knives? And the bow and arrows she'd just now noticed?

Had her grandfather foreseen societal collapse? Would she need to hunt to survive? Skin and butcher what she shot? Drive off starving neighbors?

She forced a laugh and turned to Morgan. "I know you said I'd have to learn things they didn't teach me in college. But this seems a little extreme."

And more than a little frightening.

Morgan avoided her gaze, broke open the shotgun, and slipped in two shells. "Better safe than sorry."

Rain felt an icy hand squeeze her heart. In the month since Meadow died, Morgan had changed. Always quiet, now he seldom spoke. When he did, it was more a series of grim pronouncements than conversation.

She fingered the knife and then the bow.

"Quieter than a gun," Morgan said.

The icy hand squeezed again. She wanted to demand Morgan tell her what he saw ahead for her, but she knew he wouldn't. She also knew his visions grew more unfocused as he peered further into the future.

And, for all Morgan did see, there was much he didn't—or couldn't. He once told her that long sight was selective, and the selections weren't his to make. Sometimes there were dark spots or fuzzy areas that obscured the view. Sometimes parts of images were distorted like reflections in fun house mirrors. Sometimes he saw a frame around the picture, a frame that closed in before he got a good look.

"You'll get the hang of this." Morgan thrust his arms into the sleeves of a faded denim jacket and picked up the bow and arrows. "Range is up the hill."

Rain pulled on her waterproof jacket and followed him along a set of deep muddy ruts through the orchard. "What did you drive up here, a tank?"

Morgan didn't answer. He'd been ignoring her questions often since Meadow died, but Rain had figured out a pattern to his non-responses. If a question was an attempt at humor, he didn't speak. If it was rhetorical, he didn't speak. If it was unnecessary and simply an attempt to break the silence, he didn't speak. And if it was what he considered to be stupid, she could almost feel the weight of his silence on her shoulders.

Studying the tracks, Rain concluded that several vehicles, some heavily loaded, had driven through the orchard in the week since she last visited her grandfather. Going where? Carrying what? Did Morgan's silence indicate this was none of her business? Or did it indicate she should take it upon herself to get an answer?

This land was Morgan's and he was entitled—within legal bounds—to do whatever he liked with it. But one day, far too soon, it would belong to her.

When her grandfather turned right along the fence at the top of the orchard, she stuck with the tracks and went left.

In a moment Morgan called out. "The target range is over here."

Rain didn't answer.

She could use silence too.

The track ran through a gap in the barbed wire fence—a gap created by cutting the wire and pulling out a post. She walked faster, staying between the ruts.

"Rain," Morgan shouted.

37

The track ran into the stand of Douglas fir where Motley had disappeared a month earlier. Rain followed as it curved uphill, noting piles of limbs and sprays of sawdust where trees had been felled to allow vehicles through.

"Rain!" Morgan shouted. "Not yet."

The primitive road emerged into a clearing she remembered from childhood explorations. She'd imagined then that the hillside had halted to take a few quick breaths and enjoy the view before pushing upward again. Years later she learned the forces of erosion were responsible. Wind and water had broken out a sharply defined L in the rock. The same forces had filled crevices in the perpendicular wall with barely enough soil to support tufts of grass, hardy shrubs, and half a dozen scrawny trees.

The only easy way to reach the clearing was from the south, the way she'd come. On the east, the ground sheered away. On the west the slope was more gentle, littered by a jumble of huge rocks that gave way to a tangle of blackberry vines. To the north, the earth seemed to leap for the sky except for a sliver on the eastern edge where that leap had fallen short and the slope was less severe.

Piles of building material outlined the clearing—studs and floor joists, roof trusses and shingles, a stack of pipe and a tarp-covered heap of what looked like sinks and toilets. A foundation of gray concrete blocks took up most of the center. Permit signs were posted here and there.

"I got so focused on the weapons I forgot you'd see the ruts," Morgan panted. "Now it won't be a surprise."

"It may not be a surprise," Rain said. "But it's a puzzle. Why are you building a house?"

"You'll need it."

"I have a house."

"Apartment," he scoffed. "No bigger than my kitchen. No dogs allowed."

"But I don't have a—"

Rain remembered Motley and the dogs that came before him, remembered her grandmother's words, "There will be a dog."

And, if it was like the others, it would be a large dog. It would obey, but also have a mind of its own. It wouldn't want a leash clipped to its collar. Getting a bigger apartment wasn't the answer. Few managers would allow a dog as large as Motley had been. And neighbors would complain or call the police if they encountered a dog running loose.

Rain nodded slowly and gazed along the track through the trees, then turned her head to peer between branches to the south, across the Columbia Gorge. Through the mist and fog that hung over the river, she spotted a faint silver vertical line— one of the waterfalls that plunged from the top of the basalt cliff and dropped to a plunge pool far below. Unlike the farmhouse, tucked into a fold of land for protection from the relentless wind funneling through the gorge, this house would have a view down to the water and both ways along the river. On a clear day, she could squint through a pair of binoculars and spot tourists admiring the falls and viewpoints. She'd be able to see their cars strung along the highway and appearing, from this distance, to be jewels on a long necklace.

"Okay. I get that I'll need to move. But why can't I live in the farmhouse?"

"Spoken for."

Rain felt her jaw drop. Who else was there to "speak for" the house? As far as she knew, she was the only family Meadow and Morgan had—except for her mother. "Is my mother—?"

"No." The single word contained a world of regret and loss, anger and frustration. The two-letter word was definite. Final.

"Then who? A renter?"

Morgan brushed that aside. "This place will be more secure. Better locks." He pointed to the sharp slope beyond the foundation. "Hiding places."

"Why do I need better locks if I have a dog?" Rain asked with a hollow laugh. "And why do I need an arsenal? Why would I need to hide?"

Morgan's lips set in a tight line.

Rain felt that icy hand on her heart again.

Her grandfather had never acted like this. What had he seen—or not seen—that shook him? He and Meadow said those waiting on the beach at Nightfall Bay wouldn't hurt her. So his vision had to be of earthly danger.

The grip on her heart tightened.

Each of those stranded at Nightfall Bay had information, perhaps the key to unlock a mystery. Many on this earth longed for the truth, for mysteries to be solved. Some had appealed to Meadow to do that. But—and Rain never considered this before—there must be others who feared a solution would be revealed, feared justice would be done and they'd pay for their crimes.

Rain shuddered.

Morgan laid a hand on her shoulder.

"Meadow had you," Rain whispered. "But I'm alone."

Morgan said nothing.

Rain stroked his gnarled fingers, then turned her back on the clearing and headed down the track. "I better practice with those guns."

CHAPTER 6

February
Pierce

Pierce swiveled in a black leather chair, alternately peering through the rain-streaked window to study traffic on the access road to the airport, and watching Marlin Simmons pace and thump the edge of his fist against a map that filled most of one wall of the boardroom. Yellow pins indicated where women had been taken, presumably by the Peddler. Black pins indicated women whose remains had been found. Red pins marked burial sites. Lengths of string connected the burial site pins to the pins for the women whose bodies had been found there. Distances were indicated with thick black numbers on clear tape. Arrayed on two sides of the map were photographs and information about the victims. Beneath the map was a timeline of the Peddler's activities going back more than three years.

Marlin respected computers for their speed and ability to sort and refine data, but when it came to maps and displays, he was old school.

Pierce liked that.

And Marlin said exactly what he thought. Usually at the moment he thought it. He had no filter.

Pierce liked that too.

He'd spent far too many years with people who masked their opinions and intentions with banal comments and false smiles. The old man, of course, had been the exception. But Pierce had never wanted to be on the same team with the old man.

Marlin pounded the map again. "Hundreds of towns and cities. Thousands of square miles of hunting grounds. Millions of women to choose from. Why these?"

It was, of course, a question they'd kicked around a thousand times. But Pierce delivered the simple answer. "He saw them. He wanted them."

Marlin growled and shook his fist in the air. "Yes. But *where* did he see them? *How* did he see them? As far as we can tell, except for general age and intelligence, not one thing links these women. Not one."

Not one they'd discovered.

Yet.

But Pierce didn't say that.

Marlin might see it as questioning his thought processes and investigative abilities instead of as a reminder that the door of possibility was still open. Besides, Marlin didn't need reminding. Along with juggling ideas and refusing to marry any one theory, he was all about leaving doors ajar. Still, it was clear to Pierce that Marlin not only wanted to close the door labeled RANDOM CHANCE, he wanted to lock and bolt it as well.

"They never lived in the same towns, attended the same schools or events, vacationed at the same resorts, shopped at the same stores, or belonged to branches of the same organizations. Their husbands and boyfriends and hairdressers and doctors and plumbers and cleaning and yard services have no connections." Marlin slammed the map so hard a pin jumped loose and pinged against the arm of a nearby chair. "Even their dogs and cats don't have connections."

Pierce held in a smile. That's how thorough Marlin was. Wondering if dog and cat breeders might provide a link, he'd checked the backgrounds of family pets.

"So he sees them. And he wants them." Marlin jumped to that simple theory. "He's where they are. But why? They're all over the map. What brings him to where they are?"

Another rhetorical question.

They'd kicked around theories for months, picking them apart, shooting them down, and resurrecting them again. There was, of course, the traveling salesman theory. In spite of technology, there were still people out there knocking on doors selling everything from cleaning solutions to makeup to bronze baby shoes. But the territory the Peddler traveled was huge. Representatives of every company questioned claimed it wouldn't be cost-effective. Not if the company had to foot the bill for motels and meals and mileage. Maybe he was an independent, they suggested. Perhaps someone who drove a vehicle large enough to camp in, someone who cooked his own meals and lived on a shoestring.

Marlin and Pierce both liked that component of the theory. A small RV or van or a truck with a camper shell would allow the Peddler to hide his victims within moments of taking them.

A camper vehicle also fit with other theories—like the traveling writer or photographer theory. The carnival worker theory. And the homeless drifter with a vehicle theory.

They'd plowed through published travel articles and photographs featuring the region and found only tenuous links to a few of the areas where victims resided. They'd tracked circuses and carnivals and companies supplying rides and attractions. Again, they found no firm links to all victims.

What didn't work with the homeless drifter theory was their belief that the Peddler spent time watching his victims, casing their homes, planning abductions. He did that without drawing attention to himself in city condo complexes with security gates, and in suburban neighborhoods with well-kept yards. A homeless drifter would have to dress to fit in and perhaps change his clothing and appearance often. And to run a vehicle and clothe and feed himself, he'd need money. Panhandling might draw attention, and stealing would add another element of risk.

Pierce didn't doubt that risk excited the Peddler and was an integral part of his grisly game. But he'd concluded the Peddler had a source of income—either an inheritance or savings, or regular paychecks. A chunk of money in the bank widened the range of possibilities. At the same time, it also expanded his hunting ground. With enough money, the Peddler could hunt anywhere, even abroad.

Yet, comparing reports of missing women from around the country, they'd found only two cases that matched abductions in this region. Both of those cases had been solved—one when the husband confessed, and another when the woman returned home after a fling.

The Peddler, it seemed, hadn't struck outside the Northwest. And Pierce believed that was because he worked in the region and/or was familiar with it.

But, as sales managers had pointed out, it was a huge region. What would take someone from California to Idaho to Oregon, from Washington to Nevada? He'd considered the possibility that the Peddler might be following the harvest, working in oil and gas exploration, or coordinating fundraisers.

Marlin pounded his fist in a circle around the region. "What the hell does this guy do when he's not hunting?"

The answer, as far as Pierce was concerned, was that the Peddler was *always* hunting. Maybe he worked a job that let him get out and about where he might spot potential victims. Maybe he made enough when he worked that he could afford to take time off—a few days or weeks—to stalk and plan and capture his prey. Perhaps he was an independent contractor—

"He's paid on commission."

Marlin stopped pounding. "We've been down that road."

"Right." Pierce stopped swiveling. "We've been down that road in a small-change way, thinking he's an independent salesman hawking vitamins or laundry detergent. What if he's in a profession where the payout for his services is larger?"

"What kind of a profession?" Marlin gave an exasperated sigh and spoke as he might to a failing student. "If you were paying attention, you'd remember we already ruled out the real estate connection. And car sales. And travel agencies. And insurance. We even looked at yacht sales, asphalt suppliers, signage companies—all kinds of crap."

Pierce closed his eyes and tried to re-create his train of thought before he'd derailed it by speaking. There was something—

"Sorry to interrupt." Claire Dawson extended a manila envelope. "I thought you'd want this right away."

Marlin scowled.

Claire waved the envelope, her gold nail polish catching the light. "It's the preliminary report on the body in Wenatchee," she said in a teasing voice.

Marlin's scowl gave way to a frown. "Bring it here."

The task force researcher did, but at a snail-like pace that exaggerated the hitch in her gait as she swung her right leg into position to take her weight. A former Vancouver police officer, she'd been wounded while responding to a domestic violence call, returned fire, and took down the man who shot her. Pierce liked the way she managed Marlin, making it clear she wasn't intimidated by his blustering attitude. Occasionally she even maneuvered him into a display of good manners.

As if making it clear he wouldn't be manipulated, Marlin lunged and snatched the envelope from her hand.

"I made two copies. And you're welcome," she said with a dazzling smile, her teeth bright against her dark skin and lipstick that glowed purple in the fluorescent lighting. She held the smile for the count of three before turning to Pierce. "Good morning. Can I get you a cup of coffee?"

Pierce shook his head.

Truthfully, another hit of caffeine would be great, but he knew her offer was made to annoy Marlin. Shortly after she was hired, she'd made it clear she was a contributing member of the team, not a waitress. But now and then—when Marlin was being especially surly—she offered to fetch coffee or tea for someone else as a way of showing him the benefit of respecting her.

"Thanks, but I'll pass." Pierce shot her a wink. "Good work getting the report."

"It's all about making friends with the little people." Claire cast a glance at Marlin. "Fortunately I'm a little person myself, so it's not the challenge it would be for others."

Marlin, fumbling with the metal clip on the envelope, didn't seem to hear. Pierce turned a thumb up, making a mental note to bring her a gift later in the week—a box of cookies or a bouquet of tulips or a gift certificate to a nail salon or the funky jewelry store where she bought many of the dangling earrings she was so fond of. Along with shepherding Marlin toward what she called "a condition approaching human," she'd made Pierce genuinely want to perform small acts of acknowledgement and kindness.

Such etiquette had been required of him from childhood—mostly for purposes of financial or social gain. Ariel, of course, had scoffed at the rules and conventions of polite behavior, and ridiculed those who followed them. But Pierce, now that he

46

made his own rules, found he enjoyed showing his appreciation.

"I'll leave you to it." The scent of cinnamon wafting behind her, Claire hitched her way to the door and closed it with a sharp click.

Marlin tore open the envelope, dumped the contents, and tossed a stapled copy of the report to Pierce. "Let me know if there's anything you don't understand."

Pierce didn't rise to the bait. He'd read hundreds of forensic reports—probably more than Marlin himself—training himself to see what was there and what wasn't. It was, he thought, not much different from the way the old man taught him to evaluate a potential business acquisition.

He bent over the report, scanning blocks of text, then reading like a school kid, sounding each word in his mind, pausing at the end of each phrase. As he absorbed the terms, he translated them to layman's language—leg bones smashed at the ankles, four fingers chopped off, front teeth pulled out, multiple shallow wounds, hyoid bone broken.

"Hobbled. Tortured. Strangled. Scrubbed. Dumped." Marlin slapped his report on the table and sat. "Not one damn thing we didn't have before. I thought because we found her so much sooner we'd get something to work with."

"The stomach contents are interesting," Pierce said in a soft voice.

Marlin flipped pages. "Beef. Potato. Strawberries. What's so interesting about that?"

"Maybe nothing. But it made me think of what someone on death row might order for a last meal."

"Huh." Marlin traced the lines of information with his forefinger.

"The small intestine was empty." Pierce kept his voice low, his tone almost questioning. Sometimes his mind leaped ahead too fast and too far, jumping to faulty conclusions. Marlin, more of a plodder, examined every inch of terrain ahead before he jumped. "And the fecal matter was dry and hard."

Marlin flipped back a page. "She weighed about . . . maybe 20 or 25 pounds less than when he took her."

Pierce said nothing, but he knew from the intensity with which Marlin examined this section of the report that he would make the leap. The Peddler hobbled Mona Bernstein, then tortured and starved her. And he saved a final act of cruelty for last. He served her a meal—perhaps allowed her to think she'd go free—then he snuffed out her life.

Execution was too good for this monster.

CHAPTER 7

March
Rain

In the month since she discovered the foundation and materials, Rain bore down on her editing projects during the week and visited her grandfather every weekend. Each time, she was amazed by the way the house was coming together. Morgan must have been planning the build for many months, perhaps even for years. The roof was on—shingled in green and brown and gray to blend in with trees and rock. The walls were up and the exterior painted in forest camouflage colors. Wiring had been run, poles set to bring in power, pipes and drains put in place, and a septic field laid.

During the past week, workers had installed the windows. The two upstairs in the loft bedroom were stained glass, the one in the east wall depicting a sunrise over the ocean, the one in the west wall depicting a sunset. Downstairs, the south-facing windows slanted inward at the bottom. Morgan claimed they would reflect sunlight toward the ground and be less visible from a distance. Rain wasn't certain that would work, but thought it was worth a shot.

"Place won't be big," Morgan said. "But it will be all yours. Free and clear. I worked it out so you should have plenty of room for the basics plus a few bits from your place and the farmhouse. And plenty of storage—drawers and shelves and cabinets."

Rain hadn't checked the woodshop, but she suspected he was already at work on all he'd mentioned. After years spent crafting such things for others, he wouldn't hire a stranger to design or build them for her. She inhaled the tangy scent of cedar boards delivered recently as she followed him to the rear of the structure.

"Toolshed. Pump house." He pointed to a lean-to. "Spring's up the hill."

That answered a question that had occurred to her in the night.

"Sweet water. Might dry to a trickle by August, though."

Rain nodded. Autumn would bring rain nearly every day— driving rain, pelting rain, rain mixed with sleet, rain giving way to snow that gave way to freezing rain. But weather patterns shifted as days lengthened, and there might be summer months when few drops fell, when dust devils danced along dirt roads, when gardens had to be watered if plants were to survive. "I'll conserve. Will the person living in the farmhouse allow me to draw from the well if I need to?"

Morgan didn't answer.

Rain reviewed her question. It hadn't been an attempt at humor or meant to fill silence, hadn't been rhetorical, and hadn't been—by her definition—stupid. But asking why he hadn't answered wasn't likely to get a response. So, as they walked to the farmhouse, she went with a question he might answer. "How did people who wanted answers from Nightfall Bay find grandmother? I never asked because . . . well, because I never thought to. But if I'm worthy of the gift and I accept it, how will they find me? How will they ask—?"

"Word of mouth," Morgan said. "Letters."

Letters made sense. Meadow began traveling to Nightfall Bay more than 50 years ago, in an age when computers were mammoth contraptions in the hands of government and corporations. Even now there wasn't a computer in the farmhouse. And, growing up, Rain had seldom heard the phone ring. When it had, the person on the other end had almost always been a neighbor offering to share a bounty of blueberries or wanting help corralling a cow.

Word of mouth also made sense. Advertising would have brought hordes—people in genuine pain and need of an answer as well as those curious about family history, secrets, and hidden money.

Morgan led her up a narrow staircase off the farmhouse kitchen and to the slope-ceilinged room on the second floor. "Letters she went through are in here."

He opened a closet to reveal half a dozen cardboard boxes. "We kept it locked up when you were with us. Hung a quilt on the wall so you wouldn't see too much too soon."

Like her mother had.

Rain studied the boxes. The one on the bottom was labeled 1960-1975. The years marched up the stack from there.

Somehow, Rain had expected more. Last year she'd edited a manuscript that centered on a woman who had disappeared. Curious, she'd surfed the Internet and found there were far more missing people in the U.S. than she'd imagined—as many as two-thirds of a million cases reported every year. Many of those cases were solved relatively quickly. But thousands weren't. And that meant friends and relatives searching for answers. Even with the limitations of word of mouth and the requirement of writing a letter, she'd expected enough boxes to fill the garage.

"Were there . . . are there others like grandmother? Others who go to Nightfall Bay to find answers?"

51

"Meadow never mentioned meeting another seeker. But there are plenty who claim to lift the veil in their own way." Morgan scowled. "And plenty more who deal from a pack of lies to profit from pain."

People like that would give those who were genuine—like Meadow—a bad name. Suspicion and mistrust might explain why there were fewer letters than Rain expected.

"Aren't many professionals who ask for help," Morgan said. "Or many who accept it."

Meaning law enforcement. Rain guessed detectives received plenty of calls from people who claimed to have dreams or visions or gut feelings. If a substantial percentage of those panned out, investigators might seek psychic assistance on a regular basis.

And maybe they did. Maybe they kept it quiet.

"Did Meadow ever help the police?"

Morgan shook his head, then paused. "Got a call once. No, twice. Wanted to send Meadow information on the computer."

And her grandparents had seen no reason to have one.

"Told them we needed letters."

"But they didn't write?"

"Letters never got here if they did."

Morgan sighed, perhaps thinking about a chance missed, a case unsolved. "Still get one every few days." He pointed to a small table by the window and a stack of letters. Thirty or so.

Rain crossed to the table and laid her hand on top of the stack expecting— What? Expecting to feel pain or longing or fear?

What she felt was only paper.

She flipped through the stack, spotting return addresses from Pennsylvania, Georgia, Alaska, and even London. "How did she decide?"

"She took in the words. Studied the pictures. If she felt a pull, she'd set that one aside for a day or so and read it again."

Morgan sat in a worn easy chair beside the day bed and closed his eyes as if speaking so many words had exhausted him. "She wouldn't go unless she felt a connection. Fact is, she believed she *couldn't* go unless she drew on the strength of the person who wrote."

"Strength?"

"Perseverance. Tenacity. Longing." Morgan spread his hands. "She thought of herself as, well, a last resort. She had to know they'd tried as hard as they could to find answers in *this* world."

Rain straightened the stack of letters, half longing to feel a connection, half afraid she would and the gift would be upon her before she was ready.

Would she ever feel she was ready?

How would she know when she was?

"Some letters came with checks. Some with cash— sometimes big bills. Money never swayed her." Morgan pointed to the stack. "Go through those when you get a chance. Tell them Meadow's gone on. Tear up the checks. Send the cash back."

Glancing at the stuffed boxes in the closet, Rain pondered the cost of envelopes and stamps. And then there was the time Meadow spent writing letters to those she helped, and those she couldn't. Rain's mind drifted to her freelance editing business, to expenses, income, and deductions, to money due for taxes after it all shook out. Her grandmother, apparently, hadn't had to worry about yanking on budgetary ends until they met.

As she had many times before, Rain wondered about her grandparents' financial situation. Morgan built beautiful custom cabinets for a select group of builders. Each year they sold a portion of what the orchards brought forth. And neither

53

was extravagant. But all that didn't seem to balance the cost of food and utilities and taxes.

"Your grandmother felt charging a fee would be taking advantage of grief. Sometimes, though, she'd accept a gift afterward. But only if she felt it came from the heart and not from a sense of obligation. And if the giver didn't sacrifice too much." Morgan pointed to an oil painting mounted on the wall above the day bed. "That was her favorite."

Leaning across the bed, Rain studied the seascape. The terrain was much the way she imagined Nightfall Bay. But she saw no shapes huddled in the distance, and the setting sun flung out banners of color that seemed to speak of joy and peace, of another day coming and another chance to enjoy the splendor of the world.

Examining the scrawl in the lower right corner, she made out the name of the artist, a name she was familiar with. "Wow."

"Worth a wagon load of money. I'll hang it in your house when there's a wall to hang it on. Unless you want to sell it."

"Never."

"Easy to say. But if a day comes you're down to your last can of beans, do what needs to be done. Meadow would have."

Morgan stood, his legs trembling a little. He'd lost weight since Meadow died. And he'd had only a few pounds to spare. Rain guessed he'd been working many long hours and wondered, not for the first time, if he knew the day he'd depart.

Then another thought nagged at her. Was her grandfather trying to hasten that day? Was this willing horse trying to work himself to death, to a reunion with his wife?

Perhaps.

But he wouldn't go until the house was complete and she moved in. He'd hang on until she proved proficient with the weapons he'd chosen. After that he'd see no reason to stay.

Well, she'd make the best of the time they had. And try to keep him healthy so the end didn't come sooner than he anticipated.

Blinking away tears, Rain took Morgan's hand. "I'm hungry for a grilled cheese sandwich with bacon and tomato." Plenty of calories in that, a few of them actually good for him. "And potato chips on the side. And some of those chocolate chip cookies I saw in the freezer."

Morgan flashed a smile that indicated he knew what she was up to, but he followed her to the kitchen.

CHAPTER 8

March
Pierce

Pierce had lost track of the number of times he'd read through the information compiled on the Peddler's victims. He'd memorized details about height, weight, hair color, choice of car, address, educational level, and a hundred other characteristics. But on this gloomy Friday evening, with an empty weekend ahead, he felt it amounted to nothing except busywork for a mind frustrated by lack of progress.

Closing the binder stuffed with information on the life and disappearance of Collette Chambers, he paced the length of the map. Marlin had left an hour earlier, so Pierce felt free to touch each of the pins and trace highways with his fingers. Marlin was territorial about the map and once, as Pierce reached out to point at something, karate chopped his arm.

Pierce halted, his forefinger making a circle around Anacortes, his mind drifting to a college lecture, to a quote that stuck with him: "The map is not the territory." The name of the scholar noted for those words had also, to his surprise, stuck. Alfred Korzybski.

Storm-driven raindrops spattered the window. A plane, its shape distorted by the wet glass, vaulted into the sky from the nearby airport.

Pierce tapped the map. Except for the scene of Ariel's abduction and the burial sites in Wenatchee and Anacortes, he'd experienced the cases only through photographs and written descriptions.

"Pictures and words aren't the territory."

He gathered the binders he'd spread on the conference table, stowed them in a cabinet in Claire's office, and locked them away. In his own office, he removed dry cleaning bags from two shirts and a pair of slacks, and folded the clothing into the gym bag he kept stocked with spare socks and underwear. A few minutes later he was at the airport studying the electronic departure display, and considering the relative warmth of his waterproof jacket. Two hours later, fueled by a burger and a beer, he buckled the belt on a no-frills seat, and listened to a flight attendant convey information about exits and oxygen masks. Two hours after the plane took off, he parked a compact rental car outside a chain motel on the north side of Medford and entered a room smelling vaguely of carpet glue and banana peels.

Tossing his bag on the lone chair, Pierce considered his situation and laughed.

If the rental car had been the last one on earth, his father would have chosen to walk. If the motel room was the only one available in the universe, his mother would refuse to enter it.

Their loss.

Pierce flopped across the bed with his shoes on, the slick spread sliding and bunching beneath him. In his opinion, their dismay and disapproval made the car and the motel seem special, almost exotic.

But they were part of the real world, the world where he was comfortable, content.

He fell asleep imagining his mother massaging expensive cream into the crease between her eyes, the one she blamed on his many embarrassing shortcomings and failures. He dreamed of the old man spinning, spinning, spinning in his lavish casket in a cemetery plot that may have cost more than this motel.

The next morning, after a diner breakfast of eggs and greasy hash browns that would have made his mother gag, he drove to the former home of Tanya Harter, one of the women dumped on the hillside in Anacortes. The house was empty and up for sale. Shortly after the funeral that followed an extensive autopsy, her husband had moved across the country to take a job in North Carolina. The faded sign on a post leaning many degrees from vertical indicated that, despite a more-than-fair price, no one had made an acceptable offer. The market was slow. With no special touches, the six-year-old ranch-style home was much like others in the development. And there were plenty of homes for sale that hadn't been occupied by one of the Peddler's victims.

Pierce didn't blame Tanya's husband for leaving. After all, he'd decamped from the condo he'd shared with Ariel.

Peering through the windows, he saw that Brian Harter had taken little with him. A sofa and chairs occupied the living room, pots hung from a rack over the stove, and canisters lined the countertop. Cataloging the few empty spaces he spotted, Pierce concluded that a recliner, TV, coffeemaker, and bookshelf had made the move east with their owner.

"It's a bargain," a voice said.

Pierce turned from French doors leading from a low deck to the master bedroom. A young woman in a hot pink sweatshirt and bright green leggings stood a few yards away.

She wore the combination well, completing her fashion statement with streaks of blue in her blond hair.

"I have the keys to the back door." She jingled a set threaded onto a piece of green garden twine. "If you want to check it out. Measure the closet space and stuff like that."

"Sure." He'd come with the intention of scoping the territory and talking with neighbors. And this was an opening. He thrust out his right hand. "I'm Pierce Jennings."

"Bethany Lemmert." She stepped forward and shook, her grip strong, three silver rings sparkling in the sunlight. "Do you know what happened here?"

Pierce hesitated, wondering which response would net the most information. He abandoned the house-shopping charade and went with the truth. The whole truth. "Yes. I'm on a task force investigating this case and others like it."

She took two steps away, suspicion clouding her brown eyes.

Pierce dug out his wallet and handed over a business card.

She studied it, holding it by the edges as if to preserve fingerprints.

"You're right to be cautious," he said. "That card proves exactly nothing. I could be the killer returning to the scene of the crime. But if you call the police here and ask for the chief, she'll vouch for me."

"Don't have my phone on me. Besides, it's quicker to round up a posse for protection." She jingled the keys once more. "That is, if you still want to see the inside."

"I wouldn't mind. But only if it's convenient."

"Don't worry about that. I'll seize any excuse to put off running."

She faced the house across the street and flipped her fingers, beckoning. A curtain fluttered at the window to the right of the front door. Another fluttered at the window to the

59

left. In a moment the door opened and a gaunt white-haired man emerged, a cane in one hand, a leash in the other. At the end of it, chewing on the leather, bounced a dachshund puppy. A sturdy woman in a flowered apron followed, her cheeks pink with what Pierce guessed was the embarrassment of being caught spying.

"My posse," Bethany said. "Sylvia and Tom. And Herbie."

"Tom might do some damage with that cane," Pierce observed. "But Herbie's about as threatening as a marshmallow on a grill."

"That marshmallow has puppy teeth like needles. So watch your ankles."

Bethany introduced her neighbors and Pierce handed them a card and said he hoped to get a better sense of Tanya Harter and her killer if he saw her home. Tom grunted agreement, and they trooped around to the rear, Sylvia explaining they'd been at the windows because they were expecting a package, Pierce suggesting that was wise because thieves often trailed delivery trucks.

Inside, Pierce found more evidence that Brian Harter had taken items that were his alone or bore no strong link to his wife. A quick survey of the master bedroom showed he'd left the bulk of his wife's clothing, cosmetics, books, and small possessions behind. Spaces in an array of photographs on the dresser and in the rows of books on the shelves indicated he'd packed only a few of his favorites. A darker rectangle on the wall opposite the window hinted at a painting he couldn't leave behind.

Pierce was surprised that the agent listing the house hadn't arranged to have clothing, cosmetics, and photographs boxed and stored. Perhaps, guessing this would be a hard-to-sell property, he or she hadn't made the effort.

"It makes me sad to see her clothes hanging there." Sylvia wrung her hands in her apron. "Knowing she'll never wear that pretty red dress again."

Bethany slid the closet door closed, grasped Sylvia's elbow, and steered her from the room. "Sylvia loved Tanya," Tom muttered. "Everyone did."

Except the Peddler, Pierce thought. Unless you define love in a sick and perverted way.

"And none of us saw a damn thing the day he took her." Tom sighed, bent with agonizing slowness, pried the leash from Herbie's jaws, picked up the tiny dog, and followed his wife. "Of course, we weren't as vigilant back then. We thought this neighborhood was safe."

Pierce, knowing it had all been done before and by experts, opened dresser drawers and peered into the corners of the closet looking for— What? He had no idea. And worse, he suspected he wouldn't know what he had when he found it. Or didn't find it.

Disgusted with himself and his spur-of-the-moment plan, he followed Tom to the kitchen and out to the patio where Sylvia was wiping her eyes with the hem of her flowered apron. "She wore that red dress when she and Brian had that little party for me when I turned 80," she sniffed. "Not long before she disappeared. Remember?"

Bethany shook her head and locked the door. "That was before I moved in, Sylvia."

"That's right," Tom said. "The landslide was a couple of months after the party. Maybe longer."

Pierce studied the gently sloping terrain surrounding the development. "Landslide?"

"Bethany's a writer. Stories for kids with dragons and elves. She lived way out in the hills." Tom made a vague gesture that covered 180 degrees. "She lost everything."

61

"Which wasn't much," Bethany told Pierce. "A one-bedroom cabin limits your hoarding ability. And thank goodness for the magic that lets you save what you write up in the ozone or wherever."

"Still," Sylvia said. "You lost your car and your computer. All your clothes. Everything you had."

"Except my life," Bethany reminded her. "Others weren't as lucky."

Sylvia pressed her hands together in prayer, and they were all silent for a moment.

"And the insurance came through." Tom winced and pulled his thumb from Herbie's mouth. "Surprised the hell out of me."

"Yeah," Bethany agreed. "Thanks to my dad buying the extra policy, I had coverage. But I still expected more of a fight. It was almost like the adjuster was working for me instead of the company."

Pierce heard the chime of a distant mental bell.

Sylvia grasped his arm and insisted he join them for coffee.

The bell went silent.

Driving toward Redding that afternoon, Pierce replayed conversations in his mind, hoping the far-off bell would ring again.

It didn't.

CHAPTER 9

April
Rain

Rain drew the bowstring, aimed, and released.

"Again," Morgan ordered. "Faster."

She groaned. If she didn't rush, putting an arrow close to the yellow circle in the center of the target wasn't impossible. But her accuracy decreased as Morgan, stopwatch in hand, badgered her. At least today he hadn't made her wear the dark glasses that simulated night, or shoot at the moving target he'd rigged.

Small mercies.

They hardly balanced the string of negative comments he subjected her to.

At first, she'd bridled at his criticism, but then she'd heard the fear beneath his words. Pressing him to tell her what he saw ahead got her nowhere. "Seeing isn't a science. It's not like astronomy," he'd said. "I can't adjust the focus or get a better lens. And what I see right now may not come to pass if others' courses are altered."

Thinking about that, Rain felt her hands tremble. Morgan had seen that she would survive what lay ahead, but he doubted his vision. And so he was pushing, pushing, pushing.

She released the arrow.

"Good," Morgan said. "Hardly fast enough, but in the target."

High praise.

Rain reached for another arrow.

"Leave it be for now." Morgan pointed up the slope. "Time to work on boltholes."

"Holes?" Rain thought of a rabbit running for cover. Was that how Morgan imagined her? "Holes in the ground?"

"In the rocks." Morgan pointed to the hillside above her cabin. "In case you're out of the house when trouble comes. Or you have to leave it."

What would make her leave the house? And what would make her go to a hole instead of the safety of the farmhouse or a neighbor's place?

She gripped Morgan's arm. "What did you see? Did you see me cowering in a hole?"

"No." His voice seemed too loud. Was he angry at himself and the limits of his sight? "But better safe—"

"I know." Rain plucked arrows from the target and helped Morgan carry everything to the barn. "What do we have to do to the boltholes? Hang curtains? Install wall-to-wall carpet?"

She hadn't expected Morgan to answer, and he didn't. Instead, after they stowed the gear, he walked to a stack of white plastic tubs near the door and raised one to his shoulder. "Grab the next and follow."

Rain obeyed, hoisting the tub to her shoulder and balancing it as he had. It weighed about 20 pounds, and rattled as the contents shifted. Dried beans? Spare silverware? There was no point in asking Morgan. He wouldn't answer. She'd have to wait until they arrived at their destination and she pried off the lid.

Trudging the rutted track, they reached the house, now nearly finished on the inside. Another few weeks and she'd give up her apartment. She no longer resisted the move, but still weighed the pros and cons. She'd miss the convenience of living near the center of Vancouver, miss restaurants and opportunities for entertainment. But, although she had acquaintances and movie buddies, close school friends had drifted away over the years. And, consumed by her job and the knowledge of the gift, she hadn't made deep connections with others.

So, as the house took shape, the idea of moving took root. Two days ago she'd scavenged boxes from a supermarket. Not that she had much to pack. She'd lived in the cramped apartment for three years, but never thought of it as home or tried to make it one. Perhaps she'd suspected it was only a stopover.

This place on the earth had been home once. Soon it would be home again. "Do you think my car will make it up this hill?"

His laughter coming in labored puffs, Morgan skirted the yard littered with sawed off chunks of board, sections of pipe, and other debris. "Your car wheezes on the rise to the farmhouse. You'll leave it in the garage. Gonna get you one of them all terrain vehicles. Make less of a mark on the track."

And it would be fun to ride.

Except in the rain.

But he had a point about making less of a mark. He'd designed the cabin to blend in and he planned to seed the track with grass and wildflowers once the workmen finished. He'd told a neighbor that was to preserve the scenery, but Rain guessed he felt obscuring the road gave her another degree of protection.

Morgan zigzagged up the less severe eastern edge of the rock wall, making his way around outcroppings and thickets

65

and across narrow crevices. Rain's heart pounded and her leg muscles screamed, but she bit her lip and kept up.

Finally he stopped. "Here's the first one."

Rain peered around but saw nothing except the rotting trunk of a fallen fir tree. Ferns sprouted from moss-covered bark. Along the bottom, claws had ripped away rotted wood and the earth was dug over. "My bolthole isn't a bear's den, is it?"

Morgan smiled. "I thought you liked wildlife."

"Small wildlife." Rain set her tub on the ground.

"Skunk size?"

"Yes, but without claws. And without scent strong enough to make my nose fall off."

"Then you better hope that guy doesn't come back for another helping of whatever he dug out."

"Noted. Where's the hole?"

"Behind the tree."

Rain squinted into the tangle of saplings and shrubs. She saw nothing resembling a hole.

Morgan thrust his chin to the right. "Go around. Don't break limbs or leave tracks."

Like she had the skills of a mountain man.

Lifting her feet high and placing them with care, she toted the plastic tub to the tip of the fallen tree. Branches had long since dropped away, leaving stubs protruding from the trunk and a litter of broken twigs, rubbery from years of rain and rot. She backtracked to a spot opposite Morgan, but still saw no evidence of a bolthole.

"Get down," he instructed. "And crawl into the thicket."

Hauling in a deep breath, Rain set the tub aside, squatted, and peered into the maze of shoulder-high evergreens. She still saw nothing but, lowering her head, did as Morgan said.

The mat of dead leaves and needles was cold and damp against her hands and knees, and each small branch she pushed against released the scent of green growth. In a moment she was through the screen of saplings and in a cleared area—a space Morgan had created by sawing off saplings level with the ground and weaving them to create a rough screen straight ahead.

"Go around the screen to the left," he called.

She did and found the hole—more of a crevice that offered only inches to spare as she squeezed through. Closing her eyes for a moment, she fought off a tight feeling in her chest and a few moments of dry-mouthed claustrophobic panic. By inches, she extended her arms to the sides and above, then opened her eyes to see a space larger than the bathroom in her apartment. Daylight pierced the ceiling in five places as if someone had stabbed the rock with a sword. The faint light revealed walls smoother than she'd anticipated and a floor free of dust and debris.

Morgan slipped through the opening, angling a plastic tub in front of him. "How do you like it?"

"It's a palace. All it needs is running water, electricity, a sofa, and a few throw pillows."

He snorted and set the tub against the far wall.

Rain laughed and patted his arm. "I've never been in a bolthole before, but I bet this is a cut above most."

Morgan snorted again. "Get your tub."

"Yes, sir." Rain gave him a mock salute and obeyed.

When she returned, he'd fired up a camp lantern. The light revealed a number of climbing pitons driven into cracks in the rock at about head height. Bungee cords dangled from most of them. He hung the lantern from one. "Stow your gear."

Rain opened her tub and found a sleeping bag, several cans of spaghetti, several more of orange slices, a flashlight, a folding

67

knife complete with can opener, candles, and several packets of matches. Morgan's tub contained rope, tin plates, a tiny stove, jars of instant coffee and creamer, wet wipes, plastic bags, a poncho, boots and spare clothing in her size, a bucket, and several nylon mesh sacks.

"How long do you think I'll have to stay in here?"

Morgan shrugged. "Can't say."

He packed the canned goods and coffee into a bag and hung it. "Next trip you'll bring the weapons."

So Morgan saw her doing more than simply hiding from danger. He saw her using the bolthole as a fort.

But who was the enemy? When would the attack come? And would she recognize him? Or her? Or them?

"After that, prep the second bolthole." Morgan hung the last bag and headed for daylight. "I'll show you on the way down."

The second hole—slightly below the house, beyond a jumble of large rocks, across a slope littered with slabs of stone, and through a thicket of blackberry canes—was darker and smaller. The opening was low and narrow and the interior was more of a wide crack in a pile of fallen rock than a cave. It had a rough and tilted floor Rain couldn't imagine trying to sleep on, but it offered shelter from the weather and provided space to store supplies.

Morgan gave a few curt orders about camouflaging the opening, driving in pitons, and stowing weapons for easy access. Then he left her to finish. "If I haven't seen you by dinner time, I'll blow on that conch shell we used to call you in with when you were a kid."

When she returned to the farmhouse hours later, she showered and climbed to the room from which Meadow had launched her journeys. She felt close to her grandmother here, felt almost as if Meadow's spirit swung by occasionally and plumped the pillow on the bed or straightened the stack of letters on the table. In fact, this afternoon she felt as if she'd missed her grandmother by a matter of seconds.

As she had several times before, Rain shuffled through the fresh letters, half hoping to feel something, half fearing a tingle or jolt, a burst of cold or heat. She'd asked Morgan exactly what the pull was Meadow felt when she connected with someone, but he didn't know. He remembered her saying only that she knew it when she felt it.

When Rain came downstairs, she found Morgan stirring chunks of chicken, onion, peppers, garlic, carrots, and zucchini in a frying pan. She was happy to see that. An interest in food might mean a renewed interest in living.

Her grandmother had been a good cook, but without many flights of fancy. Rain always felt she prepared meals not because she enjoyed creating, but because that's what women of her generation did. Morgan, on the other hand, never cracked a cookbook. He worked with whatever was available, and without a culinary net. He'd had resounding successes and spectacular failures, but what he'd tossed in the skillet today didn't appear to be shaping up as another for the failure category.

"I can go Asian or Italian," he said. "Depending on whether you choose rice or noodles."

"After lugging those tubs and whacking down brush, I could eat both." Rain opened the pantry door and peered at the boxes and sacks inside. She knew brown rice and whole wheat pasta were healthier choices, but they didn't deliver the comfort-food taste cultivated in childhood, so she reached for a package of old-fashioned egg noodles and plunked it on the counter beside the stove.

"Kinda the way I was thinking. Red sauce or white?"

"White. With extra parmesan. And don't skimp on the butter."

"Never. I'll balance it out with spinach and a few cherry tomatoes at the end."

Rain filled a large pot with water and set it on a burner, then lined up the ingredients he'd need and set the table. After phrasing and rephrasing the question in her mind, she launched it. "Before the new occupant gets here, should we pack away everything in Meadow's room upstairs?"

Morgan didn't glance her way. "You feel we should?"

"No. If I have a choice, I'd like it to stay as it is. I . . . well, sometimes I feel like she comes there now and then."

"I feel the same." Morgan's voice tightened. "I've smelled the lemon soap she liked. And I swear I caught a glimpse of her at the top of the stairs two days ago."

Rain felt a surge of relief. She wasn't crazy.

Or, at least, she was no crazier than her grandfather.

"Won't the next occupant want to use the room?"

"He might want to, but the shape he's in he'd have to sprout some powerful wings to get up there." Morgan sliced a stick of butter in half and put one part in a saucepan to melt. "But he'll make a good watchdog."

Although Rain teased for more information, that was all he said.

CHAPTER 10

April
Pierce

Knowing Marlin lived to pick apart anything he presented—from a theory about the crimes to suggestions about catering companies for task force meetings—Pierce did plenty of homework before he laid out his thoughts about where and how the killer spotted his victims.

It had been on the flight from Sacramento that the distant mental bell he'd heard in Medford rang again. Trying reverse psychology on his subconscious, Pierce pretended he didn't hear it and had no interest in going over his notes. He'd even gone so far as to admire the photographs of three gap-toothed grandchildren displayed on the bright blue sweatshirt worn by the woman beside him.

The bell had seen right through that ploy.

It went silent.

Pierce had laughed at the idea of fooling himself, assured the woman his laughter wasn't directed at her or her son's offspring, and summoned a flight attendant. A glass of wine soothed his traveling companion and a double gin and tonic lulled him to a numb-brained state where he was able to smile and nod through what seemed like an endless array of photos stored on her phone, each accompanied by a lengthy story.

Giving himself a mental kick for stepping in conversational quicksand, Pierce had ordered another drink. As he sipped, still nodding and smiling, he wondered whether she realized how tiresome her meandering tales were to a man who—as he'd told her when she asked—was without a wife or children.

It had taken him about ten seconds to conclude she didn't. The kids were the center of her universe. To Pierce it seemed like an extremely small universe, but it was hers. And obviously she was happy with it and its inhabitants. Perhaps far happier than he was.

Considering grandchildren led him to wonder if he'd ever have children. Ariel had made it clear she didn't have the least interest in motherhood. And his parents had provided some of the worst bad parenting examples on record.

No, not merely bad. Atrocious. Abominable. Disastrous.

The mental bell had rung, punctuating the last item on the list.

It had rung louder.

But only once.

Pierce found himself slapping his tray table in place and rising to pull his laptop from the compartment above his seat. Then he'd thought better of going through his notes, apologized to the woman beside him, said he had a cramp in his leg, and paced the aisle pretending to work it out.

When his memory was ready to deliver the thought that rang the bell, it would. Until then, he'd court it with disinterest.

And he had.

For three long days.

Until TV news reports on flooding in Texas rang the bell once more.

72

This time he went though his notes. Then he spent hours at the computer, combing the months before each victim disappeared, searching for natural disasters, house fires, and even car accidents. Then, saying only that he'd be off for a few days, he flew to Reno and Boise. Again, he talked with neighbors. Or, rather, he let them talk to him about the abduction of women they'd been acquainted with, and about other traumatic events in their lives.

For the first time ever, he was grateful to his father. If nothing else, by telling him to shut up so often, the old man had made him a good listener.

Eventually, he'd struck a vein of what he hoped would turn out to be gold.

Unfortunately, he didn't have time to mine it.

Several months earlier he'd agreed to fly to San Francisco for two weeks of meetings, dinners, golf, tennis, and small talk. He thought of himself as little more than a figurehead for the corporate fleet, sailing only until his mother died or requested a buy-out that would free him to sell off businesses or turn them over to the employees who made them run. But Mal, the corporate guru, was convinced stockholders and managers looked to him for approval and assurance. Since Mal hadn't been wrong before, Pierce hadn't argued for more than a few minutes. He'd booked a hotel to spare himself a stay at the family mansion, bought a plane ticket and a few new shirts and ties, got a haircut, and packed sports gear and suits.

With only a few hours to spare, he took a copy of what he had to the office and flew it by Marlin.

As Pierce anticipated, Marlin attempted to shoot it down before it cleared the runway.

"We ruled out insurance agents." Marlin limped back and forth in front of the map, chopping the palm of his left hand with the side of the right as if tenderizing a steak. "We ruled them out the first week the task force was up and running. First week."

With an expression he'd practiced in front of a mirror, Pierce played dazed and confused. "Oh. Right. I guess we did."

"No guessing about it. We did." Marlin switched hands and hacked at the other palm, his weakened left hand sliding more than chopping. "There was no common thread. No thread."

With a mock wince of embarrassment followed by a hunch of his shoulders, Pierce shuffled the papers he'd laid out on the conference table. "I'm sorry I bothered you. It's just that I didn't find anything in the files and I couldn't remember whether we— Well, it's probably nothing. Never mind."

Marlin's hands dropped to his sides. He nibbled at the bait. "Never mind what? What?"

"It's nothing." Tamping down his frustration with the slow process of steering Marlin toward his goal, and reminding himself his mental leap might have overshot the evidence, Pierce carried on with what seemed to be blatant manipulation. "A waste of your time."

"Then stop wasting it and get to the point."

Pierce focused on the table and spoke in a near whisper. "Um, when we ruled out insurance agents, did we rule out adjusters too?"

"We ruled out entire companies." Marlin's tone was patronizing, his delivery as measured as if he spoke to someone from a foreign land or distant planet. "Only two of the victims used the same company, and they lived 500 miles apart. There was no connection between their agents or other employees. No connection."

Pierce shuffled papers again, giving Marlin time to dismount from the high horse he was so fond of riding. "Okay. I wondered because sometimes adjusters are independent, so they might not be listed with regular employees of a company."

He closed the file folder. "But I guess if you're satisfied, there's no point in—"

"Independent?"

"Right." Pierce stuffed the file folder in the canvas messenger satchel he favored over a briefcase.

Marlin cleared his throat twice and coughed once as if finding it difficult to swallow his pride. "What does that mean exactly? What?"

"They might work for several companies in different states. They often work catastrophes. Disasters." Pierce flipped the flap, closing the satchel. "But, like you said, there's no point in—"

"Hold on." Marlin gripped his arm with his strong hand. "Don't get your shorts in a bunch. Tell me. Tell me what you came to tell me."

Pasting a resigned outward expression over an inward smile, Pierce pulled the folder from the satchel and emptied the contents on the conference table once again. Then he started at the beginning, knowing Marlin often preached that skipping steps might mean skipping over vital information. He explained about wanting to see the territory to broaden his understanding of what was displayed on the map. He explained his snap decision to go to Medford because it was close and likely to be warmer and drier than Portland.

Sparks of impatience flashed in Marlin's eyes and his jaw clenched, but he took his chair at the head of the table. Then, although he tapped the point of a pen against a yellow pad and glanced at the clock, he said nothing.

Pierce told him about visiting the house where Tanya Harter had lived and meeting Bethany Lemmert. "She moved to the neighborhood after Tanya was taken. She'd been living in a cabin in the mountains, but a landslide destroyed it."

Sparks of impatience gave way to flashes of interest in Marlin's eyes. "A landslide?"

"Right. She lost everything," Pierce went on. "But she had extra insurance. And she got a decent settlement."

Marlin's pen stopped tapping. In small letters, he printed "insurance adjuster" on the yellow pad.

Pierce wasn't dismayed by the size of the print. He told Marlin about going on to Redding and meeting a woman who knew a man who lived a block away from the house where Mona Bernstein had lived, a man who had lost his auto repair shop in a wind-whipped blaze that claimed ten homes and three other businesses. The insurance settlement had been enough to convince him to take his wife's advice and retire.

Marlin drew a line under the words he'd printed and sat up straighter. Pierce allowed himself a sliver of a smile as he explained that he'd found no insurance links in Sacramento, but met a couple in Reno who had been flooded out. "They moved to an apartment in the same complex as Melissa Foster."

Marlin drew another line. "And they got a settlement? Got money?"

"Not much. They fought and argued with the guy who came around, but he made it clear their policy didn't cover the event."

"The guy who came around. Did—?"

"No. She couldn't remember his name."

"And the others? Did any of them get a name? A name?"

"Bethany Lemmert tossed out all the papers once she got her check. She thought the adjuster's name might have been Stan. Or maybe Steve. Or Stewart. She said he was handsome and helpful and kind. She felt he was on her side."

The flash of interest in Marlin's eyes brightened. They'd speculated that the Peddler had charm. "Think she dodged a bullet?"

"Maybe. She's his type. But I doubt he'd target a client. Too obvious."

Marlin aimed a finger and opened his mouth, then nodded. "Possible. What else?"

"The guy who lost his auto repair business bought a camper trailer," Pierce said. "He's somewhere on the road seeing parks and monuments and places that sell rubber tomahawks and stale candy. He doesn't have a cellphone. Doesn't want to be in touch."

Marlin slammed the flat of his right hand on the table and cursed under his breath.

"I have his full name and address. Maybe Claire can find him. Or find his insurance records."

Marlin grunted. "What else you got? What else?"

Pierce shoved a paper in front of him. "A list of events around cities where women were abducted or near the dump sites—fires, drought, storms."

"Events an independent insurance adjuster might have worked. *Might* have."

"That's my guess. But I'm not the expert in the room."

Marlin accepted the compliment with a lazy flip of his left hand.

"Anyway, I've got business commitments in San Francisco for the next two weeks." Pierce tapped the papers until the edges were aligned and stuffed them in the folder. "I can leave this in my office if you have any interest."

"Might as well." Marlin yawned, not bothering to cover his mouth. "No point in lugging it down there. You'll be too busy with fancy dinners and money meetings."

Regrettably.

"Can't promise I'll get to it." Marlin yawned again, this time adding a stretch. "Got a lot of tips to check on. Lot of tips."

Promises of anonymity and rewards brought a steady stream of calls to a dedicated line. But not, Pierce knew, enough calls to occupy Marlin for the two weeks he'd be away. "Understood."

He dropped the file on his desk, suspecting Marlin would paw through it before the elevator doors closed.

CHAPTER 11

April
Rain

Warped by heat and moisture, the knotty pine doors on the cabinets above the stove in the farmhouse kitchen fought Rain's efforts to open them. She tugged harder, teetering on an ancient metal chair that converted to a step stool. Its red paint was faded and flaking, and one leg was bent. Rain had seen new chairs like it advertised as retro. This one, she thought, was simply old. But still functional. *If* she was careful to keep her weight toward the rear.

"Probably nothing up there," Morgan said. "Meadow kept what she needed on the low shelves."

"Maybe there's something up here she didn't need often."

Or ever.

When Morgan had instructed her to go through the farmhouse and take whatever she wanted for her own place, Rain thought the task wouldn't take more than a few minutes. Although the cabin had many drawers and shelves and cabinets, the actual living space was small. There wasn't room for much after she brought the furniture from her apartment.

This morning, as she'd admired the drawers Morgan had built into the steps leading to the sleeping loft, she asked whether his vision of her future had influenced the design. "Did you see me living alone for . . . a long time?"

He hadn't answered.

She hadn't expected him to.

But she'd found herself measuring spaces with her eyes and hands, wondering if two people could share the compact kitchen, work area, and living room. And share without rubbing each other's nerves raw. Was there enough room in the bathroom cabinets for the supplies a man needed to shave and shower and whatever else men did to prepare for bed or to meet the day?

In her college days she'd had a number of relationships, but none had been of the long-term live-in variety. She'd never shared a bathroom or bedroom. In fact, she'd never spent the entire night with a man, never fallen asleep and awakened beside him with light streaming through her windows. Or his.

Had Morgan sensed that?

When he herded her to the farmhouse to sort through the kitchen, she'd put those questions aside.

She didn't *need* anything from Meadow's kitchen, but there were a few items she wanted—a sugar bowl shaped like a stubby lighthouse, and a serving platter with a pattern of morning glories around the edge. Never mind that she didn't take sugar in her coffee and couldn't imagine cooking anything substantial enough to need a platter. The bowl and platter reminded her of holiday feasts with neighbors, and coffee and conversations that came when the table was cleared and the dishes washed.

Those memories brought to mind salt and pepper shakers shaped like tiny log cabins. Hunting for them, she found a butter dish painted with butterflies. She also found dust and a few greasy fingerprints. Morgan insisted he'd wipe up later, but she tossed a few rags in a bowl of soapy water and got to work.

"No point in cleaning that high cabinet anyway," Morgan said.

"You know I can't do the rest and leave this one."

Her grandfather beamed. "You might put a chore off for seed, but you never walked away and left a job half done. Even when you were no bigger than a minute."

With a grating squeal of wood and hinges, the doors gave, releasing the scents of dust and stale coffee and old paper.

"See anything?"

"No."

Rain balanced on the seat of the chair, stood on tiptoe and slid her hand across the bottom of the cabinet, expecting to feel nothing more than grit or—hopefully not—mouse droppings. But her fingers touched metal. A smooth surface, a sharp corner, and another surface. "There's a box of some kind. I've got to stand on the counter to get it."

Morgan moved in to steady her. Frail as he'd become, she doubted he could break her fall without also breaking several bones. But she didn't argue. Stretching, she wiggled the dusty gray box to the edge of the cabinet, grabbed it, executed a cautious turn, and handed it to him.

"Never saw this before." He set it on the table and wiped it with a paper napkin.

Rain clambered from her perch. "Maybe it was there before you moved in."

"Possible." Morgan scratched his head. "The place belonged to my great uncle. Never married, though my mother claimed there were plenty who would have had him and been happy with the bargain. Deeded the property to me on condition I work the farm and take care of him."

He hooked a chair with his foot and sat, gazing out the window to the orchard. "Old guy died the day after I married Meadow. While we were on our honeymoon."

81

"How sad. And troubling, to have a relative die at a time when you're starting a new phase of your life."

Morgan shrugged. "He was ready to go. Told me before the wedding I'd learned all he had to teach me. And Meadow didn't see it as a bad omen. She liked him. And he thought she hung the moon."

He pointed to the box with a wavering finger. "Doubt that's his, but let's find out. Open it."

Rain pried at the top. It gave with a pop and a scatter of rust. The inside was packed with papers, some stiff card stock, some flimsy, most frayed at the edges. Tipping the box, she shook the contents onto the table. Morgan reached for a folded paper and examined it.

"Recipe. For cornbread."

Rain unfolded what turned out to be a three-page letter written on onion skin paper. In places it was pale blue, but much was now a dirty white. Spiky handwriting swooped across the pages, letters sliding for the margins. "This one explains how to make cinnamon bread."

"Meadow made the best cinnamon bread I ever tasted." Morgan licked his lips. "I remember her standing right where you are, kneading the dough, flour covering her arms to the elbows."

Rain followed the sloping lines to the second and then the third page, noting the signature. "Did the bread have raisins and walnuts in it?"

"Sometimes apples and pecans. Once or twice she put in dates." Morgan's hands moved as if slicing and buttering bread.

"Well, if this is the recipe, she got it from her grandmother." Rain set the pages aside and picked up a card with another set of precise and detailed instructions. A page from a lined tablet was filled with more directions. "Did she make peach butter? Or applesauce?"

"Every fall." Morgan frowned. "Are those all recipes?"

"Looks like."

"I used to brag that she had a magic touch and could cook anything she set her mind to. And all the time . . ."

He shook his head, a frown creasing his forehead. "She got a lot of letters from her grandmother. Fat ones. I thought it was because they were so close, or because she was offering advice about using the gift. I used to say we never had a secret between us." His voice dropped to a whisper. "But we did."

"It wasn't a harmful secret."

In five steps Rain rounded the table, slid a chair beside his, and hugged him. "And it wasn't like she lied. Except by omission."

Morgan flipped the cornbread recipe aside and picked up three more. "Beef stew. Banana bread. Chicken and dumplings. All these years I thought what she put on the table came from her imagination."

"And maybe it did." Rain took the recipes and tossed them toward the box. "Maybe she added new spices or ingredients. Maybe she made them her own as time went on."

"But why wouldn't she tell me?" Morgan hunched in the chair as if he'd taken a series of bone-crushing blows. "What did it matter that it wasn't all her own?"

"Maybe it didn't after the first year or so. But people had different attitudes toward marriage and the roles of men and women when you were young. She may have felt insecure. She may have believed—even just a little—that if she wasn't a good cook, she wouldn't be a good wife."

Rain hugged him tighter.

"I would have loved her if she couldn't boil water without burning it," he muttered.

"I know. And I believe she was certain of that." Rain stood and shuffled the recipes into a pile and wedged them in the box.

"I don't think she hid these because she doubted you. Maybe she did it because she was embarrassed. Or because she didn't want you to know how hard she was trying to be everything she thought she should be."

She shoved the last letter inside and closed the box. "I know that sounds silly. Meadow was strong and capable, but she was also very young when you married. And, of course, she was a woman. Women get a lot of messages—from their friends and relatives, from TV and movies and books and magazines—about what it means to be female and how they should relate to men."

"Mostly a lot of baloney."

"It is." Rain set the box next to the platter and sugar bowl. Later she'd go through the recipes. Maybe she'd attempt to make cinnamon bread and do it the old way, kneading the dough with her hands instead of using a bread machine to get it started. "But until we get old enough to understand that, the messages all seem true and vital and . . . we make mistakes."

While Morgan mulled that, she climbed on the counter again and wiped down the high cabinet, trying to keep her mind off the mistakes she'd made with men. Many sprang from a need to fill the hole ripped in her soul when her mother abandoned her. The sexual encounters had been satisfying in the way cool water slakes your thirst, but not in the way hot chocolate warms your fingers and tongue and belly and awakens your senses. She'd plunged in too fast and too far, hadn't listened, hadn't heard, hadn't known enough. Until she knew too much.

Nothing injured except my heart.

And my pride.

"Tell me about the long sight," she said to pry him from dwelling on what he seemed to view almost as a betrayal. "When I was a kid I never asked you about it except to beg you to use it to see if I'd get an A or a date or something stupid. And when I got older it seemed you didn't want to talk about it. You'd change the subject or ignore my questions."

She sat beside him again and folded his blue-veined hands in hers. When had his skin become so thin, so translucent? "Is it like Meadow's gift? Do you have to have intention to use it? Did you have to work to develop it, or did you always have it?"

She kissed his cheek, the skin sunken, his whiskers prickling her lips. "I know I'm pestering, but there are so many things I never asked Meadow. And now she's gone and you say you're going soon, so . . ."

"Pour me a glass of cider and bring it out to the porch. Should be a bit of sunshine there."

He stood, rubbed the small of his back with both fists, and headed for the door, his legs straight, his torso canted forward. Rain poured cider for both of them and joined him. He'd appropriated the chaise—something she'd never known him to do—and lay with his chin tipped toward the sun.

"Used to feel that if I talked about it, then I might lose it."

"Ah."

Rain set his cider on a low table beside him and eased into a rocker that was ancient when she first came to live here. Great globs of glue, yellow and shiny, held the rungs in place. A spiral of wire locked a splintered leg together. Despite that, the chair was comfortable, still rocked, and was so low she didn't worry about injuries if it gave up the ghost while she was aboard.

"Thought it might shut down if I used it too often, or tried too hard." He sipped at his cider. "I probably could have done more for others, the way Meadow did. Probably should have."

Rain patted his arm.

"But the thing is, the way it works for me, I can't tell you when the earth will shake or slide, or the ocean will rise up, or a volcano will blow. Not unless I have an emotional bond—a strong one—to someone in the way."

"Maybe you need their energy. Like Meadow did."

"Likely that's so." He drained the cider, tipped his chin to the sun again and closed his eyes. "Think I'll sleep for a bit. You go on up with your kitchen gear and check on the cable they ran in yesterday."

"Cable?"

"For your e-mail and phone. Can't run a business if your clients can't get in touch."

Until that moment, Rain hadn't considered the issue of communication. Cellphone reception was iffy up here. She often got a signal on the east side of the farmhouse, but she hadn't attempted to connect from the cabin. She also hadn't thought about what it would cost to remedy that problem. A lot. A whole lot. Morgan would have had them run cable all the way from the state highway.

He and Meadow had never seen the need for cable. Their TV was ancient, purchased at a yard sale when Rain was a child. Twisted wire hangers, on a good day, brought in the signals from two TV stations. When she was a teenager, Rain had chafed against the limitations and complained about the shows she "needed" to watch because all her friends did. But her grandparents held firm, saying there was a world of difference between wanting and needing, saying one day she'd realized how little she'd missed. Their entertainment came in the form of sunsets, the flight of birds, rabbits on the lawn, conversations, and shelves laden with books.

She wondered if their response had been a way of avoiding the subject of money. If they'd said they couldn't afford a new TV and cable service, she would have felt selfish and guilty for pestering.

But if money was an issue then, why did it seem to be no problem now? The cabin, compact as it was, had too many unique touches to be cheap. And then there was the all terrain vehicle.

"Ran cable in here, too. Figured the watchdog would need it for his computer and what all." Morgan tugged at her long hair. "Cable will bring you TV, too. So you don't miss those mystery shows."

Rain ducked her head. She was addicted to any variation on the theme of Sherlock Holmes. And, because she frequently edited mysteries, she told herself watching shows heavy on procedure and analysis came under the heading of research. Beyond that, most mysteries ended with justice—in some form—being done, and with cases being solved, closure being achieved. In the real world that wasn't always the case. She was reminded of that with each letter addressed to Meadow.

"Your grandmother sometimes read romance novels. And I'm fond of a good western or a yarn set in outer space. We all have our guilty pleasures." Morgan hooked his thumb toward the cabin. "Now you run along and see that everything's hooked up and working so you can enjoy yours when you want to."

CHAPTER 12

May
Pierce

His cellphone rang as Pierce stepped out of the shower on the final Friday of what he thought of as indentured servitude.

Claire. Breathless. Sobbing. Her voice hollow. "Marlin's dead. Murdered."

"When?" Pierce grabbed a towel. "Where? How?"

"Last night. At the office building. I found him in the stairwell. I . . . I think he was strangled."

"I'm on the way."

Claire sucked in a breath. "Thank you. I called it in. I'll stay with him until . . ."

Her voice broke.

"I'll be there as soon as I can." Pierce disconnected, imagining her in the institutional-gray stairwell, standing guard over Marlin's body, making sure the scene wasn't disturbed.

And crying.

That was the part he had difficulty imagining, even though he'd heard her sobs. Had he come to see her more as a professional than a person? Had he assumed—because of what she'd come through, because she doubled up on physical therapy exercises, took martial arts training, and hit the gun range every week—that she was too tough for tears? Or, had he assumed she wouldn't grieve for Marlin because of the way he'd treated her?

As he dressed, he called Mal, secured a corporate jet, and arranged with the concierge to have his possessions packed up and shipped to Portland. In the cab, he called the members of the task force, told them what he knew, and said he'd provide more information later.

When he was buckled in, he called his mother. To his relief, her secretary told him she was playing tennis. He left a message apologizing and canceling plans to join her for dinner. He doubted she'd been looking forward to the obligatory meal any more than he had. Since he arrived, he'd seen her only once, at a welcoming cocktail party. She'd seemed much as always—too brittle, too bright. She'd delivered an air kiss and brief comments about how well he appeared and how she hoped they'd have time to catch up. Then she'd waved at someone across the room and left in a cloud of flowery perfume.

A tanned man with the hungry but hesitant manner of a feral dog followed in her wake. That she hadn't introduced him told Pierce the man wouldn't be in her wake much longer. A month ago, according to Mal, she'd been planning a romantic round-the-world sailing trip—just the two of them. Pierce had laughed and said they'd be back in less than a day.

Sailing involved work, and Pierce often thought Diane Donovan Jennings had labored only twice in her life—the night she conceived and the day she gave birth.

Closing his mind to both of those images, he concentrated on two things—willing the jet to go faster, and making a list of the questions exploding in his brain.

Before the cab came to a stop, Pierce threw a few bills at the driver and opened the door. He spotted Claire on the sidewalk in front of the office building, staring up at the sixth-floor windows. Her short springy hair was silvered with mist, her pale green sweater soaked. Without wondering if it was right, he gathered her in his arms.

"I always take the stairs," she blurted. "Trying to make my leg stronger. If I hadn't, who knows how long he might have been there."

Her voice cracked and she sobbed against the shoulder of the pin-striped suit jacket Pierce had yanked on over a T-shirt and jeans. He held her closer, thinking of a dozen platitudes and murmuring none.

When she pulled away, he dug a crumpled cocktail napkin from his pocket and blotted her eyes. "You're freezing." He removed his jacket and wrapped her in it. "Let's go inside."

"We can't go up to—"

"I know. But we can wait in the lobby."

She hesitated, glancing at the cluster of police vehicles. Her gaze lingered on a van Pierce suspected might be waiting to transport Marlin to an autopsy table.

"Marlin would say you don't have enough sense to get in out of the rain." Pierce turned her toward the door. "And I don't have enough sense to insist. Or maybe he'd say I'm not man enough."

Claire whimpered and let Pierce steer her through glass doors to a small lobby apparently designed to discourage lingering. The lone sofa needed little more than a few spikes to qualify as a medieval torture device, and if the chairs had been crafted to support bodies, they certainly weren't human bodies. The place smelled of old plastic and even older magazines. A trail of damp footprints led to the elevators where a young police officer frowned and pushed off from the wall he'd been leaning against.

"At least it's warm." Pierce guided her toward the sofa, then had a better idea and detoured to the ground-floor office of a financial advisor. He got her settled in one of several leather club chairs selected, he assumed, to convey a sense of competence and money to be made. The advisor was out, but a young secretary—either sympathetic or bored or perhaps both—listened to Pierce's explanation, gasped, and hurried to get coffee, a stack of paper towels, and a collection of men's socks she kept on hand for the days the advisor showed up wearing ones that didn't match. When Pierce slipped a large bill into her hand and suggested she round up a few sandwiches and keep the change, she lingered only long enough to lock the inner door and ask if he'd like soup as well.

Claire dried her hair, pulled off her low-cut boots and sopping gray socks, and slipped on a pair of navy blue ones with bright red and yellow arrows. "Marlin would have hated these."

"Too much color," Pierce agreed. "Marlin was all about gray and black."

"And white shirts. I never saw him in anything else. Not even beige. Or gray." Claire sniffled into a paper towel. "Thanks for coming so fast. I know your business—"

"My business needs me like the Dead Sea needs more salt." Pierce pressed the mug of coffee into her hands. "Drink this down and tell me everything."

Claire drank, stopping only once to breathe, and set the cup on a glass coffee table layered with slick brochures. "He was on the landing for the fifth floor. I knew he was dead as soon as I saw him. His head was twisted around."

She crossed her arms at the wrists and raised her hands to her throat, her gaze locked on Pierce. "There were marks on his neck like he'd been choked."

"Like the Peddler's victims?"

91

"Yes. At least that's how it appeared." She leaned closer. "I should have called it in right then. But I had to see—"

She glanced around and lowered her voice. "I went to the fourth floor and took the elevator up and checked the office. It was torn apart. File cabinets pried open, files dumped, computers smashed, the map ripped to pieces."

Pierce grunted. What she'd seen as ruin, he saw as confirmation. They'd tugged on a strand of the Peddler's web. And, like a spider, he'd come for them.

"What was Marlin working on while I was gone?"

"He wouldn't say. You know how he was, how he kept things to himself so he felt superior. I know he went to Spokane because I booked his flight and arranged for a rental car. But he didn't say a word about why."

Spokane meant Collette Chambers, an interior decorator claimed by the Peddler a few months before. Marlin, it seemed, had been following the trail Pierce had pointed him toward. But how far down that trail had he gone? "Did he drop any hints?"

"You mean did he say anything to make me ask what he was doing so he could tell me it was none of my business?" Claire shook her head. "No. And, now that you mention it, that seems odd. He loved to lord it over me."

"And me."

She snatched up a wad of paper towels and blew her nose. "I liked him. In spite of the way he was, I liked him. I was planning to invite him over for a cookout when the weather got better."

Pierce tried to imagine Marlin standing beside a smoking grill, holding a bottle of beer and wearing shorts and a T-shirt. The elements in the picture bent and split and sliced across each other until his mental image resembled a work by Picasso.

Claire wiped her eyes. "He probably wouldn't have come. He probably would have put on that expression of disbelief and shook his head."

"I know the expression well. I saw it on his face right before I left for San Francisco."

The secretary trotted in with two paper sacks, set them on the coffee table, thrust her chin toward the door, and raised her eyebrows.

Pierce checked his watch. "I hate to interfere with your lunch plans, but we'd like to stay here for a bit. Could you lock up anything private or important and let us have this space?"

When she hesitated, he slipped another large bill from his wallet. "Your boss knows who I am. I'll explain the situation and make it clear you took all the necessary precautions."

In ten seconds she'd shut down her computer and was out the door.

"I bet she's headed for a shoe sale," Claire said. "She has that look."

"And here she works for a financial advisor." Pierce chuckled. "She'll never get rich blowing her extra cash on shoes."

"Unless she attracts a wealthy foot fetishist."

Pierce rolled his eyes, but was pleased to see Claire's sense of humor returning. He cocked his head toward the upper floors. "How long do you think it will be before we're allowed in the office?"

"Hours." Claire shrugged. "Days. Unless they want us to sort through the wreckage and figure out what's missing."

"Is there any way we can make that happen sooner rather than later?"

She stared at him with a puzzled frown.

"Anyone you know who might suggest that, if this is connected to the Peddler, it would be an act of idiocy to waste time?"

Her eyes sparkled and a slow grin lifted the corners of her mouth. "You have a devious mind."

She dug her cellphone from her purse and tapped the screen a few times, her fingernails—today sparkling silver—flashing. In a few moments she was deep in conversation with one of the state patrol officers who sat on the task force.

Pierce unpacked the paper sacks and arranged sandwiches, bags of chips, and cardboard containers of soup on the coffee table. Eating didn't feel like the right thing to do with Marlin dead upstairs, but he'd had nothing except coffee for breakfast, and passing on lunch wouldn't change the situation.

In a calm voice and with precise sentences, Claire described the bruises on Marlin's neck, and explained the office had been trashed and she'd been ordered to remain downstairs. "Maybe I'm way off base, but if the Peddler did this, we need to know if he took anything, especially anything connected to recent research."

Pierce heard an indistinct rumble of words and then she disconnected. "I think he at least nibbled on the bait. But I don't know how hard he'll push." She turned the phone in her fingers. "I could call—"

"No. At least not yet. Don't want to make it too obvious we're trying to pull strings." Pierce opened a container, releasing the soothing aroma of cream of mushroom soup. "Try a little of this."

"I'm not—"

"You are." Pierce held out a plastic soup spoon. "You're hungry. And you're human. You can't bring Marlin to life by depriving yourself. And you know he'd say you're too stupid to live if you pass up a free lunch."

"You're right." Claire blinked, sniffled, and accepted the spoon and the carton of soup. "But it seems so . . . wrong."

"I know. I had the same argument with myself while you were on the phone." Pierce pulled the wrapper from a sandwich—egg salad with spinach on whole wheat—and took a huge bite.

"It appears you lost that argument." Claire sipped soup. "Or won."

Pierce swallowed. "I fought myself to a draw. Now fuel up. When we get into the office and start digging around, you won't stop until you drop."

"Like you will?" Claire snatched the other half of his sandwich. "We're close. Marlin got to him somehow. We have to figure out how."

"I have an idea about that."

She paused, about to take a bite. "Tell me."

"I will. But not until you finish your soup and sandwich."

CHAPTER 13

June
Rain

Rain set her coffee aside and devoted her full attention to the lengthy on-line article about the murder of Marlin Simmons. Essentially, it was a recap of what she'd read in previous stories, but with more information about the regional task force. It also included photographs and brief bios of the women taken by the serial killer known as the Peddler. Twelve of them. One from across the river in Portland.

So close.

Rain shivered and slid her chair into the sunlight pouring through the east windows of her cabin. A quote from Pierce Jennings, the man who put together the task force after his wife was taken, caught her eye. "Before he died, Marlin Simmons discovered something that brought him close to identifying the man we call the Peddler. We believe that drove the killer to take an enormous risk, to murder Marlin Simmons, and remove materials crucial to our investigation. We hope to reconstruct our files and follow the thought process that set Marlin Simmons on a collision course with death. In the meantime, if anyone saw anything suspicious in or around the office building where Marlin Simmons was killed, or if anyone reading this has an idea about who the Peddler might be, call our tip line. We're offering substantial rewards for information. Every call will be taken seriously."

Resting her fingers on the computer screen along the margins of a photograph of Pierce Jennings, Rain stared into his eyes. He looked serious, as if he considered everything with intense focus and contemplation. Before his wife was taken, had he laughed and joked and been easy with himself? She stared deeper into his eyes and thought not. The pain she saw ran deep and wide and long. It had been with him for a lifetime.

She lifted her hands. Felt a tiny shock that made her fingers tingle. Like static electricity on a dry winter day. But this was June, it had rained much of the night, and sunlight drew twists of mist from tree trunks and rocks.

Perhaps the damp air was responsible, had somehow drawn electricity from her laptop through her fingertips. Was that possible?

Or perhaps the laptop was the source of the shock. Perhaps she should have it checked.

"Imagination."

That was a more likely explanation. She'd been responding to letters that still came for Meadow, and wondering about the gift and how it would feel to connect with someone who asked for help.

"Definitely imagination."

Rain finished her coffee while reading the remainder of the article. Pierce Jennings had added more to the reward fund. Claire Dawson had been named to replace Marlin Simmons as task force coordinator. Her eyes also brimmed with torment— part physical, part mental. And they held a mix of frustration, anger, and what Rain suspected was a sharp and stitching pain—the kind she felt when she bit down on her lip and tried harder. Claire Dawson, Rain thought, would always try harder.

97

Before she headed to the farmhouse, Rain washed her mug and set it on the drain board. She hadn't always done that in her apartment, but the cabin was so well organized even one dirty cup in the sink felt like a violation.

"You'll get over it," she told herself with a laugh.

And she had no doubt that she would, once she'd been here two months instead of two weeks.

She zipped her fleece and pulled up her hood as she hurried down the track to the farmhouse. The gorge wind was relentless. On a hot day she'd appreciate it, but this morning it sliced at her exposed skin as if trying to peel it off. The one consolation was that it would have felt worse if she'd driven what she referred to as "the big toy on wheels."

When she let herself in, she found Morgan slumped at the table, his head resting on his folded arms, his eyes staring across the landscape of the tabletop. She suspected he didn't see the beehive-shaped pot that held honey, the blue glass pepper and salt shakers, or the bottle of vitamins she'd bought last week. Was he using his long sight? Or was he imagining Meadow nearby, young again, and hunting for a recipe in the box she'd hidden? Did she know they'd discovered her secret? Would she and Morgan talk about it when they were together again?

"You ready for breakfast?"

"Not hungry."

Exactly what he'd said every morning for the past two weeks.

So she did exactly what she'd done since his first denial. She made coffee, warmed up the skillet, and poured him a small glass of orange juice. "It's a pretty day. I thought I'd refill the hummingbird feeders and do some weeding."

Morgan said nothing.

Rain melted butter to fry the French toast she'd set to soak in egg batter last night. "How did you sleep?"

"Didn't."

She doubted that. But Morgan napped so often during the day it was possible he slept little at night. "When I can't sleep, it's usually because my mind won't turn off. I make lists and plans, or remember things I should have done. Then I get mad at myself. And that makes the situation worse."

"Usually does."

Rain forked dripping bread slices into bubbling butter. The scents of vanilla and nutmeg filled the room. Morgan's gaze shifted to the stove and he sniffed and swallowed, betraying the claim that he wasn't hungry. When she set a plate before him, he might eat. But not much. Just enough to make her think that today she might change the course he'd set, the one that would take him to Nightfall Bay before long.

Given his age, his gaunt frame, and his determination, Rain guessed he intended to depart by the end of the month.

She poured the egg mixture remaining in the bowl across the slices of bread in the skillet. "Tell me about the man who's coming to live here."

Morgan said nothing while she washed the bowl and flipped bread with a sizzle to reveal golden brown cooked sides. Then he took a single sip of orange juice, pushed the glass aside, and muttered, "Watchdog."

Rain thought of Motley. "You said that before. Will he have a dog with him?"

Morgan made a rusty and uneven sound that might have been a chuckle. "No dog. He'll keep an eye out and an ear open. He's like that."

"Nosy?"

"Professionally."

She hoped he'd elaborate, but he rested his head on his arms again and closed his eyes. While she pulled plates from a cabinet and took syrup and a bowl of strawberries from the refrigerator, Rain thought about professions requiring varying degrees of nosiness—gossip columnists, corporate headhunters, apartment managers, background checkers, detectives. Was the watchdog a former cop?

The question reminded her of the long article she'd read. If her grandmother was alive, if she knew about the murder of Marlin Simmons and his efforts to get justice for the women taken by the Peddler, would she have been tempted to break with tradition? Would she have traveled to Nightfall Bay to find Marlin Simmons and the women whose murders he'd been working to solve?

The scent of scorching toast interrupted her speculation. She served Morgan and settled at the table with her own plate. "Try a little. I followed a recipe from the box we found, but I didn't make the bread from scratch, so I know it won't be as good as Meadow's."

At the mention of her grandmother's name, Morgan's eyes opened, but when he raised his head and glanced around, he seemed to be lost in a dream. Rain poured a puddle of syrup beside his toast and pressed a fork into his hand. "Try a little. Please. So my feelings won't be hurt."

Morgan blinked, forked off a corner of toast and dipped it in syrup. Then he stared at it, as if wondering what to do next. Rain closed her eyes to contain her tears and drew in a long breath. Was this the day she'd been dreading, the day when mental determination overpowered physical hunger, the day he wouldn't eat at all?

After a moment, Morgan brought the toast to his mouth. He brushed syrup on his lips, but that was all.

Rain closed her eyes to hold in a welling of tears, then turned her attention to her breakfast. To distract herself, she told Morgan about the murder of Marlin Simmons and the cases he'd been investigating. He pushed his plate aside and rested his head on his arms once more, but cocked an ear in her direction. Occasionally his fingers traced the edges of a series of dark knots in the pale pine table.

"When I was cooking the toast, I wondered if Meadow might have wanted to break with her tradition of waiting for letters. I wondered if she might have volunteered to help find this killer."

"Doubt she would have heard about it," Morgan muttered. "TV hasn't been on for years. Probably dead as a doornail. And you know we don't take a paper."

Rain had been a teenager when her grandparents cancelled their subscription. "There's more bad news than good," Meadow had said. "People fighting everywhere. Over everything. And it seems nothing can be done about it."

After that, Rain borrowed papers from a neighbor to complete high school assignments on current events. She didn't mention the subjects of those assignments when dinner conversations turned to school and what she'd learned.

"We know the world is out there and we can't shut ourselves away," Morgan had told her. "We know a war or a drought or a flood halfway around the globe can affect us, and we accept that. We know there are horrors and misery and injustice, but we don't need to start the day reading about them. Not when we can watch deer grazing on the meadow or birds at the feeder."

"But if she had heard about the case," Rain persisted, "do you think she would have at least wondered—?"

"No. She said the only way to keep from wearing herself out too soon was to stick to her rules, her system."

That sounded like Meadow had thought—at least once—about pursuing a mystery on her own. Perhaps that was part of the reason for cancelling the newspaper. Perhaps the longing to try to help had been so strong she'd decided to limit her access to a world growing closer and more terrifying. Or perhaps she'd gone to Nightfall Bay without a letter of request. Perhaps the journey hadn't gone well.

"Don't want to talk." Morgan lurched to his feet and shuffled toward the bedroom. "Tired."

Rain's first impulse was to run after him and say she was sorry. But Morgan was a man who seldom apologized, and seldom had the patience to listen while others did. So she kept still.

Morgan didn't come out of the bedroom for lunch or dinner. He didn't respond to her calls. When she entered the room, he didn't open his eyes or acknowledge her.

The rise and fall of his chest told her he was breathing and the set of his jaw and small wrinkles around his eyes spoke of concentration. He didn't touch the sandwich or soup or oatmeal cookies she left on the nightstand. He drank none of the milk or cider, sipping only water, and only a little of that.

Gulping sobs, Rain scrubbed the kitchen walls and floor, washed and ironed the café curtains over the sink, straightened the pantry, and cleaned the windows. She moved on to the bedroom that had once been hers. She dusted and vacuumed, washed and scrubbed. With a heave, she flipped the queen mattress and made up the bed with fresh sheets. She hoped the man Morgan called a watchdog would sleep in here. She wasn't ready to have anyone else occupy the bedroom where Meadow had died and where Morgan intended to.

By the end of the day, her eyes and nose were raw, her head ached, and her arm muscles throbbed, but she'd attained a level of peace. Morgan had decided the time was right. He was ready to depart. Nothing she did or said would change that. She could only prepare for the arrival of the watchdog. And prepare for the rest of her life.

The next morning, she found a stack of documents on the kitchen table.

Heart pounding, she ran to the bedroom.

Morgan lay on the bed, his cheeks shaved, his hair combed, Meadow's rainbow quilt pulled to his waist.

Was he breathing?

She crossed the room and bent over him.

He opened his eyes. "Fresh water?"

Rain scurried to bring a brimming glass. No ice. Morgan always said water from the well was cool enough. He raised his head, sipped, and lay back. Sometime during the night he'd put on a fresh shirt, a new one, sky blue with white stitching, smelling faintly of fabric sizing.

"Go over the documents," Morgan whispered. "Lawyer said they're easy to understand. Call him tomorrow first thing."

Tomorrow?

Rain stumbled backward, felt for the arm of the rocker, sat so hard her teeth clicked together.

When she walked to the cabin yesterday evening she felt prepared for Morgan's death. But now? Now she saw how far she was from acceptance. She wanted to force food and drink down his throat. She wanted to take him to the closest hospital and have him hooked up to drips and monitors.

As if he read her mind, Morgan shook his head.

Admitting defeat, she sighed.

"Open the window wide," Morgan croaked. "Light fresh candles when dusk comes. Then go on home."

"No." She raised her head and straightened her spine. "I won't let you die alone."

"I won't be alone." He lifted his gaze toward the window. "Meadow is on her way. And the dogs are coming. They'll be with me in the night."

The flesh on the back of Rain's neck tingled. She stood and walked to the window. Peered out. Saw nothing.

"I don't . . . I don't want *you* to leave *me* alone . . . like my mother did."

Morgan patted the edge of the bed and she sat beside him and clutched his hand. "The watchdog will be here soon. Don't know the day or hour—he keeps his own clock. But soon. You'll be alone for just a blink of time."

A blink?

How long was that?

The child inside her insisted the amount of time wasn't the point.

"But I don't know him. I know you. I love you. I'm . . . I'm afraid. I'm afraid I'll get the gift before I'm ready. I'm afraid I won't know *whether* I'm ready. Or *when*. And I'm more afraid I won't receive it, that I'll let you and Meadow down."

"Be a fool if you weren't afraid." He gazed at her a long moment then closed his eyes. "Open that window and leave me for a bit. Clean some if you must, though I guarantee the watchdog won't notice."

Rain kissed his forehead and, feet dragging, opened the window.

"Remember all we did for Meadow up on the hill and do the same for me," Morgan whispered.

"I will."

"Especially the casket. What did I say I wanted you to paint on it?"

"Horses. I've been practicing. They're starting to resemble cows more than hippos."

"Then say they're cows." He chuckled, coughed, cleared his throat. "I'll keep your secret." He chuckled again. "I'll take it to my grave."

Wiping tears, Rain returned to the kitchen to study the documents. Many were old, deeds with edges yellowing, ink and official seals fading. Others were recent. She read through a will he'd made after Meadow died. It left everything to Rain on condition that a man named Bertram Mosier would be allowed to make his home in the farmhouse, rent free, as long as he lived. A note in Morgan's spiky handwriting was clipped to the edge of the will. "Don't lend him money. Don't let him treat you like a maid or a secretary. Don't let him drop matches on the rugs and start fires if he's still smoking a pipe. Don't let him go too far off his diet if he's finally on one. Don't believe more than half of the stories he tells. Don't let him make you as suspicious and distrustful as he is."

Quite a list. Who was this man? What kind of a diet was he on? What kind of stories did he have to tell? How did her grandfather know him?

She rose, intending to ask Morgan, but decided he wouldn't answer. He seemed to enjoy teasing her with random bits of information about the watchdog while withholding anything she asked about. He wanted her to be surprised by Bertram Mosier. But his list indicated he also wanted her to be warned.

She made coffee, toasted and buttered an English muffin, and pored over financial documents. Eventually she got a handle on the convoluted legal language and gleaned that a savings account, stock funds, and certificates of deposit had been placed in a trust for her benefit, "so that she may use her gift."

Saw nothing.

The bottom line on an accounting of the trust was staggering.

If she didn't make outrageous purchases, there was money enough for a lifetime—a long lifetime.

Where had it come from?

Had Morgan used his long sight to play the market?

No, he'd told her he couldn't see the future for mountains or rivers, for non-human things. But what if he'd peered into the future for the person who would benefit from an investment? For her?

Another question she knew he wouldn't answer.

She hoped she would prove herself worthy.

Setting her mug aside, she seized dust rags and, dragging the vacuum cleaner behind her, went to the living room to make it ready for the watchdog. "Although he won't notice you're not dusty," she told the books as she wiped and replaced them on their shelves. "Although he might drop matches on you," she told the braided rugs as she vacuumed. "Although he'll try to treat me like a maid."

She laughed. She'd already assumed that role. And she'd yet to meet the man.

At dusk she heard a scratching at the door. Peering through the window she'd washed earlier, she surveyed the porch. Nothing there. Only a dry leaf tormented by a herky-jerky breeze.

She returned to the mantel, to the last chore she'd set for herself, polishing Meadow's collection of tiny glass animals and wiping the conch shell.

The scratching came again, louder, more insistent.

Again she peered through the window.

Saw nothing.

The third time she flung wide the door and called, "Come in, Motley. Come in, Mustard. And Merle. And the rest of you. Morgan's in the bedroom."

She heard no ghostly click of nails on wood, felt no swish of phantom tails, inhaled no scent of sea and sand. But she waited a few moments before closing the door and returning to the mantel. When the last glass creature was polished, she went to Morgan's room.

A broad smile lit his face, peeling away years. His arms were stretched out to his sides, his fingers scratching the heads of dogs invisible to her.

Moving slowly and giving a wide berth to Motley and his phantom pack, Rain eased to the head of the bed and kissed Morgan's forehead. "I love you."

She turned to address the rocker where she imagined Meadow might be sitting. "I love you, grandmother. I'll try to make you proud."

Then she lit the beeswax candles, closed the bedroom door, and went out into the night.

CHAPTER 14

June
Pierce

"Much as that man frustrated me when he was alive, he's got me in more of a lather now that he's gone." Claire thumped her fists on the polished surface of the conference table. "The thing is, I don't know how mad I should be. Did he keep everything in his head? Or did he write it down and did the Peddler take it?"

She'd asked those questions, in various forms, several dozen times. Pierce no longer felt an obligation to say either choice was possible. In fact, he felt no obligation to say anything. He didn't glance up from the bulging file on Collette Chambers—reconstructed from the original reports, and padded out with Pierce's notes from his recent trip to Spokane. He'd gone with the certainty that he'd find something and would know it when he found it. But unlike his earlier forays, this journey netted him nothing that moved the case further along. Disappointment had sapped his energy—both mental and physical—for days. Had Marlin also come up dry? Or had he found something that, like a tripwire, alerted the Peddler?

"I could have helped him." Claire spun in her swivel chair her dangly gold earrings flashing. "He *hired* me to help him. My *job* was all about helping him. Was he afraid I'd find out more than he would? Was he so jealous that he didn't make a single note because I might see it and get ahead of him?"

Not one of those questions was new, but last night Pierce had arrived at a possible answer. "I think he may have had another stroke."

"What? When?"

"Before I left for San Francisco. I've been wondering why he didn't put up more of a fight when he was strangled. Then I remembered his left arm seemed weaker when I met with him. And he was repeating parts of sentences."

Claire gasped. "I noticed that, but I didn't realize it meant . . ."

"I didn't, either. I thought he was doing it for emphasis. Or in a critical way."

She moaned and hugged herself. "I should have noticed. I should have urged him to see a doctor. I should—"

Pierce closed the file. "Marlin would have told you to stay out of his business. Or go to hell."

"Or both," Claire agreed with a sigh. "You're right. And he would have denied having any problems. Plus, if he had been intending to see a doctor, he might have cancelled the appointment to spite me."

"Or himself," Pierce mused. Marlin had a self-destructive streak as wide as his own. But, while Pierce was aware of his and mostly made an effort to control it, Marlin had seemed either unaware or unwilling to change his behavior. Perhaps some of that had been due to the initial stroke.

Lately, fighting the desire to cut, Pierce had wondered about his own brain and what lack of sleep, longer and harder daily runs, and churning thoughts might be doing to his mental abilities. Lately he'd found himself running his fingers along

109

the sharp edges of letter openers, metal picture frames, and even the tiny teeth on the tape dispenser.

Claire pointed at the binder. "Anything occur to you this time through?"

"Not a damn thing."

"Maybe you should go back again. To Spokane."

Pierce ran his fingers along the edge of the three-ring binder. If he pressed hard enough, he might draw blood. Only a little. Just enough to release some of his anger and his frustration.

"Maybe you'll find someone you didn't talk to before."

Hard to imagine. It seemed as if he'd talked with everyone in the city. He'd stayed for nearly a week, walking in widening circles from the upscale apartment complex where Collette Chambers had lived, from the office she shared with a woman who designed furniture and another who wove rugs. He knew he had more patience than Marlin, and more physical stamina. He'd knocked on some doors six or seven times before he found anyone at home. He'd collected names of those who had moved away and tracked them down. Either Marlin had gotten exceptionally lucky, or the connection to the Peddler hadn't been there.

Or the Peddler had somehow kept tabs on Marlin and knew he was on the right track.

Or the Peddler knew nothing of their progress but had killed Marlin to make a statement.

Or . . .

Pierce felt like a dog chasing its tail. A very short tail.

While he'd focused on Spokane and Collette Chambers, Claire had taken on the tasks of replacing the map, restoring the timeline, printing new photographs, reassembling the paper files, and rebuilding the old-school foundation of knowledge stored in the three-ring binders—one for each victim—the

Peddler had stolen. Everything on computer had been backed up, with the exception of whatever Marlin hadn't shared. But Pierce and Claire agreed that computer files seemed sterile. Paper files, even if they were only copies of original notes, seemed somehow alive.

He should, he realized, have suggested she work on his insurance-adjuster theory. He'd shared it with her. But he hadn't nudged her to begin calling and cross-referencing and trying to find connections. Had he, like Marlin, been jealous of her abilities?

"Why didn't you argue when I said we should reconstruct the files before you tackled anything else?"

"I guess I was still numb." Claire rubbed her arms. "About Marlin. About that creature coming in here and tearing everything apart. Violating our space."

"I didn't intimidate you, did I? Because I don't see you as working for me. You work for the task force."

She shook her head, linked stars and circles swaying from her earlobes. "If anything, I intimidated myself. I guess . . . No, I *know* I was afraid he'd return. Especially if we found something new, something he thought would lead us to him. When we got Marlin's cellphone records I was actually afraid to check the numbers he'd called. I thought maybe I'd ring the same bell Marlin had and . . ."

Pierce nodded. He'd had the same thought. But if Marlin had made a connection, it hadn't been by phone.

Claire shivered and rubbed her arms once more. "Even after we changed the locks. Even . . . even now. The cleaning crew comes only on the weekends, but twice I've had the feeling someone was in here during the week. And I don't have much of an imagination."

Pierce stood, came around the table, and laid his hands on her shoulders. "I have imagination to spare. Yesterday I thought I smelled something in my office, something I never smelled before—maybe cologne or deodorant or hair gel."

Neither moved for a moment, then Claire patted Pierce's hands and stood. "I know it's early, but I need lunch." She headed for the door. "You're coming with me."

An order.

Pierce raised an eyebrow, but followed Claire to her office where she grabbed her purse and scrawled four words on a legal pad: "Is the office bugged?"

Pierce almost laughed. Bugged? Like in a spy novel?

Frowning, she plucked his sleeve, and headed for the door, stuffing the paper in her purse. "I'm not sure whether I want a burger or a sandwich or soup. Or all of the above. Good thing there are lots of choices at the airport."

Shaking his head, Pierce locked the office and followed.

Neither spoke until they'd ordered rice bowls and found seats at a table in a far corner of a narrow restaurant.

"Maybe I'm losing my grip," Claire said in a tight whisper.

"But maybe you're not. Maybe that's how he knew what Marlin was up to."

"And now he's got the binders. He knows everything we knew before Marlin was killed." She blotted her eyes with a napkin.

The gutting sense of violation Pierce had felt when he saw the ransacked office returned. "We'll have the place checked as soon as possible."

"What . . . what about our cars?"

"Cars, homes, garden sheds, bicycles—whatever you can think of. You find the bug finder. I'll do what I do best and write a check."

Claire turned a thumb up and forked a piece of avocado from her rice bowl. "If he bugged us, that's more proof he's worried we're making progress. He might get careless. Maybe careless enough to get caught."

"Right." Pierce stirred peanut sauce into his rice and vegetables. "If he bugged us, how did he get in? No one had keys except us."

"And the management com— Crap!" Claire dropped her fork and clawed at her hair. "The cleaning service had keys, too. And the maintenance staff. Double crap! And I bet after they changed the locks they handed out fresh keys all around."

"We could change the locks again. Do it ourselves."

"He'll be suspicious. Besides, even though Marlin was sure he talked his way in to take his victims, I always wondered if he picked locks."

"I wondered that myself."

"So we can't change the locks or install an alarm system." Claire picked up her fork and twirled it. "And if he bugged us, he'll know we caught on if we remove the bugs."

Pierce groaned. "So we keep them in place. And we do our real work only on laptops we carry with us."

"And we don't talk about the cases. Except to say we're discouraged and the Peddler's smarter than we are."

"I hate that." Pierce gritted his teeth. "But I'll do it."

"What about creating fictional material for a few of the binders? If he's checking through them to see what's new, he might think we're riding off in the wrong direction."

"Good."

"I feel better." Claire sighed and stabbed at her lunch. "Now I'm hungry for real."

While Pierce stirred his meal to mush, she shoveled hers down and, in a few minutes, chased the last grains of rice around the bottom of the bowl. "I'll get to work on your theory right away." Claire wiped her mouth and wadded her napkin. "I'll work out of my car or a coffee shop."

"Except if he bugged us, he'll know we're not in the office and he'll suspect we're onto him."

"Crap."

Pierce pushed his bowl aside. "I may have the germ of an idea."

"Normally I don't care much for germs." Claire crammed her napkin in her bowl and leaned across the table. "But today I'm wild about them."

CHAPTER 15

June
Rain

Morgan's body had been in the ground for five days. The spectral presence of Meadow and the dogs had vanished like morning mist. The neighbors had all dropped by with casseroles and cookies. But Bertram Mosier, the man Morgan referred to as a watchdog, hadn't arrived.

The sun hung red in the west. Rain paced the freshly swept porch of the farmhouse, ear cocked toward every distant thrum of an engine, eyes aching for a glimpse of a rooster tail of dust rising from the long driveway.

He was overdue. Well, overdue by her reckoning. Morgan had said he'd be here soon. But he'd also said Bertram Mosier kept his own clock. Still, it seemed like he should have turned up by now.

Last night she'd typed his name, then deleted it before launching a search of the Internet. What if she found dozens of men with that name? How would she determine which was the watchdog? Call them all? And say what? "You don't know me, but Morgan Paxton was my grandfather and he warned me you'd drop matches on the rugs."

With a sigh, she checked once more that the note she'd written was clearly visible on the porch steps. "Welcome, Bertram. The door is open. The bedroom on the left is made up for you. Make yourself at home. I'll be back in the morning. If you need me before then, my number is by the telephone."

She was halfway to the cabin when she heard a distant rattling. Pausing where the track switched back on itself, she shaded her eyes against a low slant of sunlight and spotted a vehicle. It appeared to be half car and half truck and plucked from a documentary on the Dust Bowl. With a cough and a sputter, it came to a stop beside the farmhouse. The front fender was crumpled. Steam leaked from beneath the hood. The tires tilted inward. The load in the lidless trunk was secured with yellow nylon rope.

Metal shrieked. The passenger door opened. A huge man tumbled out with all the grace of a grizzly in a ballet class. Rusty red hair stood in two Viking-horn tufts on his head. More hair shot in spikes from his cheeks and chin. His white shirt hung loose over a pair of sagging black slacks, and the toes of both feet protruded from gashes cut in red tennis shoes.

The watchdog?

He stomped to the porch steps and read her note.

Rain headed down the track to greet him.

The man turned and bellowed, his words indistinct.

Rain paused and slid into a deep shadow to study him.

He pointed at the front door and bellowed again. The volume conveyed anger, but his relaxed body language didn't support that.

In a moment the driver's door opened and a woman got out. A tiny woman, clothed in faded denim. Gray hair streamed from beneath a green ball cap and cascaded across her shoulders. She stalked around the front of the vehicle, batting rising steam with her hand, and confronted the man with words

116

Rain couldn't hear. When she finished speaking, she thrust out her right hand, palm up.

The man reared back and bellowed again.

The woman stood firm.

The man dug at a hip pocket, removed a wallet, counted bills onto her palm. Paused. Bellowed. Counted a few more. Bellowed again.

The woman stuffed the bills under her ball cap, opened the rear door, hauled out a box, and let it drop. The side split. Papers spilled.

The man bellowed and waved another bill. And another.

The woman grasped a second box and carried it to the porch.

When she'd unloaded everything, she lugged the boxes and three large suitcases inside.

As the day faded, Rain watched the watchdog as he watched the driver. Was he tired and in pain, or simply bad-tempered and lazy? Was he naturally loud or had he lost his hearing and, with it, any concept of volume control?

When the watchdog went inside and the driver fired up her decrepit vehicle and navigated toward the highway by the dim glow of a single headlight, Rain climbed the track to the cabin. She'd waited this long to meet Bertram Mosier. She could wait until tomorrow.

At 5:00 the phone on Rain's nightstand rang. The number for the farmhouse lit up the screen. She let it ring twice more, then answered. "Good morning, Mr. Mosier."

"Nothing good about it without coffee," he boomed.

Rain swept aside the comforter and swung her feet to the floor. Then she remembered Morgan's list, and the advice about the watchdog written in sentences all beginning with DON'T.

"Cupboard to the left of the stove," she boomed in return.

And disconnected.

In two minutes the phone rang again. "Damn machine's more complicated than a super collider." The boom was gone, replaced by a huff and a wheeze.

Hardly true. It was a ten-year-old model. Simple. Basic.

"Directions are on the side."

She disconnected again.

The phone was silent for almost five minutes.

"Is whole wheat the only bread?"

This time, Rain hung up without speaking. She tried to sleep, but ground her teeth, thinking about the watchdog bumbling about in the kitchen she'd scrubbed. Right now he could be spilling coffee, burning toast, dropping crumbs. She imagined him in the front room, dumping out the contents of his boxes and suitcases, scuffing the floor, rumpling rugs, perhaps even flicking matches.

Ten minutes later, dressed in running shoes, jeans, and a cotton sweater the color of apricots, she was halfway to the farmhouse, moving at a trot. And telling herself to slow down. Morgan knew what this man was like. Morgan had invited him to stay, warning her only about matches and fire, not about damage to his possessions.

Former possessions.

Morgan had left everything behind. Left it all to her. And left her with instructions to provide the watchdog with a home.

She slowed to a walk.

A home was more than a house and its furnishings. At least it was to her. A home was about people who lived under one roof and the way they interacted and related. Morgan had invited the watchdog to make a home in the farmhouse. If this man's idea of the visible trappings of a home didn't mesh with Rain's vision, then she wouldn't let it bother her.

Or at least she'd try.

She reached the farmhouse and let herself in through the mudroom off the kitchen. A trail of brown dribbles leading from the machine to the table revealed that Bertram Mosier had managed to make coffee. A trail of crumbs, a smear of butter, and a glop of strawberry jam indicated he'd made toast. The fact that bread, butter, and jam hadn't been put away indicated he wasn't a tidy person—something Rain already grasped—or perhaps intended to have seconds.

"You're not his maid," she reminded herself. "Morgan made that clear."

But she covered the butter, put the lid on the jam, and twisted a tie on the bread bag. Then, a cup of coffee in hand, she followed a line of spatters, tracking him through a jumble of boxes, papers, and articles of clothing.

Wearing what he'd had on when he arrived, he sat in the glider swing on the porch, taking up most of it, coffee sloshing in his mug. "See the top of the cliff," he yawped by way of greeting. "Basalt across the river there. Piled up. Stuff on the bottom's 17 million years old." He drew in a wheezing breath. "Give or take."

"Uh, right." Rain wasn't sure he was right, but the tone and volume of his pronouncement seemed to indicate any effort to correct him would be shouted down.

Unless too much shouting led to respiratory failure. His breathing was loud and ragged.

She sat in the old rocking chair with broad arms and a low seat. It might collapse, but it was a good three yards from the watchdog, a distance her ears would appreciate.

"Won't get much chance to take in the scenery," he announced. "Once I get to work."

She sipped coffee, positive he'd go on without prompting. And even more positive she couldn't interrupt the flow of verbiage without slapping a plunger over his mouth.

119

"True crime book," he confided in a rasping voice punctuated by a gasp at the end of each sentence. "Hell, maybe a series. Fictionalized so they don't sue my shorts off. Nasty stuff. Nevada is famous for it."

Rain took another sip and watched a deer lead her fawn through the pasture toward the orchard. Mosier's voice didn't seem to disturb the doe or bother three rabbits dining on clover where the lawn met the drive.

"Crime reporter there. Pay was crap, but the job was meat and drink to me. Would have gone on another decade if it wasn't for that martinet of a doctor. Claims with my damn gout and high blood pressure and shortness of breath and diabetic tendencies I'm a walking heart attack. Told me to quit or die young."

Rain bent her head over her coffee and cast a sidelong glance. Bertram Mosier hadn't appeared young last night, and the early morning light revealed further signs of age and poor health—wrinkles, white hair among the red, puffy fingers, swollen feet and ankles.

"Gonna take all those seamy details and sick theories we couldn't print. Use 'em for seed. I hear you're an editor. Maybe I'll let you read through it, fix some of my grammar. Who. Whom. That kind of stuff."

Rain opened her mouth to protest, to say Morgan warned her not to become a secretary. But she quickly realized the futility. She'd cross the editing bridge when she came to it. If the state of the boxes in the living room was any indication, it might be years before he got organized enough to write more than a few chapters.

"Got a hell of a serial-killer case going on in this neck of the woods. If I was still in harness I'd get my teeth into it."

He punctuated his statement by removing a full set of dentures and clacking them.

Rain recoiled, then rolled her eyes.

He popped them back in.

"Man investigating those missing women gets taken out. Should be *some* leads. Maybe they're not digging hard enough. Or in the right places. Meadow might have set them straight if they were smart enough to ask for her help."

Rain nodded. That she agreed with.

He slurped coffee and brushed toast crumbs from his beard, relocating them to his shirt. "You always this quiet? Haven't said more than two words since you sat down."

Rain thought of a dozen comebacks.

He steamrolled on before she settled on one of them.

"Quiet's fine. I talk enough for two. Or so they say. When they can get a word in edgewise to say it."

He yanked the false teeth out and clacked them again. His belly laugh shook the glider swing so hard Rain feared for the nuts and bolts holding it together.

"Listen, kid, I know what you're thinking about me."

I doubt it.

Rain raised her eyebrows.

The watchdog nodded. "You're thinking I'm a buffoon. A fat, sloppy, loud-mouthed, dumb-ass buffoon."

Rain swallowed and struggled to keep her face neutral.

He'd nailed it. Nailed it almost word for word.

"Well I'll own the fat and the sloppy and the loud, but the rest is an act." He lowered his voice. "Cultivated it for years. Lulled people. Made them think they were smarter than me. Let me pick up on their secrets." He swiped crumbs from his shirt with the edge of his hand. "Everybody has secrets."

And this man was living proof of a secret Morgan and Meadow kept from her. "How did you know my grandparents?"

"Cousins. Second. Or maybe third. Well, Morgan was. So I guess Meadow would have been by marriage. I was a kid when they married. Used to be we'd see each other at family reunions."

He raised a hand before Rain spoke. "Before your time. Not much family left now. Just me and you."

"And my mother. Maybe."

"Right. Holly. Figured I wouldn't mention her unless you did."

The kindness seemed out of character. Perhaps the watchdog was more complex than she supposed.

She moved her chair closer. "I never searched for her and I never asked my grandparents. But from what Morgan didn't say when I asked if she'd be living here, I got the feeling she isn't coming home. Ever. That she's dead or her mind is gone."

She saw his eyes soften and asked, "Did you know her?"

"Not well. Beautiful girl. Always smiling. Met her a few times at family things. When there used to be family things. I was out in Nevada, you know. Didn't get up this way often. And then she . . ."

"Went off the rails."

"Your words. Not any I ever used. Or heard from Morgan and Meadow. She made some hurtful choices, but she must have had her reasons. The gift is a powerful burden. Not everyone is willing to lift it. Not everyone can. Some see it as a curse."

He stood with a jerk and a stumble and trundled to the door. "Well, gotta get started. Don't suppose you want to lend an old man a hand?"

Again, he beat Rain to the conversational punch with a laugh, this one so blaring it spooked the deer and set them bounding away. "Know what? I bet Morgan warned you not to be my secretary or maid. My car broke down in Winnemucca and I sold it for junk, so I hope he didn't tell you not to give me a lift to the market now and then."

"He didn't mention that. But his truck is in the garage. The keys are under the seat."

"Probably a stick," he groused. "Morgan believed the automatic shift marked the beginning of the downfall of civilization."

Rain smiled. That sounded exactly like her grandfather. "My car's in there, too. But it's small. And also a stick."

"I'll try the truck." The watchdog went inside, letting the screen door whap closed behind him, calling, "Probably tear out a few gears, but I'll manage."

Rain finished her coffee, wondering as she did what Morgan had been thinking when he called Bertram Mosier a watchdog. A true watchdog, after all, had the ability to listen.

CHAPTER 16

June
Pierce

Working silently while Claire and Pierce rustled paper or opened file drawers and banged them shut, the bug sweeper did his thing. He found two listening devices and a phone tap in the task force office. He also discovered a tracking device on Pierce's car.

When the sweeper took off, Pierce and Claire left everything as it was. They drove her car to the airport for a lunch meeting at what Claire called their usual table.

"Listening to us. Tracking my car," Pierce fumed. "That bastard knows where I live."

"And you can't trade your car in or dump it for a rental or he'll suspect something." Claire opened a paper napkin and spread it on her lap. "Unless the Peddler isn't . . ."

"Isn't what?"

"The one who did the bugging and planted the tracker."

Pierce blinked. "Who else?"

She ducked her head as if to dodge a blow. "Uh, Marlin?"

"You're kidding? Why the hell would Marlin bug my office and track my car?"

"Because his first impulse was to suspect you of killing your wife. And despite everything he learned and everything you did, he never really put that aside."

Claire reached across the table and gripped his wrist. "I think it was automatic—part of his nature." Her glittery nails pinched his skin. "I never suspected you. I've come across a lot of liars and fakers, but their eyes almost always give them away."

"How?"

She released her grip. "With some it's pretty obvious. Their eyes are too wide open or too shifty. And of course, there's body language to reinforce that. Others . . . it's hard to describe . . . it's like their eyes have a curtain or a shutter or a shadow or they're covered with a wavy piece of glass like you find in old windows."

"And my eyes?"

"Your eyes were full of pain and confusion and frustration and determination. Some of it old. Some fresh. But you don't try to hide it."

She picked up her fork and dug beans and guacamole from her bowl. "Eat your lunch. Then you can tell me about your germ of an idea."

"Tomorrow." Pierce stabbed a chunk of tomato. "Today we're getting away from that office."

"And doing what?"

"You'll be shopping for new cellphones and laptops."

"The old ones are fine. We'll have them checked and—"

"Humor me."

"Okay." Her lips twisted in a wry smile. "Consider yourself humored."

"Check. Use the new phone to contact members of the task force and tell them our security has been compromised."

"Check." Claire echoed his tone. "What will you be doing?"

"Changing the locks on my house. Upgrading the alarm system."

"Won't that make him suspicious?"

"Maybe." Pierce shoved his bowl aside. "So you and I will return to the office and have a conversation about the rise in rural burglaries to lay the groundwork. You'll suggest I upgrade. After I do, I'll tackle a few other logistical details."

"Like what?"

"You'll see."

The next morning, finger to his lips, Pierce signaled for Claire to follow him out of the office and to the stairwell. "You okay with taking the stairs?"

"I wasn't for the first week after Marlin was killed," Claire answered. "But now I'm back to my routine. Sometimes I talk to him when I get to fifth floor landing."

"Good. Because now you'll have more opportunities to chat."

They took the stairs to the fifth floor, to an office directly beneath theirs. The sign on the door had been taped over. The front room was empty. Depressions in the gray industrial carpet indicated where furniture had been placed in the past.

"Dental supply firm. Went out of business months ago." Pierce led the way to the rear and a large room with a sink and cabinets in one corner, a tiny bathroom in another, and space for a table and a couple of desks. "Think you could work here?"

"Sure. I could work in a phone booth. But won't he figure out we're down here?"

"Not if we're careful and don't let anyone see us come and go. There's no office between this one and the door to the stairwell, and nothing directly across the corridor. We'll use this space for phone calling and information sharing."

126

He ushered her into the front room again. "Mal's having one of our corporations lease the place, supposedly for space we'll require later in the year. He'll tell the building manager we don't need cleaning or maintenance. We'll furnish the back room and put a lock of our own on the door and install an alarm system. We'll leave the front room vacant so it appears no one's moved in yet."

She pointed at the ceiling. "But if he's listening. He'll know we're not upstairs. He'll suspect something."

"Yes, but I have an idea about that." He shot her a grin. "How would you rate your acting ability?"

For the next two weeks they practiced what Claire called "dysfunctional workplace dynamics" to make it seem as if they weren't getting along. They argued about everything—from the number of file folders she ordered to his failure to put paper towels on the roll the "correct" way. They slammed drawers and doors and cultivated what they hoped were tense and heavy silences broken only by the soft tapping of fingers on laptop keys, the squeak of a desk chair, or a heavy sigh. All those sounds covered the retreat of one of them to the lower office to make phone calls.

They also pretended to be disheartened and discouraged with their lack of progress.

"Maybe Marlin was right," Pierce said in a mournful voice. "Maybe I'm a dilettante playing at being an investigator. Maybe I don't have the intelligence or the drive to get anywhere."

"Well, sitting at your desk playing games on your computer won't make you smarter," Claire snapped. "Or more focused."

"Like you're focused. When you're not off at your exercise class or the gun range, you're reading an unintelligible collection of words."

"It's *Ulysses*. It's a literary masterpiece." She slammed the heavy book on her desk. "And if you won't give me direction, I might as well read."

"I made you the coordinator of the task force because I thought you had plenty of direction-finding ability. When Marlin was here you had a dozen ideas a day. I should have realized *your* ideas were all about undermining *his* ideas."

"That's a low blow," Claire seethed. "I ought to quit."

"Quitting, yeah, that's a direction," Pierce shouted. "Well, go ahead."

Claire let silence stretch between them before responding in a tight voice. "I have too much respect for the task force and its working members to walk off and leave them to deal with you or a new coordinator who might need months to get up to speed. If you want me gone, you'll have to fire me. But before you do, think how that will play in the media. There may be some who believe—like Marlin did—that you killed your wife and made it appear to be the work of the Peddler. They may think I got too close to the truth and you wanted me gone."

"You bitch. You complete and utter bitch."

Pierce stalked out, slamming the door.

When he and Claire met in the downstairs office a few minutes later, they exchanged high fives and hugs.

"The only thing new is a possible connection I made last night." She brought up a website for a firm in Tacoma, clicked to the page with a group photo, and tapped the grinning face of a man in the back row. "This guy—Bruce Mitchum—worked cases for neighbors of two of the victims. He settled the claim for the landslide woman in Medford, and for a neighbor of Annabelle Watson in Boise."

Pierce raised his hand for another high five, but she shook her head. "Unfortunately, this company isn't big on updating their website. He hasn't worked for them for about three years. No one has a clue where he went."

Bending over the laptop, Pierce peered at the tiny picture of the man with dark hair. Bruce Mitchum fit his idea of how the Peddler would appear to the world and to his victims—well-groomed, clean-shaven, handsome, friendly, approachable, trustworthy.

"His paychecks went to a post office box. The physical address he provided was here." Claire brought up a photo from a real estate site. "Big old house, rooms for rent on a month-to-month basis. Owner lives in Phoenix. His son manages the place." She laughed. "Manages it as well as the government manages to stick to a budget."

"And no one knows where Mitchum moved to?"

"Right. The manager says he traveled a lot, ate out, didn't use the kitchen, never exchanged more than a nod with other tenants. And, of course, he paid his rent with cash."

Claire brought up another website. "This is a company in Eugene. They also don't update their website like they should. But that's a benefit for us. Check out the blond guy on the far left, the one looking off to the side."

Bending close, Pierce studied the face, focused on the eyes and the shape of the mouth beneath a neatly trimmed mustache. "Is that Mitchum?"

"Or his brother. He worked there only a few months. Went by the name of Paul Reeves."

"Went?"

"Yeah. Nobody's seen him for about two years. Maybe more. Nobody knows where he might be."

"Did he work cases for any neighbors of the victims?"

"If he did, I haven't found them yet."

Pierce stalked to the window, reached for the pull to open the blinds, then remembered they'd agreed to keep the windows covered and use only minimal lighting to preserve the illusion of an empty office. "So, the Peddler might be Bruce Mitchum who might be Paul Reeves who might be anywhere."

Claire closed the laptop with a snap. "Pretty much."

"Still, great job connecting the dots." Pierce turned from the window. "Seriously. Nice work."

"It was mostly dogged determination and luck. Which got us nowhere." Turquoise nails flashing, Claire clawed at her hair. "Absolutely nowhere."

"We don't know that. Get the task force members in the loop. They have the resources to hunt for this guy—whoever he is, whoever he's pretending to be now."

CHAPTER 17

July
Rain

The headline seemed to spring from Rain's laptop screen: "The Peddler Strikes Again?" Below that, in smaller type, was a summary of the story: "Woman slain in airport hotel might be the latest victim of the serial killer known as the Peddler."

Taking in information in chunks, she raced through the article about the death of Teresa McCormack, then warmed her coffee in the microwave and read it again, fingertips tingling.

The hotel, according to the article, was only a hundred yards, only a berm and a hedge and a long parking lot, from the office building that housed the task force. Like most other female victims, Teresa McCormack had fought the killer. But she hadn't been abducted. Like Marlin Simmons, she had been strangled and dumped in a stairwell. Both police and recently appointed task force coordinator Claire Dawson had no comment on speculation that the killer selected the location in order to taunt task force members.

Rain surfed to the article she'd read a few weeks ago—the one with pictures of Claire Dawson and Pierce Jennings. Studying his face, she tried to imagine what it must feel like to commit to hunting a killer who took your wife, killed a coworker, and mocked you with a slaying within sight of your office. What she conjured was a rage that ran hot and cold. Even simply imagining the intensity of it created a rushing roar in her head and a queasy twisting in her gut.

For the first time ever, she wished for the gift, wished without doubt or fear or reservation. If she had the ability, she'd travel to Nightfall Bay, she'd find the women brutalized by this horrible man, and she'd return with information to bring him down.

Her fingers tingled once again, and she thought perhaps she'd heard a faint hissing boom in her ears, like what she'd once thought was the sound of the ocean in a seashell.

She glanced around, but saw nothing except what she expected—the interior of the cabin, her furniture, a spill of sunlight on her desk. No gray beach, no looming waves, no huddled figures in the distance.

And no dog.

If the gift arrived, there would be a dog.

She was certain of that. Meadow had told her.

What Meadow hadn't told her was how it would feel to make the tumbling, falling, jolting journey.

"I never asked. I should have."

She closed the laptop, wondering if it would be as painful as she'd heard childbirth could be. Would it be like a sneeze, over and done in a second? Or would it linger like a cold? Or a hangover?

Rain seldom drank, but she recalled a lost weekend in college, recalled the headache and nausea and regret and anger at the lack of willpower that made her go along with others when she'd been determined not to.

She gazed out the window and across the Columbia Gorge. Morgan had picked a wonderful site for the cabin. He would have enjoyed sitting on the porch, watching clouds scud across the sky, seeing their blue shadows sweep the towering rock walls on the other side of the river.

She remembered what he'd told her about how Meadow chose those she would try to help, how she drew on their strength and determination.

Was that necessary to "trigger" the gift? Would she receive it only when someone in great need appealed to her? And how, if she had yet to solve a mystery, would someone even know she existed? How had they found Meadow? Had her mother and grandmother passed along letters they received? Would one of the letters that continued to arrive for Meadow be the key?

Carrying a quartet of blueberry muffins on a plate, she walked to the farmhouse.

The countertops had been wiped and crumbs relocated to the floor where they made a gritty crunch beneath her feet as she crossed to the living room. Two boxes had been unpacked, the papers they'd contained stacked against the wall. As for the suitcases, they gaped on either side of the bedroom door, clothing spilling out.

The watchdog—she'd decided to call him Watch—sat in the glider swing, flipping through a sheaf of papers held together with several rusty staples. Yellowing newspaper articles had been stuck to the brittle pages with tape now equally yellow.

"I made muffins." Rain set her offering on a low table.

"Shouldn't have them." He snatched one and peeled away the foil cup. "Not on my diet."

"I reduced the sugar and used whole wheat flour and oatmeal." She reached for the plate. "But I'll take them away if you can't have them."

"No need." He caught her wrist as he bit off half a muffin. "I'll space them out," he mumbled.

"Space them out?"

He swallowed and pounded his chest. "One now. One for lunch. One for dinner. Confuse my digestive system."

Rain had heard a lot of theories about dieting when she was in high school and college, but never this. "That works?"

"Don't know. Don't care. Something will kill me someday."

He stuffed the remainder of the muffin in his mouth, wadded the foil cup, and tossed it at the plate. It missed, bounced off the edge of the table, and rolled across the porch. Rain moved to retrieve it, then remembered Morgan's warning and halted.

"Two letters came for Meadow yesterday." He hooked a thumb. "Put them on top of the refrigerator so they'd stay clean."

"Thanks." She turned toward the house.

"Clean is overrated, you know." He flipped a page, paper and tape crackling.

"Oh?"

"Too much cleaning, too few germs, less resistance."

Rain guessed he must have enough resistance by now to emerge unscathed from a full-body bath in a vat of sewage. "I'll keep that in mind."

"Don't think it. Live it."

Advice that could apply to many things other than cleanliness. Rain sidled to the rocker and sat. "When Meadow, uh, accepted the gift, did she ever say anything about it? About what it felt like?"

"Don't remember that she ever said. And I never asked." Watch turned his shaggy head, his eyes narrowing. "You thinking you're ready for it?"

Rain shrugged.

"Because of that woman? The latest victim?"

"I—"

"That's a lot of horror to take on, especially first time out of the gate. Thirteen women and that investigator, all laid at the door of a man as twisted as a corkscrew. And you with no experience. Might tear you up, turn you inside out. If you want my advice, don't do it."

"Maybe I don't want your advice." Rain stood, her throat tight with rage. "Someone needs to stop that man."

"I'm not arguing that point. I don't think a killer should be allowed to walk the earth as free as the wind. But you—"

"What if I went to Nightfall Bay to find just one victim? What if someone on the task force wrote me a letter and—"

"As long as they have leads to follow up on, I can't see the cops asking for help. Not from you, not from a psychic, a card reader, or anyone like that."

"But what if they did? What if they asked me to find Mr. Simmons? Only him. No one else."

"He's tied in to the others. It's one big scary-as-hell ball of wax."

"I'm not scared."

"You should be. Anybody working this case should be. Especially those two running the task force. If he thinks they're close, he'll try to take them out like he took out Marlin Simmons."

Rain sucked in a breath. "Meadow was never scared. She wasn't scared of going to Nightfall Bay and she wasn't scared of what might happen because of what she found out there."

"Are you sure?" Watch peeled the foil from a second muffin, shook his head, and returned it to the plate. "Did you ever ask her?"

"No. But she kept going. If she was really scared, she would have stopped."

His lips twitched. "You think? You think your grandmother, as gritty a gal as she was, would have put herself

135

first and walked away? Especially after your mother refused the gift?"

Rain felt her lungs compress in a sob. She sat, drawing up her knees, ducking her head, making herself small. Feeling small.

Of course Meadow would have kept on, frightened or not. But she had Morgan to protect her. Rain had this man. And a few guns. And a bow. And knives. And, when the gift arrived, a dog. A large dog.

And, although Morgan had hinted at the possibility, Rain had never noticed anything to make her sense Meadow feared someone with a black secret might try to kill her to protect it. But had Meadow ever encountered a case like this one?

"All this discussion doesn't amount to a hill of beans," Watch said. "The way I understand it, the gift decides when it's time. You can't rush it. And you can't delay it."

He picked up the muffin again and studied it. "Maybe I'm full of manure, but I have a feeling it won't be long before the time is here. And I have a feeling a letter will be the trigger."

Exactly what she thought.

She stood, no longer wallowing, feeling a sense of trust in herself and the future. "Thanks. Um, I thought you weren't planning to eat another muffin until later."

"Changed my mind. Plan was too obvious. Never would have confused my system."

He bit into the muffin, crumbs falling on his beard and gray sweatshirt.

Talk about full of manure.

Rain collected the letters from the top of the refrigerator and carried them upstairs to Meadow's journeying room. As she had several times before, she felt her grandmother had left seconds earlier and was lingering nearby. She sat at the table and cradled her head in her arms, imagining Meadow beside her, stroking her hair, telling her it would be fine.

After a few minutes she opened the letters and read each one slowly, hoping to feel the tingle she felt earlier when she read about the latest victim of the Peddler. No matter how hard she concentrated, how much she tried to open her mind and heart to the pleading words on the page, she felt nothing.

Nothing except the desire to feel something.

With a sigh, she returned the letters to their envelopes and set them on top of the stack that had arrived since Meadow died. She'd responded to most of them, except for the dozen that came since Watch turned up. His presence was like a rock tossed into a quiet pond. Disruptive ripples spread out in all directions, making it difficult to concentrate here.

Which is why I have a home of my own.

She shuffled the unanswered letters from the stack, and secured them with a rubber band. Then she gathered up a box of the simple cream-colored notepaper Meadow had used for responses and tucked a sheet of stamps inside.

Perhaps Watch was right and the police wouldn't ask for her help. Perhaps their request wouldn't bring the gift.

She wouldn't know until the letter came.

And the only way to make sure a letter came, was to write one herself.

CHAPTER 18

July
Pierce

"Nothing. Nothing. Nothing." Pierce kicked the chair he'd assigned himself in the downstairs office they called "the bunker." Upstairs he had a leather luxury model with lumbar support, cushioned arms, and levers to create dozens of adjustment combinations. To his surprise, he found he thought better in the one he purchased for the secret room—a basic model with a cloth seat and back and plastic armrests. His old man wouldn't have consigned it to the lowliest intern.

But, although he had more thoughts and ideas in the low-rent chair, few had been clear or logical. In the days since the Peddler took his latest victim, a fog seemed to fill his brain. The mental mist was an evil yellow cloud with tendrils that found their way into every crevice and drove his thoughts in tight circles until he wanted to lower his head and charge the nearest wall. If he knocked himself out, he might have some rest, some peace, a few hours without choking on anger. "We've got nothing."

Eyes closed, Claire might have been a statue carved from obsidian. She made no attempt to halt his rampage, didn't tell him he was acting like a child.

"He gets in. He gets out. He doesn't leave a trace." Pierce lifted his right foot and kicked the seat of the chair, slamming it against the card table at which Claire sat. She didn't move. Didn't open her eyes.

Why should she? She'd seen it all before. From him. And from Marlin.

Marlin!

The name was like a splash of icy water. It cleared the fog.

Pierce swung the chair about and sat. "I apologize."

Claire didn't open her eyes. "The more you lose it, the less I need to."

"Glad I have a purpose."

"You also sign my paycheck. Although lately I'm thinking I'm not worth even a tenth of it. I haven't found a single trace of Mitchum or Reeves or anyone resembling them at other insurance agencies. And I haven't found a connection between them and any other victims."

"Neither has anyone else."

"No consolation."

They were both silent for several minutes, Pierce tapping his fingers on the black plastic armrests, Claire plucking at her upper lip with her right thumb and forefinger, her red nail polish glittering.

"We know where he hunts. And we have an idea of how he hunts. But where does he take them?"

He didn't expect Claire to answer the question they'd asked every day since the task force was formed.

"City or country?"

Another question they'd kicked around for months, but this time Claire answered. "City. More people packed in less space, but there's more going on, more coming and going. They might not notice the guy lugging a rolled-up carpet in or out of his house every few months. Or, if they noticed, they'd assume

139

he was some kind of a decorator, or figure it was none of their business."

"But there's so much lonely space outside the city." Pierce thought of the long road through the forest to his home. "So many isolated houses. And a lot of abandoned properties."

"But not as many ways in or out. Fewer people, but more focus." Claire shifted her gaze to the blinds covering the windows. "And I think he's close."

More ground they'd gone over so often Pierce felt he now crossed it in ruts almost as deep as he was tall. "How close?"

"Close. In Portland. Or the suburbs." She turned her attention to the map on the wall, a replica of the one upstairs. "I feel like—don't ask me why—he found a place he thought was safe enough for a long-term base of operations. Maybe he got a job in the area or came into an inheritance. Maybe settling here had something to do with you forming the task force."

She clenched her fists and pounded them gently on the table. "I think he spent a lot of time scoping out this building, watching us come and go. And even though no one at the hotel recognized the pictures of Mitchum and Reeves, I bet my next paycheck he took a room there."

"Registered under another name. With his hair dyed red or black or purple." Pierce groaned and dug his fingers into the back of his neck. "I'm sick of waiting for him to make a mistake. How the hell do we catch this guy?"

His question hung in the air, pressing on his shoulders, making breathing a chore.

"I don't know," Claire admitted. "I'm as sick of waiting as you are. Somehow—and don't ask me how, because I have no idea—we have to think outside the box."

"I don't even know what the box is. Or where I am inside it. Or how to raise the flaps." Pierce stood and kicked the chair twice, sending it spinning across the room. "I'm not one of you, remember? I don't have your training. I'm just a guy who wants to know what happened to his wife, a guy who wants to move on with his life."

He leaned on the table, looming over her. "Show me the damn box and I'll break it to pieces. I'll chew through it if I have to."

Claire said nothing, but in a moment she sighed, closed her eyes again, and folded her hands in front of her.

Pierce retrieved his long-suffering chair, and rolled it to the table. "Sorry."

"No problem. If you lose it—"

"Then you don't have to." He groaned. "I know. I know."

"Okay, then on the subject of 'outside the box' and what that means, we got this letter and I thought it was bunk, but I keep rereading it." Claire drew the folded piece of cream-colored notepaper from a manila folder and passed it to Pierce across the card table. "I don't know why. But I've read it twice a day since it arrived last week."

Pierce opened the note and read the few lines. "The women in my family have a gift, the ability to go to a place where the dead wait for the living to find answers. Only then can they be released to cross a dark sea. During her lifetime, my grandmother traveled there many times to find answers for friends and relatives of the missing or murdered. I hope to receive my gift soon. I also hope to be of service to the task force if you request my assistance. As long tradition dictates, such a request must be made in the form of a handwritten letter."

A laugh caught in Pierce's throat. He coughed and read the note again. On one hand, the letter seemed like the work of an off-the-rails nutcase. On the other hand, the complete sentences and formal phrasing—"as long tradition dictates"—

seemed to indicate just the opposite. It felt as if she was trying to draw them in, but hold them at arm's length as well.

"See what I mean," Claire said. "There's something about it. It has such a matter-of-fact style. The woman who wrote it totally believes in this gift and this place the dead wait for the living to get answers."

"Like limbo."

"More or less, but I get the impression this isn't a religious thing. But I'd be the first to say I'm not an expert on religion."

"I'm even less of an expert. The only thing my family worshipped was profit. If the old man ever prayed it was for the stock market to multiply his loaves and fishes."

Pierce slipped the note into the folder. "Do detectives ever use psychics?"

"Now and then."

"Does it help?"

Claire waggled her right hand. "Now and then."

"How would you feel about calling in someone to— whatever it is they do—read tea leaves, hold a séance, throw bones, disembowel some poor creature and pick over the entrails?"

Claire grimaced. "Except for the entrails part, I guess I'd be okay with it if we weren't counting on a breakthrough. And if we didn't have to believe—or pretend to believe—anything too far out there."

"Which would give them an out if their prediction came to nothing." Pierce leaned back in his chair, the spring squawking. "They'd claim our negative energy drained off their positive energy. Or our auras confused the spirits. Still . . ."

Claire cocked her head. "Still what?"

"It's an avenue we haven't gone down." He drew the note from the folder and turned it in his fingers. "And what do we have to lose?"

142

"Our reputations?"

"Yours, maybe." He smiled. "I'm a dabbler, remember? A dilettante. My reputation might actually improve if I listened to spirits rap on tables and watched candle flames flutter in a spectral breeze while waiting for a woman in a flowing gown to emerge from a trance."

His smile broadened. "In fact, maybe I'll do that. I'll make the rounds of psychics and mediums and astrologers. I could use some time away, and I bet you'd like time away from me. If I don't return with anything else, maybe I'll have some stock market tips to pass on to Mal."

Claire offered the note. "You might as well start your grand tour with this one."

"No. That's yours."

"Mine?"

"You're the one who wasn't able to stick it in a file folder and leave it there. I'll be happy to help you craft the letter. But you write it. And you deliver it. By hand."

CHAPTER 19

July
Rain

The cabin's landline rang as Rain groped for a gentle way to inform a budding author that, although his plot had promise, she felt his writing was flat and his characters two-dimensional. She glanced at the number displayed on the handset—the farmhouse—and let it ring once more. If Watch had overloaded the dryer again or put the wrong soap in the dishwasher for the third time, he could deal with it himself. She'd never missed a deadline yet. She'd promised the analysis of the first 100 pages of this mystery by tomorrow, and she meant to have it written up and e-mailed off before midnight.

The phone stopped ringing.

Good.

It rang again. The farmhouse number appeared.

What would he do if she ignored this call? And the next? And the one after that? Would he be worried? Or would he surmise that she was asserting herself? Would he attempt to muscle Morgan's truck up the track? Or would he hike?

She laughed at the idea of Watch hauling his bulbous body up the grade, cursing with each stomping step. If he didn't collapse along the way and reached her house, he'd open fire with every verbal bullet in his vocabulary.

The phone stopped ringing.

And started once more, displaying the farmhouse number.

Give him credit. He was persistent. She bet he'd been good at his job. If he lived long enough, maybe he *would* write a book.

She snatched up the handset. "What?"

"Visitor," Watch barked.

"Who is it?"

"Woman from that task force."

A woman? Rain felt a slight sting of disappointment, felt herself flush with the guilty realization that she'd hoped, if someone responded to her letter, it would be Pierce Jennings. "Claire Dawson?"

"Has a letter. Won't leave it with me."

Rain felt a sizzle of excitement in her chest.

Was this the day the gift arrived? The day the dog appeared? The day she journeyed to Nightfall Bay?

"Show her the path."

"Not smart."

"Why not?"

"Think about it. Then come down. We're on the porch."

He said nothing more. Rain knew him well enough by now to realize he wouldn't change his mind. She'd probably never know what Morgan had told him, but apparently it had been enough to make him take the job of a watchdog seriously. Was there something about Claire Dawson that made him feel he couldn't trust her? Or was his concern more about faceless future danger?

"I'll be there in a few minutes."

She saved her job, closed the file, and brought up the article with the photo of Claire Dawson. Again, she was taken by the flinty determination in the woman's eyes. This was a woman on a mission. She knew what she wanted and she'd go the distance, whatever the distance might be.

Rain's gaze shifted to the photo of Pierce Jennings. He would also go the distance. He'd go because of a sense of responsibility and duty. But mostly he'd go to end his pain.

Rain powered off the computer, drained the last of the cold coffee in her mug, and caught her hair in a clip. Careful to lock the door behind her, she headed for the farmhouse.

Although the calendar clearly indicated summer had arrived and sunlight sparkled on leaves still wet from a morning shower, the wind coming from the east was sharp. It plucked at the sleeves of her denim shirt.

She accelerated to a trot. Then slowed to a walk, thinking of her grandparents. Morgan would tell her not to rush toward her destiny. Meadow might say the gift would be there when she was ready.

Was she?

Was her desire to find the killer a sign that she wasn't?

Watch certainly thought so.

She continued at a stroll, passing the garden where the tomato and pepper plants she tended seemed to huddle in their metal cages, fighting the chill. Raspberry canes whipped at the wires that held them upright. The berries were fat, but still pale pink and days from being ready. As a child, she'd thought of raspberries as summer on a stem. She loved them warm, right from the garden. She'd often lie on her back and wiggle her way beneath the bushes to pick berries that hung out of sight. Perhaps it had been her imagination, but they'd seemed fatter and darker than the rest. She remembered insisting their flavor was deeper.

Morgan and Meadow had never argued with her pronouncement or asked what she meant. And neither had ever

146

knelt to reach among the canes to pick the berries she claimed as her own. They'd been good about letting her find her own way and have experiences that were hers alone.

But should she take that as proof they would have approved of sending a letter to the task force?

Watch would say "No."

Meadow might have said, "What's done is done."

Her grandparents hadn't second-guessed decisions or actions. They'd cleaned it up if they could, and sucked it up if they couldn't. And then they'd gone on.

So would she.

She came around the side of the house and, before she focused on Claire Dawson, felt the woman's gaze slide along her body, halt at her feet, and begin another sweep.

I'm not what you expected.

Rain held in a smile.

Planting her right foot to the side, Claire leaned forward, pushed off with her left, pumped her arms, and rose from her chair—a low folding canvas model without armrests. It had stood sentry on the porch for years. Morgan often used it as a footrest, but Rain couldn't remember anyone sitting in it unless all the other seats were taken. Had Claire selected it, or had Watch directed her to it? Rain suspected the choice was the result of the collision of two strong wills.

Claire smoothed her gray pantsuit and settled the strap of a huge black leather purse on her shoulder. Flakes of glitter glinted in the red polish on her fingernails. Her eyes, so icy and filled with determination in the photo, held a wavering uncertainty in their depths.

With a nod to Watch, Rain mounted the steps, her hand thrust out to meet Claire's, her body braced for what might come.

Claire's grip was powerful.

147

Rain's fingers and palm tingled. She felt the porch shift beneath her feet and wind whirl about her head. But then it settled and there was nothing more. No distant barking. No sense of falling. No glimpse of Nightfall Bay.

Claire released her hand. "Nice to meet you."

Rain shook off her disappointment. "Same here. Would you like coffee?"

"*I* would." Watch thumped his empty mug on the low table beside the glider swing. "And maybe a few biscuits. With jam."

"Not on your diet," Rain said.

Watch snorted.

"Coffee would be good," Claire said. "If it's no trouble."

"No trouble at all." Rain laughed. "Well, no trouble beyond washing the pot and mugs."

Watch tapped his pen on the arm of the glider and rattled a sheaf of brittle paper. "Some of us aren't obsessed with cleaning for no good reason."

"Disrupts the ecology of the kitchen if you kill off too many germs," Rain told Claire as they entered the house.

"Why I live alone," Watch called after them.

"Why you always will," Rain shot back.

"That's the plan."

The papers in the living room were neater and seemed to have been arranged in some kind of order. But the suitcases still gaped and bits of clothing lay on the floor and across the chairs and sofa. Some of it appeared damp and Rain suspected Watch had managed to overstuff and overheat the dryer.

Claire pressed her arms against her sides as if fighting an urge to fold and straighten.

"The kitchen is worse," Rain said. "It literally makes me itch. But my grandfather left me strict instructions not to be his maid, so I come around only when I have to. And then I do my best to clean up as little as he does. Which, as you can see, is darn little."

They surveyed the kitchen. Splotches of grease covered the stove and long trickles of something reddish brown had dried on the oven door. Shreds of lettuce and cheese littered the countertops between dirty dishes, and most of the cabinet doors hung open. The floor, however, had been swept. But not well. In fact, Rain thought it looked more like he'd used the edge of the broom to plow furrows in a field of dirt and crumbs.

"I don't mind loading the dishwasher," Claire offered. "And wiping the counters."

"Suit yourself." Rain tossed a coffee filter filled with soggy grounds into a compost bucket in the cabinet under the sink.

Claire set her purse on a chair and opened the dishwasher. "Ugh. Smells like sour milk and bacon grease." She peered inside. "Is that a pork chop bone in the catch basket?"

"Wouldn't surprise me."

"At least it's a clean bone." Claire fished it out, tossed it in a close-to-overflowing trashcan, and began rinsing dishes and loading the racks.

While the coffeemaker gurgled, Rain got a fresh dishrag from a drawer and scrubbed three mugs, then wiped the counter. "Can't help myself. My grandmother always kept this place neat as a pin."

"Your letter said she died recently." Claire dropped her chin and paused for a few seconds. "I'm sorry for your loss."

"Thank you."

"The man on the porch—is he your grandfather?"

Rain laughed. "No. My grandfather would be insulted by that, but it's his fault Bertram Mosier is here. He's a distant cousin. Under the terms of Morgan's will, he can live in the farmhouse for the rest of his life."

"So your grandfather also died recently?"

Rain considered the question and Watch's reluctance to direct Claire to the cabin. Claire hadn't asked where Rain lived and whether she lived alone, so this question probably arose more from human interest than from intent to probe her situation. "A few weeks ago."

"I'm sorry."

"We all expected it." Rain lined up the mugs. "You had a loss, too. Marlin Simmons."

Claire's lips compressed, she drew in a halting breath, and her eyes closed for a few seconds. She bent her head once more, her hair bronze in the light of the long fluorescent bulbs in the three fixtures on the ceiling. The high windows in the kitchen were too close to the eaves to allow in much sunlight and the one over the sink was small so, when their eyes began to fail, Morgan and Meadow had removed the hanging lamps and installed these. One step above what Morgan called shop lights they were, as Meadow said, "Not pretty to look at, but first-rate shadow-chasers."

"Marlin was a complex man. Smart, relentless, driven, tireless, sometimes not in control of his temper. And jealous. He . . . we believe he found something. If he'd told us . . ." She halted, gulping air.

"You have a letter for me." Rain poured coffee.

"Yes."

"But you haven't offered it to me yet."

"You aren't what I expected. You're . . . younger . . . and you don't seem, well, serious—at least not serious to the bone."

If thanks for that were to be doled out, they'd go to Watch. He annoyed her but was, somehow, also a source of amusement. He was demanding and argumentative and unyielding. But without him she might wallow in a swamp of grief, holding her losses close.

150

"Have you had a lot of experience with people who communicate with the dead?"

"No. None." Claire wedged a bowl into the bottom rack of the dishwasher and mock-punched herself in the head. "I broke Marlin's prime rule. I made an assumption without evidence."

"And he never did the same thing?"

"Of course he did. But he was the boss." Claire drew a manila envelope from her purse. It was at least an inch thick, the contents straining the metal clasp. She held it toward Rain. "This contains information on all the cases. And our response to your letter. We'd like you to help if you can."

The coffeemaker spit the last drops of water into the filter.

"And I *want* to help. *If* I can. *When* I can." Rain filled the mugs. "But I haven't received the gift yet."

Claire turned the envelope in her hands. "So . . . should I take this away when I leave?"

"No. I want to know more about the cases."

"And I want to know more about the gift." Claire held the envelope against her chest.

"Fair enough." Rain picked up one of the mugs. "Let me take this to his majesty, and then we'll go upstairs."

For the first few minutes, Rain felt as if she might be violating her grandmother's space by bringing Claire Dawson to what she thought of as the journey room. But Claire was respectful, touching nothing, sitting in the small chair at the table, her eyes showing interest without judgment as Rain opened the closet and revealed the boxes of letters.

Claire seemed to recognize the pain contained in those boxes. She told Rain about working on the case of a young boy who'd gone missing from school—a case never solved. She put her hand over her heart and said it hurt every time she wondered what might have become of him.

151

Rain found herself trusting her and wanting to tell her more. Was that because she was lonely? Because she missed Meadow and Morgan?

By sending the letter to the task force, she'd opened the door to her world. Now Claire was here, and Rain found both pleasure and relief in talking with her.

She told Claire about her mother disappearing down a rabbit hole of addiction, leaving her nameless child on the steps of a church. She spoke of growing up in the farmhouse, aware of boundless love and the knowledge that her grandparents were different. She explained, as well as she could, how her grandmother used the strength of victims' friends and families to journey to Nightfall Bay.

"How do you get there? What's it like?" Claire asked. "And how will you find the person or persons you're searching for?"

"I guess I'll ask. Somehow."

She described what she'd been told about the well and sky and sterile shore, the huddled figures waiting to be released. She told about the dogs that appeared and disappeared over the years and how they returned to escort Morgan. She didn't mention Morgan's insistence she practice with a range of weapons, or explain about the boltholes she stocked. But she spoke about Morgan's long sight and his certainty that she would receive the gift and that using it would put her in danger.

"You'll survive?" Claire asked. "Or didn't he see that far?"

"He said I'd come through. But he also said the courses of others could affect mine." Rain gazed at Claire's injured leg. "Not every survivor is able to heal. Completely."

"Yes." Claire stood and touched her leg and then her forehead. "The pain never really lets go. And the scars . . . well, they're deep, they bind. They change you."

She laid the envelope on the desk. "I'll leave this here. But I warn you, it's not for the faint of heart. What he did to the women we found is . . . well, you'll see." She lifted her purse and set the strap on her shoulder, the gold chains in her ears swaying. "When I put together the file, I didn't include information on a person of interest, a man we know had a connection to neighbors of two of the victims. He'd used the names Bruce Mitchum and Paul Reeves when he worked as an insurance adjuster."

She drew a pen from her purse and wrote the names on the outside of the envelope along with the names of the insurance companies. "These companies have websites. His pictures are on them in group photos."

Would checking the photo of a suspect affect what she might learn if she journeyed to Nightfall Bay to speak with his victims? Rain chewed her lip. Had Meadow ever been confronted with a situation where a friend or relative of the victim passed along a photo of a person believed to be responsible?

"Anyway," Claire said, "thanks for sharing so much."

"Thank you for not laughing." Rain held out her hand, nurturing a frail hope that when her skin touched Claire's she might feel more than when they shook earlier, might feel something she could take as a sign.

But she felt only the smooth coolness of Claire's skin and the strength of her grip.

CHAPTER 20

August
Pierce

Pierce shaded his eyes, peered across the narrow valley in the mountains of Southern Oregon, and studied the broad scar in the earth where Bethany Lemmert's cabin and other dwellings once stood. Near one edge of the landslide, yellow tape defined a rectangle. Inside it, a tent shielded the forensic team from the blazing summer sun.

"Why here? If the Peddler wasn't an insurance adjuster and wasn't using the identities of Mitchum and Reeves, why bury the bodies here? Why at the site of an insurance claim?"

"Are you playing devil's advocate?" Claire asked. "You want me to answer that?"

"Yes."

"Okay, well, if he didn't have first-hand knowledge of this site, maybe he read about the landslide in the paper or on the Internet. Or saw a story on TV. Landslides make for great pictures and interviews."

"Sure. But why this one? There have been others that affected more people and would have received more coverage."

"Maybe he picked this because it's remote."

"But it's a one-way-in-and-out situation. There's more chance of being seen. And plenty of other sites are easier to access. With the road barricaded half a mile back, he had a long hike lugging dead weight."

"Unless they were alive." Claire's voice dropped to a whisper. "Unless he made them walk to their graves."

The image of four women walking to the place where they'd go into the ground was like a punch to the gut. Pierce turned aside, pressing his face against the rough bark of a spruce, swallowing the acid that seared his throat.

Why hadn't he thought of that? Was he unwilling to credit the Peddler with an act of such depraved inhumanity? Or was he unwilling to delve too far into his own dark imagination?

"How long before we have IDs?"

"Officially several weeks." Claire offered a bottle of water she pulled from her purse. "Unofficially, based on the details from my sources, there's no doubt in my mind. Patricia Crane. Caroline Egan. Martie Rush. Yvette Nelson."

For a second Pierce felt almost weightless with relief. Ariel wasn't in that grave.

Then he plunged into a pit of anger and despair. She was dead and buried elsewhere. Buried where she'd never be found. "Not Ariel?"

"No."

"They're sure?"

"Not 100%. But as sure as they can be until the autopsies."

Pierce swished water in his mouth and swallowed. This wasn't about him. This was about the women in the grave and the man who killed them. He drank half the bottle before the vile taste in his throat dissipated. "Any unofficial opinions on how long they've been here?"

"Just guesses right now based on the accumulation of leaves and needles and other debris on top of the gravesites. Six months. A year. Eighteen months." She used the edge of her boot to push together a heap of cones and leaves and needles, then used her heel to create a furrow in the earth. "If there hadn't been so much rain last week, and if the soil hadn't slid and fractured, the geologist checking the slide wouldn't have seen a thing."

But cracks had opened and a foot had been revealed. When the forensic team uncovered another body, the local sheriff called the task force office. Claire alerted Pierce. He chartered a plane in Seattle, picked her up in Portland, and got them here shortly after the crime scene team uncovered body number four.

"The simplest theory—at least to me—is that the Peddler used the names Mitchum and Reeves," Claire said. "He worked Bethany Lemmert's insurance claim—"

"But she didn't recognize him."

"It's been more than two years since she saw him." Claire shrugged. "And you have to admit she's kind of an airhead. She threw out the papers. And her memory of his name was all over the map."

Pierce felt himself bristle, then acknowledged the truth of that with a nod. He'd liked Bethany Lemmert, but he wasn't sure he'd hire her for a position where organizational skills counted for more than creativity.

"So," Claire went on, "he was familiar with this place, and he brought the victims here over a period of a year partly because it's remote and partly to taunt us if we figured out the connection."

Pierce drained the remainder of the water and crumpled the bottle. "I'd sign over everything I've got for a sharp knife and ten minutes alone with this sick bastard. And I wouldn't spend half a second worrying what the legal system might do to me when I was finished peeling the skin from his body."

"Take a number." Claire pried the bottle from his hand and stashed it in her purse.

"What do we do now?"

"Go to the office. Respond to calls from the media. Work any tips that come in."

"In other words, twiddle our thumbs."

"If you must. But before you start twiddling, I have information about the woman who sent that letter. And I want to hear about what you found."

"As soon as I collect my car from Seattle and get my notes in order, you'll get an earful."

"Here it is, all neat and tidy and formatted with headings and bold type to make it appear there's actual content." Pierce slid a manila folder across the card table to Claire. "It's a good thing I don't have to account for my spending to anyone but myself or I'd be drawn and quartered by now."

Claire flipped open the folder, ran a finger down the first page to the number after the dollar sign, and slapped a hand to her chest. "You spent all that on psychics? In two weeks?"

"Not just psychics. Mediums. Card readers. Tea-leaf readers. And a man who swore the pattern of broken shells and wrack left by the tide would reveal the Peddler's address."

"Since you're sitting here and not out with a team making an arrest, I assume it didn't."

"Never thought it would. But—give the high-tide guy credit—he had a persuasive line, a vivid imagination, and an endless supply of excuses. And not one of them was, 'The sun is in my eyes.'"

"Impressive. Does he make a living from wrack reading?"

"If you define 'a living' as eating beans and living in a van with three dogs and a collection of sea glass." Pierce tossed a couple of sand-polished chunks on the table—one dark blue, the other green. "Guy seemed content, though. Happier than some I know who have a hell of a lot more."

Claire didn't comment, but Pierce suspected she was thinking he was one of those.

"There's no point in reading the whole thing. The last two pages summarize my findings, and I doubt there's even a whiff of possibility."

He watched her face as she read, gauging where she was by whether her expression revealed she was considering possibilities, wondering if she'd read something wrong, or reeling with amazement at a ridiculous theory. And some of them were exactly that. The Peddler had gone to South America like Butch and Sundance. The Peddler had performed brain surgery on himself and had no memory of what he'd done. The Peddler, to atone for his crimes, had hiked to a remote area on the slopes of Mount Rainier and taken his own life. The Peddler would become a campaign manager for a presidential candidate. The Peddler would be captured at the Oregon State Fair. The Peddler would be revealed to be the man funding the task force charged with finding him.

Claire's eyes widened and she glanced at Pierce.

"The last one is my favorite," he said. "Although, I suppose it wouldn't be if I didn't have alibis for most of the abductions and killings."

"I take it you didn't tell any of these people about—"

"No. I didn't mention Ariel or that I was with the task force. All I said was that I was interested in the cases, felt for the victims and their families, and wanted to think—and pay— outside the box. Not one of them recognized me or sensed anything beyond that."

He gathered the chunks of glass and tucked them in his pocket. "Speaking of that damn box, what did you think of the woman who sent us the letter about wanting to help when she got her gift?"

"Rain Paxton. She's not what I expected and . . . I think she definitely believes the women in her family had the ability to consult with the dead. She calls it a gift, but what she told me makes me believe she sees it as an obligation, an opportunity to provide closure and healing."

Claire told him about her visit to the farmhouse and her long conversation with Rain.

Pierce listened, leaning forward in his chair. "So, basically, she can't help us because she has no idea when—or if—she'll receive this gift?"

"Right. And even if she had it, she might not be able to help. She needs to feel a connection to a victim and the person who wants answers. She needs to draw on their strength." Claire massaged the skin beneath her eyes. "I remember thinking it was like a jump-start."

"And she didn't feel a connection to any of the cases? Or to you?"

Claire studied her right hand. "I thought maybe she felt something when we shook hands. Her fingers twitched and her eyes—well, she had a look that was a mix of expectation and hope and fear. But then that faded."

"Hmmm."

"I can't explain it. I only know I didn't provide the spark." Claire closed her hand. "Maybe *you* would."

"I doubt it. I'm not a sparking kind of guy." Pierce laughed. "Besides, I've had enough of walking on the weird side for the time being."

CHAPTER 21

August
Rain

The last plant in the row yielded five more ripe tomatoes and filled the old woven basket Meadow had always used to carry what she picked. Rain grasped both handles, bent her knees, and hoisted. A muscle in her lower back tugged, and she could almost hear Morgan's voice telling her to make two trips. Not that *he* would have.

In the kitchen, she tipped the basket and spilled tomatoes on the newspaper spread across the table. A dozen green peppers and onions lined up on the countertop beside a few bulbs of garlic. When the sauce was nearly done, she'd toss in red pepper flakes and fresh basil.

Steam rose from a pot of simmering water on the stove. Rain flipped on a fan she'd brought from the garage and plucked at her over-sized T-shirt where it stuck to her damp skin.

Watch wandered in with a mug of coffee and a crumpled paper napkin.

"Set those on the counter I cleaned and sanitized," Rain warned, "and I'll fetch a set of pliers and pull your ears off."

He laughed. "Sometimes you sound so much like your grandmother I think she's still with us."

"If she was, she'd say, 'Mug in the dishwasher. Napkin in the trash.'"

"Yes, ma'am." Watch flipped a mock salute and complied. "Okay if I sit and watch?"

Rain chose a knife from the block and got a cutting board from a cabinet. "Don't you have a book to write?"

"Taking a break."

Rain rolled tomatoes into a colander for rinsing. It had been days since she'd seen him with a sheaf of papers or file folder or notebook. He hadn't been at his laptop, either. "How long a break?"

"Hard to know." He pulled out a chair and sat, wooden legs and rungs squeaking as he shifted his bulk. Less bulk, Rain noted, than when he arrived. He moved with more ease and his breathing was quieter. Lately he'd gotten out two or three sentences without sucking air. "Never worked without a deadline before."

"Or been your own boss?"

"Huh." He scratched his chin, an easier task since he'd started making regular visits to a barber shop to have his beard clipped and shaped. "Hadn't thought of that. Guess I need to be a more demanding boss."

Rain cut an X on the bottom of a tomato and dropped it in the pot of boiling water. "You mean, tee off on yourself like you do on me?"

"Can't help that you're the sensitive type," he groused. "And hung up on excessive cleanliness."

"And I can't help that you're not." She slipped more tomatoes into the boiling water, counted off the seconds, and moved them to one of three bowls filled with ice water.

"Seems we rock along okay in spite of that."

161

"Oh, yeah." She incised Xs in another batch of tomatoes and popped them in boiling water. "We get along like a sack full of badgers."

Watch snorted. "Morgan used to say that about a couple of old uncles on his mother's side. Fight? Tell you what, those two could go six rounds before breakfast. Argue over anything from politics to the right way to toast a bagel. Never married. Never moved apart."

Rain wouldn't live that way. She didn't want a relationship with someone spineless, someone who would turn aside from confrontation of any degree. But she didn't want constant skirmishes, either. When she imagined a future with a lover, she imagined discussions rather than arguments, and stretches of companionable silence broken by a smile or a touch.

"Want me to give you a hand?"

"No need." Rain transferred tomatoes to the second bowl of ice water. She doubted he'd be anything except in the way and, to be honest, she'd hoped to be alone in the kitchen. Last year she and Meadow had made gallons of tomato sauce and packed it in the chest freezer in the mudroom. If Watch returned to the porch, she might be able to imagine her grandmother's spirit was with her. Since she'd read about the latest gravesite and the bodies buried there, she'd yearned for a sense of Meadow's presence as much as she yearned for the power to find the killer. "It's a small kitchen and I have a routine. But thanks."

"Doubt I'd be much help anyway. Clumsy and messy as I am."

"You're not all that clumsy," Rain said in a jesting tone. "But you *are* a clutter magnet."

"Always have been. Saving grace is I know where all my stuff is."

Between tomato transfers she washed peppers and onions and considered his still-unpacked suitcases along the wall in the living room. "I'll take your word for that."

He grunted and rolled a tomato between his hands. "Wish you'd take my word about the world of hurt you'll inhabit if you mess with that killer."

His voice was soft, almost wistful, but it lit Rain's fuse. "I'm not 'messing' with a killer."

"I saw your face when you shook hands with Claire Dawson. You were expecting to make a connection, hoping to get involved in the hunt."

Rain ignored him. Or, rather, wished that was possible.

"Morgan would say you're trying to put the pedal to the metal to meet your fate sooner."

"I'm not!" She spoke without facing him. "I'm not over in Portland at the task force office. I'm right in front of you, making tomato sauce. When I'm finished, I'm going to my place and starting my next editing project."

"Yes, but you're thinking about those cases."

She turned, pointing the paring knife at him. "So what? I bet you are too."

"You're right. I am. But I don't have your gift."

"In case you haven't noticed, I don't have the gift either. And I don't know when—or if—I will."

"It will be soon," he said in an ominous tone. "Morgan saw it. And you feel it. You're wearing a gun."

Rain plucked at the T-shirt again. This morning she'd threaded a holster onto her belt and pulled her small revolver from her nightstand. She'd blamed a vague feeling of looming evil less on the Peddler than on the most recent manuscript she'd edited—a paranormal thriller. Feeling foolish, she'd worn a baggy shirt hoping to hide the gun from Watch. "Morgan trained me to defend myself. I'm prepared for whatever comes."

163

Watch blew air between his lips. "Did Morgan skip the part where he said thinking you're prepared can make you careless?"

"No." Rain jabbed the knife into a tomato. "He told me that all the time."

"And you listened?"

"Of course I listened." She tossed the tomato into the pot of boiling water, sending a wave hissing onto the stovetop. "Why are you on my case?"

Watch stood, kicking aside his chair. "Because I think 'on your case' is where your grandparents would want me to be. Because I think Morgan sent for me to make sure you kept your safety in mind."

"He should have had a sign made. A whole bunch of signs." She scooped tomatoes from the boiling pot and slammed them in the cooling bath. "Then you could have stayed in Nevada."

Watch's response was to grin. He held it for an annoying five seconds. "If you looked at yourself in a mirror right now you'd see your jaw set in a way that would have worried Morgan."

Rain grabbed a tomato, cocked her arm, sighed, and let it drop. "When he invited you to stay here, what did he ask you to do?"

"Be your watchdog."

"What does that mean? What's the job description?"

He beamed that annoying grin again. "Well, I have no experience with firearms or knife fighting or martial arts. But I can watch for trouble coming down the road. And if you show me that file Claire Dawson left, I'll have a better idea what I'm watching for."

Rain blinked. "*What*? *What* you're watching for? Not who?"

"Whatever he looks like, he's a monster in a man's skin. Don't think of him as human. Not even for a second. You do and it gives him an edge."

She thought of the photographs on the insurance company websites. After wrestling for days with the question of whether to look at the face of the man Claire Dawson suspected, she'd opened her computer and done it.

Now she wished she hadn't.

Yes, after studying the photos, she felt she could recognize the Peddler.

But could she think of him without an ounce of empathy? Could she view him the way he viewed a potential victim?

CHAPTER 22

September
Pierce

Leaning back in his long-suffering basic office chair, Pierce pounded his fists on the cracked plastic armrests, stared at the replicated map, and considered all the ways to say the investigation was making no progress. Sure, the official news-release statement claimed detectives were studying evidence from the bodies at the landslide site, following fresh leads, and considering all tips. But the truth was, when you added that up, it amounted to nothing. Nada. Zero. Zilch. Zippo.

The Peddler was a careful man. The victims had been scrubbed like the others. The tarps in which they were wrapped were sold almost everywhere. An analysis of stomach contents revealed beef and potatoes and lettuce that could have been purchased almost anywhere. Not a single fingerprint had been discovered. Not a single bit of blood or saliva or skin.

Nothing. Bupkis. Goose eggs.

He glowered at Claire's empty chair.

With each day that passed, his mood grew bleaker, blacker. He criticized every suggestion she made. She avoided him whenever possible. She went to the gun range more often, and made fewer trips to the lower office. She didn't offer to make

166

coffee and didn't come to work with a sack of pastries purchased on the way. She passed along updates—all amounting to a complete lack of progress—in writing. And she disappeared at lunchtime without a word. They hadn't been to their "other office" at the airport restaurant in weeks.

Over the years, the old man or his mother or Ariel had called him a failure so many times he'd lost count. In their eyes, he was a bust at business, networking, conversation, socializing, and being a husband and lover. He'd never bought it. Until now.

He rolled up his left sleeve and contemplated the scars on his arm. The urge to cut was stronger than hunger, as powerful as the need to breathe. He surveyed the table, but saw nothing sharper than a pen. Placing his fingertips in the spaces between scars, he dug in his nails until his fingers throbbed.

"What's the point of continuing this charade?"

He put the question to a stain on the ceiling that bore a passing resemblance to a famous photograph of the Loch Ness Monster.

The stain, much like Nessie might, didn't acknowledge him.

"I'm about as much help around here as a broken stapler."

The stain didn't argue.

Pierce rolled down his sleeve.

He should walk away. Right now. Send Claire a text. Tell her she was a solo act from now on. And—

And what?

Go back to San Francisco and get involved in running the empire again?

He'd get in Mal's way, drive him crazy. More than that, he'd drive himself crazy.

Start a new enterprise?

No. He lacked the imagination.

167

Fund and manage an organization to facilitate projects in emerging nations far away from here?

That he *could* imagine.

And his departure wouldn't create even a tiny ripple in the smooth running of the task force. Claire was the brains and the guts of it. She'd carry on. In fact, like Mal, she'd probably do better without him. She wouldn't give up. If there were connections to be made, she'd make them. If there were boxes to be thought outside of, she'd find them. And, if there was an arrest to be made, she would have earned the right to be on hand to witness it.

But he wouldn't be there with her.

Not if he quit.

He pounded the armrests once more, pinching the edge of his fist in a crack.

Yelping, he freed himself, stood, and kicked the chair into a corner.

Well he wouldn't walk away.

And he wouldn't cut himself in frustration.

And he wouldn't buy another chair to replace the one he'd brutalized. He'd suffer along with it.

And he'd humble himself.

In fact, he'd start right now, start by apologizing to Claire, inviting her to dinner, and asking if there was anything he could do, anything at all.

"There's nothing," she told him as she sipped the brandy he'd insisted she have when she ordered chocolate mousse and cherries for dessert. "There's nothing we can do except check out the calls on the tip line, coordinate the flow of information, and hope we get a break."

Pierce stabbed a slab of peach pie with his fork, sending bits of crust and crumb toppling onto the starched white tablecloth. "Doesn't seem to me there's much information flowing. I thought we'd have more on Mitchum and Reeves by now."

"So did I. But it's like they're ghosts." Claire took a larger sip followed by a long breath drawn in over her tongue. "We might try to kindle more media coverage and hope we get more tips."

"Increase the reward fund. That might make reporters bite."

"It's already at $50,000."

"Double it."

She took another sip and another breath. "I don't think I'll ever get used to the fact that you have so much money you can say something like that without pausing for even two seconds to think it over. Were you always so free and easy with your money?"

"Not when I had to account to the old man." Pierce forked off a chunk of pie. "But then he put himself out of my misery, and I learned the trick to letting go of big chunks."

He worked on the pie, savoring the meld of sweet and salt and butter and fruit, letting the conversation hang. Claire asked him to explain with a waggle of her fingers.

"I imagine that spending his money for any reason beyond the pursuit of business and profit sets the old man spinning in his casket. I imagine that the more I spend, the faster he spins." Pierce moved his hand in circles above his plate, causing a passing waiter to frown and beckon to the whippet of a man serving their table. "At first it would take me a few minutes to make a decision, but now it's instantaneous."

He snapped his fingers. "Want me to triple the reward fund?"

Claire raised a hand, palm out. "Double's great."

169

"If you decide you need more, don't even ask. Imagine the old man spinning. Then increase his RPMs."

She shook her head. "I can't do that without asking. It's your money—even though you mostly refer to it as your father's."

"Force of habit. I was raised to think of it that way." Pierce flipped his fingers, sending the hovering waiter away, and forked up the last bite of pie.

"But you worked for what you have. You earned it."

"I *earned* damned little, Claire. Not in the traditional sense. It was dumped in my lap because the old man needed an heir and my twin didn't live." He shoved his plate aside, reached for his snifter, and gulped, letting the burn serve as penance.

"I . . . I didn't know."

"Few do. The irony is that I was the sickly one." He drained the brandy and told her about being renamed and constantly compared to the dead brother who would have made the family proud. Urged on by brandy and the sad disbelief in her eyes, he unbuttoned his cuff and shoved up his sleeve to exhibit his scars. "Cutting is how I coped."

Claire said nothing for a few moments, then reached across the table and touched one of the bruises between the scars. "And those?"

"I do that so I won't cut." He yanked the sleeve down. "Pain relieves some of the anger and frustration. Although not for long."

"I'm not in your league, but I have my own self-destructive coping mechanism. I go for snack food. Salty, crunchy stuff. Ate three bags of potato chips this week. Big bags. Barbecue, cheddar, and dill pickle." She puffed out her cheeks. "I feel like a blimp."

Pierce laughed. "Forget it! You're not snookering me with a variation on 'Do I look fat?' I'm beaten before I begin. Let's talk about the Peddler, the task force, and what we can do."

"All right. But, honestly, except for what we already discussed, I'm out of ideas."

"What happened to thinking outside the box?"

"Not including the sea glass you brought from the beach," she said with an apologetic smile, "that was an exercise in futility. An expensive exercise in futility."

"But I bet the price tag really set the old man rotating." He rolled his snifter between his palms. "What about that woman with the gift? I got the impression you didn't feel that was entirely futile."

"It is until she accesses the ability to help. And who knows when that will be." Claire tugged at a dangling earring, a series of gold circles linked together. "And even then, the way she explained it to me, she has to connect to the case and draw power from those who ask her to intervene. And I somehow doubt she'd connect with the kind of charm I've seen you turn on for politicians and the press. In fact, it might drive her away."

"I agree, even though we both know that charm is counterfeit and makes me uncomfortable." Pierce drew a credit card from his wallet and beckoned to their waiter. "I'm not surprised you changed your mind."

"About what?"

"About me providing what you called a spark to jump-start Rain Paxton's power."

"I forgot I said that." Claire cocked her head, considering. "Anything's possible. She suffered a huge loss at an early age. I think she might relate to you. You're also a wounded creature."

Pierce tapped his arm and shot her a jaunty grin. "Finally. Those years of cutting pay off."

"I was thinking of the wounds from your parents. And Ariel."

His grin collapsed in a rush of emotions. Sometimes, lately, he almost forgot about Ariel. No, not forgot, but shoved memories of her to a corner of his mind and focused on the other victims. He assumed that was some kind of mental self-preservation strategy. Perhaps it was even normal. But he hadn't pursued that with a therapist. In fact, he hadn't seen a therapist since the task force got off the ground. "Of course. Ariel."

"I'm sor—"

"It's okay. You're right. That mystery is my deepest wound."

He added in a mammoth tip, signed the credit card receipt, and stood, amused by Claire's surprise when the waiter drew back her chair and offered his arm to help her to her feet.

"I'm not someone's elderly aunt," she hissed as the door closed behind them and they faced the early autumn night. "I can get out of a chair fine if you give me an extra second."

"He was showing his appreciation for the tip."

"Next time he can do that by bringing me a dessert to go." She settled herself in the passenger seat of his car. "So, are you free tomorrow for another leap outside the box? Want to head up to see Rain Paxton around nine?"

"You're not sending me alone?"

"No way." She snapped her seatbelt. "If something *does* happen, I don't want to miss it."

CHAPTER 23

September
Rain

"Company's coming," Watch called from the porch. "That woman from the task force. And a man."

A man?

Pierce Jennings?

Rain felt her cheeks flush and chastised herself. What was she hoping for from this man? Was her heart fluttering because he might be the connection that channeled the gift? Or did she feel another kind of link because of all she'd seen—or imagined—in his eyes? In a photograph, no less.

"Stop it," she whispered. "You're acting like a fool."

Bertram Mosier would notice. And tease her.

Setting aside her paring knife and the apple she'd been about to slice, she splashed cool water on her face and took a series of deep breaths.

Watch's footsteps—lighter and faster than when he arrived—crossed the living room. Then he was in the doorway, stroking his short beard and surveying the apples piled on the table and the flour, butter, salt, brown sugar, and cinnamon lined up on the counter. "You're in the middle of something. I'll tell them to buzz off."

"I'll be in the middle of something from now until half past the first hard frost." Rain tightened the band on her ponytail. "If they're willing to peel and chop, they can come in."

"Don't know why you're going to all this trouble," he grumped. "Kitchen torn up every day. More food in the freezer than we can eat in a decade."

Rain snatched up the paring knife and pointed it at him. "In the first place, even 'torn up' as you call it, the kitchen is in better shape than when you've been in here doing what you claim is cooking. In the second place, when January comes, you'll be glad there's apple pie in the freezer. And in the third place, it's good to have extra so we can invite neighbors for dinner now and then."

Mumbling about the political leanings and social skills of the neighbor who'd brought over two cans of sauerkraut as a welcoming gift, Watch returned to the porch.

When he was out of sight, Rain smiled. The picking, cooking, canning, and freezing routine was less about putting food by for later than about feeling close to Meadow. Until this harvest season, they'd worked together. And Morgan had stood in the doorway and "complained" that the kitchen was a disaster area and the freezer was overflowing.

Two car doors slammed and Rain heard indistinct voices. She washed apples, sliced a lemon, and squeezed the juice into a large glass bowl. The voices grew louder. The screen door whapped closed. Footsteps crossed the living room.

"Claire Dawson's here again," Watch announced from the doorway. "Guy with her is Pierson Jennings."

He nodded at the man behind him. The word "average" leaped to Rain's mind as she studied him. Tall, but not too tall. Not heavy, but not thin. Not exactly handsome, but not hard to look at. And not—in jeans and a long-sleeved blue-and-white-checked shirt—what she thought would be considered dressed for success in the world of business from which he came.

"Call me Pierce, please." He maneuvered around Watch, crossed the room, and thrust out his hand.

Rain raised hers, a knife in one, an apple in the other. "I'm too sticky to shake right now, but it's nice to meet you."

He flashed an okay signal. "Likewise."

"Mr. Mosier says we have to pay to play," Claire said. "What would you like us to do?"

"Whatever you're comfortable with. Peeling and chopping. Making the crumb topping. Tackling the crust."

"Oh, no." Pierce raised his hands in surrender and backed toward the door. "I've read scathing reviews about crust that was too dry or tough or thin. I'm not brave enough to attempt it. Give me a knife and a chopping board, and a promise that you won't be surprised by what hits the floor instead of the bowl."

"Promise made."

"Well I'm brave, but I'm not foolhardy," Claire said with a laugh. "I'll take a run at the crumbs. Where do we wash up?"

"Follow me. I'll get you a clean towel." Watch led them to the bathroom, instructing them to use plenty of soap and the nail brush because "certain people who don't even live here are obsessive about cleanliness."

Smiling, Rain set up a workstation at the table for Pierce, made a space beside the stove for Claire, and propped one of Meadow's recipe cards against the flour canister. Then she removed the holster from her belt and set the revolver on top of the refrigerator. Wouldn't want them to think . . . well, she wasn't sure what they'd think.

When they returned, Pierce with fingers scrubbed pink, Rain pointed out the ingredients and the recipe to Claire. "If you multiply that by six, it should work out right."

"Only six?" Watch asked. "Seems you have enough apples for sixty pies."

"They cook down," Claire told him. "And there's less after you peel and core them and cut out the bruised and wormy parts."

"Cut out the wormy parts?" Pierce jabbed a brown spot on an apple. "And waste all this protein?"

"We'll put what you cut off out for the birds and squirrels. It won't be wasted." Rain took a chair beside his, quartered an apple, removed the seeds and peel, and cut away bad spots. Sitting this close, she expected to smell his cologne above the scent of apple and lemon, but she sniffed nothing except the soap he'd washed with, soap smelling faintly of coconut and vanilla. She found that endearing and, like his clothing, exactly the opposite of what she'd expected of a man who came from wealth and privilege.

"This is how I clean and slice them." She demonstrated, flipping slices into the bowl as she cut. "But if another method is better for you, go for it. As long as the slices are about the same thickness, it doesn't matter what they look like."

His gaze tracked every slice she made, then he glanced up and smiled. "I'll go with your method."

"Never heard him say that before," Claire muttered. "At least not to me."

"Now that we got this pie stuff underway," Watch said. "Let's get down to those old brass tacks. Why are you here?"

Pierce glanced at Claire, but before she spoke, Watch went on. "No, don't try to blow a fast one by me. I know why. You're dead in the water and you think maybe Rain can whistle up a wind."

Claire whirled toward him. "We don't—"

"You're right," Pierce interrupted. "We're stalled. We're frustrated. And we're angry."

Watch's eye's narrowed and his cheeks flamed. "And you came to dump all that on Rain? Try to push my girl to grab for her gift before she's ready?"

"We only thought if we—"

Watch silenced Claire with a chopping motion. "You send her to that place searching for all your victims and you'll drain her. She might never come home."

Could that happen?

Rain flashed on an image of a gray beach, grasping waves, a setting sun. Dizzy with dread, she gripped the edge of the counter. Could she be trapped there? She'd never asked Meadow if that was possible.

She raised her head, saw Pierce's eyes mirroring her fear and saw Claire's brow furrowed. She faced Watch. "How do you know I could be stuck there? Did Meadow tell you?"

"No. But it stands to reason when you consider the evidence."

"What evidence?"

"The fact that Meadow went after only one victim at a time. And when she returned from some of those journeys she was so weak she could hardly stand."

Rain chewed her lip, remembering times her grandmother did little more than sit by the fire or in the glider swing. Morgan often read to her, stories with wishes coming true and happy endings. Motley, or one of the dogs that came before, would rest his head on her knee and pace close beside her when she walked.

"You gave her that file." Watch leveled a finger at Claire. "You hoped she'd get close to those women."

"I never meant—"

"Sure you did." He pointed at Pierce. "One of those women is your wife. You meant for all this to be under Rain's skin like it's under yours."

177

Pierce set aside his paring knife and stood, his voice gentle and filled with regret. "We should go."

"Yes." Claire dusted flour from her hands. "We're asking too much. I'm sorry. We want answers and, to be honest, I want revenge, especially for Marlin. But I had no idea this was so dangerous."

"No one has any idea," Rain said softly. "No one who hasn't been there and come home again. And the way it was for my grandmother may not be the way it is for me."

"That's a fool's argument," Watch warned.

Rain felt dread and fear swirl into an anger that filled her chest. What did he truly know about any of this? "If I went after only one person, if I went after Mr. Simmons, he'd know who killed him and all the others, right? Then it wouldn't be as dangerous."

Watch laughed. "No more dangerous than skinny dipping in a lake of fire."

Indignation boiled in Rain's brain. "And what business is it of yours?"

"Morgan asked me to watch over you."

"Yes, but he didn't mean you should make decisions for me!"

"If the decisions you're making could kill you, then maybe that's exactly what he intended."

"I'm sorry." Pierce stepped between them. "We shouldn't have come. We're leaving."

"Good riddance," Watch shouted. "Don't even think about coming here again."

"No, don't go." Rain plucked at Pierce's sleeve. "Please. Don't listen to him. Stay."

He shook his head, his eyes solemn. "I think the best thing for all of us is that we go. Everyone's upset. Maybe some time in the future we—"

178

"No. Stay."

She clutched at his hand.

Felt a needle of pain. As if she'd been stung by a wasp or touched a live wire.

And then she was in a well. Falling. Falling. Falling.

And hearing Meadow's voice. "There will be a dog."

CHAPTER 24

September
Pierce

Pierce caught Rain as she slumped. "Something zapped me. Shocked both of us. I think she fainted."

"That's no faint," Watch said. "She got the gift. She's gone to Nightfall Bay."

Pierce lowered her to the floor and Claire knelt by her side, feeling for a pulse in her neck. "What should we do? Can we bring her back?"

"Not one of us has the power for that. All we can do is make her comfortable." Watch settled in the chair Pierce had vacated. "But first, let the dog in."

"Dog?" Claire frowned. "I didn't see a dog when I was here before."

"There's one now. Big one." Watch nodded toward the living room. "Wants in. Bad. Wants to be with her."

And then Pierce heard it, an insistent scratching that made the screen door rattle in its frame. He brushed a strand of hair from Rain's cheek and stood. His father had railed at the expense of a having a pet. His mother had insisted dogs were filthy creatures. "I, uh, don't know much about dogs."

"If he's like the others before him," Watch said, "he'll be a law unto himself. But he won't bite. Unless he has to."

Not exactly what Pierce hoped to hear.

Conscious of Watch's gaze, he feigned confidence and strode to the door. The dog, a shaggy gray and black creature more than a yard tall at the shoulders, raised its head and stared at him through the screen. A white blaze started even with blue-gray eyes and ran between its ears and along its back, narrowing to a point at the base of a tail as long as Pierce's arm.

"Want to come in?" Pierce asked.

The dog pawed at the door.

"Sorry. Of course you do. You want to be with Rain." Slowly, Pierce pushed the door. The dog made way, its eyes seeming to size up the opening until it lowered its head and charged through.

When Pierce returned to the kitchen, it was lying beside Rain, its chin on her shoulder. Claire squatted on her heels, watching. "It's huge, but it seems gentle. Where did it come from?"

"I'd tell you if I ever got an answer when I put that question to Meadow and Morgan. Could be they didn't know." Watch picked up the paring knife Pierce had abandoned and went to work on an apple. "Could also be they didn't think I'd be inclined to swallow the truth."

"Meaning that this dog isn't, uh, real?" Pierce asked.

Claire stretched to stroke the dog's side. "It feels real."

"He," Watch said. "Probably. The rest were males."

"I'll take your word for it." Pierce had seen enough dogs to know how to determine sex, but he saw no reason to attempt that now, no reason to mess with a dog that had a job to do. Especially one with jaws powerful enough to tear through skin and muscle and break bone.

181

"We can't leave her here. Even if she doesn't feel how hard the floor is while she's, um, gone, when she returns she'll be stiff and sore." Claire reached for Pierce's hand. "If you helped, we could carry her upstairs to the room Meadow used."

"Will the dog let us?"

"Might not," Watch said. "And it won't be easy getting Rain up those stairs. They're as steep as they are narrow and there's a turn in the middle."

"That's true," Claire said.

"Put her in the best bedroom, where Morgan and Meadow slept."

At Watch's words, the dog stood, walked to the doorway to the living room, looked over its shoulder at Pierce, and whined.

"If you help me get her up," he told Claire, "I can carry her."

"You sure?"

"She's tall," Watch said. "But there's not much to her."

Claire helped lift Rain to her feet and positioned her right arm around Pierce's shoulders. He lifted, cradling her against his chest, inhaling the scents of her hair and skin, shampoo and soap, honey and lemon. As Watch said, she wasn't heavy, but his legs trembled and he felt beads of sweat pop out on his upper lip. He leaned back and took short, quick steps.

"The door on the right," Watch told him.

Claire went ahead, moving a wing chair aside, kicking at a heap of clothing, and tweaking a wrinkle out of a braided rug. Panting with the effort, Pierce bent to lay Rain on the bed. Claire plumped pillows for her head, removed the band from her ponytail, and fanned her hair. Pierce arranged Rain's arms by her sides. When he stepped aside, the dog took his place, resting his chin on Rain's right hand and closing his eyes.

"I don't know why," Claire said, "but I have a feeling the window should be open."

182

"Go with it," Pierce said. "We're in strange waters here. Trust your instincts."

Claire nodded, crossed, the room, and pushed up the sash. "And I think we should light a candle. Or maybe several candles."

Watch spoke from the doorway. "Plenty of candles in a wooden box on the bottom of the long bookshelf."

"See if any are beeswax," Claire ordered. "If not, bring me anything with a subtle scent."

"Should I salute before I fetch and carry?"

"Never mind," Pierce said in a tight voice. "I'll get them."

"Hey." Watch raised his hands. "Just trying to relieve a little tension. Snapping at each other won't ease her way."

Claire sighed. "He has a point."

"Much as you hate to admit it." Watch turned and went after the candles.

Pierce slumped against the wall beside the window and rubbed his hand. "She touched me. That's all."

"That's all it took." Claire polished a stubby brass candlestick with a tissue.

"It electrified me. All the way to my toes. And now I feel like I gave about a gallon of blood." Pierce slid down the wall and sat on the floor, legs outstretched. "Gave blood and didn't get a cookie."

"She musta tapped your energy, son." Watch laid several candles on the bureau.

"I'll make a sandwich for you. And then I'll clean up the kitchen." Claire wedged a candle in the candlestick, set it on the nightstand, and issued a command to Watch. "Get this lit. And bring some water for that dog."

"Likes to give orders, doesn't she?" Watch observed.

Pierce was grateful the question didn't need an answer and that Watch didn't ask another. The simple act of breathing

183

seemed to siphon strength from his muscles. Including his brain. His thoughts swelled and then rolled across desert sand in slow motion, the way they had when he was ten, came down with the flu, and ran a fever for days.

If Rain had depleted so much of his energy to journey to Nightfall Bay, how much of her own would she burn?

And would she have enough to return?

CHAPTER 25

September
Rain

The narrow stone well shaft seemed to go on forever. Then she struck water so cold it might have melted from a glacier moments before. In a second she broke through and, buffeted by wind and hail, plummeted through fog. She landed with a bone-jarring thud on a sloping dune.

Waves broke on the gray sand and retreated, hissing. Black water stretched to the horizon, and a wintry sun hung low in a leaden sky. Weak, weary, and anxious, she struggled to her feet and peered up and down the beach. Sloping dunes—sand the color of ash and without a single tuft of grass—stretched in either direction. Huddled figures massed at the base of the dunes. Some sat, some crouched, some bent into an insidious wind blowing from the sea, a wind that carried no scent of salt or seaweed, carried no scent at all.

Rain hugged herself, trying to control her shivering. And her fear. "You're here. You have the gift. This is what you wanted to do."

Her teeth chattered. This is what she *thought* she wanted to do. But being here, seeing this place, drained away every ounce of bold conviction.

"Don't be a baby. Meadow did this. Her mother did this. And her grandmother. You can do it."

But how? Where did she begin? Should she walk right or left? And what would she say if, somehow, she found Marlin Simmons?

The task seemed daunting, impossible. All those . . . people. She had to remember they were people. How had Meadow done it? How had she found the one she sought?

Once more, she peered to her right and then to her left. Neither direction appeared more promising. There was no difference in the dim light, no difference in the terrain, no difference in the number of the forlorn who waited and watched.

Waited for what?

Watched for what?

Had she ever asked Meadow if she knew?

She couldn't remember.

Greek myth called for Charon to ferry souls in his boat. But she didn't think Charon had to cross an ocean of black water.

She recalled that his service wasn't free. Believers buried their dead with coins to pay for passage.

Were earthly justice and closure equivalent forms of payment?

Again she looked left and right. There seemed no end to the huddled figures and, she supposed, no end to their misery. She might trudge along the shore for miles, for days, and never encounter Marlin Simmons or anyone who knew him.

Were miles the same here?

Were days?

Would she need to return to this spot in order to get back to the farmhouse and to life? Should she mark it in some way? Draw something in the sand or leave her shoes?

So many questions she should have asked Meadow.

She plodded toward the water, stood out of reach of the waves, and studied the tide line. She saw no bits of shell or rock, no gull feathers or seaweed.

What she did see were paw prints in the damp sand. Prints the size of her hand. Leading off to her left. They reminded her of the prints Motley made in the driveway after a storm.

"There will be a dog."

Meadow's voice.

Rain cocked her head. Real? Or in her mind?

She looked around, but saw no sign of her grandmother.

Waves licked at the prints, filling a dozen of them.

Rain took off at a trot, following the trail marked for her.

Unswerving, the tracks led along the narrow strand between lapping waves and those who waited. Rain hesitated, stumbled, then plunged on, close enough now to see that beneath thick gray blankets shielding them from the wind, each wore unique clothing. She imagined these were the clothes they died in. Some had heavy jackets, others summer dresses or pajamas. One, a young man, was naked.

She tried to put that from her mind, but failed. And she tried to keep her gaze on the tracks, tried not to glimpse faces from the corners of her eyes, faces that bore striking expressions. Some grimaced with pain, some stared wide-eyed in terror, some wore faint smiles of hope. Other faces were tight with anger or slack with resignation. One face had no eyes. Another was little more than pulp.

Trying to control a rising sense of fear and horror, Rain followed the tracks away from the water and into the crowd. She remembered her grandparents said those who waited couldn't hurt, might only frighten. But she told herself not to look. And not to think about how far the crowds stretched in either direction.

187

She understood why Meadow needed to draw on the strength and determination of others. And she understood why her mother took a road that, although dangerous and degrading, didn't lead to Nightfall Bay.

The dog's tracks threaded their way through the crowd and Rain followed, gaze locked on the sand. Each of those who waited seemed to be alone and isolated, closed off from the others. Although some stood or sat close together, she saw no signs they were comforting each other—no hugging, no clasping of hands. Rain wondered if their deaths were connected, if they had died in a fire, on a capsized ship, or in an avalanche.

When the tracks led through a close tangle of those who waited, she hunched her shoulders, drew in her arms, turned sideways, and made herself as small as possible. Still, contact was inevitable. She felt the rough fibers of the blankets—wool perhaps. She felt the slight give of flesh. But she felt no drawing away, no movement at all.

She apologized each time, but heard no response. It was as if they were numb and didn't feel her pressing against them. And, although she drew in both short breaths and lung-filling ones, she smelled nothing. It was as if these people, like the beach, had been scrubbed clean of the life functions that created scent and sound.

Her fear and anxiety gave way to a sense of familiarity, to detached acceptance.

The paw prints broke from the crowded area and led through a band of widely spaced souls. Yes, souls. No matter what Meadow and Morgan told her, Rain wasn't able to think of these as people.

Did it matter?

If she asked that question, would someone here answer?

The tracks disappeared a few feet from a male figure sitting close against the steep slope of the dune. Unlike the others, he wasn't still. His legs shifted forward and back, jerking from the knees, his heels plowing furrows in the sand. His hands were level with his neck. His fingers twitched and clawed.

Rain didn't need even a one-second glance at the face with its bulging eyes and open mouth to know this was Marlin Simmons, reliving his final moments.

Had others also re-enacted those moments until, like battery-powered toys, they ran down and were still? How long before Marlin Simmons was little more than a statue? And—a larger question—how was she supposed to communicate with him?

Meadow hadn't said there was a trick to this.

But Rain had never asked.

She felt like a dim-witted, thick-headed fool.

So that's where she began.

Kneeling before the soul that had been Marlin Simmons, her gaze directed at the sand because she couldn't force herself to meet those terror-filled eyes, she apologized. "Mr. Simmons, I'm sorry to intrude. You don't know me. My name is Rain Paxton and I inherited a gift that allowed me to travel to this place and find you. Pierce and Claire came to me because the case is stalled and they don't have any fresh leads and they hope you can identify the man they call the Peddler. But I'm not sure you can hear me or if this is even the way I'm supposed to communicate with you. I sort of assumed everything would fall in place when I got here, and I didn't ask Meadow the—"

"Enough."

The voice filled her mind.

She raised her gaze to the face of the soul before her.

"Get to the point."

The lips didn't move. But the voice was clear. Was it Marlin Simmons? From what Claire had told her, he had been quick-tempered and hadn't suffered fools gladly.

"Sorry. Um, okay, did you see the person who, um—?"

"Killed me? Just say it, girl. I'm dead. Pussyfooting around won't change that."

Apparently dying hadn't altered his personality.

"Right. Okay, did you see who killed you?"

"No, damn it. I was at my desk. He came up behind me."

"It was a man?"

"I said so, didn't I?"

The voice was so filled with rage that Rain reminded herself Marlin Simmons couldn't harm her. "Yes, but I wanted to be sure."

"Now you are."

"Sorry, I never did this before."

"You said that."

Rain reminded herself that Claire and Pierce had put up with this every day they worked with Marlin Simmons. If they were here now, what would they ask? She wished she'd made a list of possible questions for him—or for any victim—before she received the gift. She should have prepared. She should have—

"When he jerked me from the chair, he pulled me against his chest. He was about my height, maybe wider in the shoulders."

His statements seemed to turn on a row of mental lights in Rain's mind. "Did you see his clothing or shoes?"

"He wore a ski mask. And rain jacket. Black. Black jeans and shoes."

"Did he say anything?"

"No."

"Did you smell anything? Hair gel? Cologne?"

"Foul stuff Pierce used to wear until I called him on it."

"Did—"

A dog barked, the sound deep and insistent.

Rain got to her feet, glanced around, saw nothing.

The dog barked again and paw prints appeared, leading along the face of the dunes, leading back the way she came. She glanced over her shoulder at the ocean. Only a knife-blade of sky remained between the wintry sun and the black water.

She told herself she wasn't afraid of this place, but the idea of spending a night—however long a night might be—among the dead made her shiver.

If she stayed too long, would the way home be closed?

She turned to the twitching figure and spoke in a voice she hoped was filled with confidence. "I have to go, Mr. Simmons. Claire and Pierce haven't forgotten you. They'll get the Peddler. And then you can leave here and go across the water."

The dog barked a third time, the sound fainter, farther away.

The sun slipped.

Its rim touched the water.

Rain ran.

CHAPTER 26

September
Pierce

Pierce woke to find himself on the braided rug beneath the bedroom window, his head cushioned by a pillow, a quilt covering him. Except for candles burning on either side of the bed, the room was dark. Rain lay as he and Claire had placed her, but covered with a rainbow quilt. Her skin seemed as white as the pillowcase. The dog also hadn't moved. His chin lay on Rain's right hand. His bowl of water was untouched. Watch, snoring, sat in the rocking chair near the bureau. Claire leaned in the doorway, sipping from a mug.

Every muscle, Pierce discovered as he flexed his fingers and toes, resisted movement with painful spasms.

"You're awake." Claire saluted him with her mug. "Coffee?"

"Please."

She turned a thumb up and hitched toward the kitchen.

Pierce rotated his ankles, stretching calf muscles that seemed to bind and catch and seize. How long had he been asleep? He rolled his shoulders and massaged the back of his neck. He felt like he'd been dragged behind a tank across an obstacle course, dumped in a ditch, and covered with rocks.

Claire returned and set two mugs on the bureau. "Need a hand?"

"What I need is a crane." He rolled to his side and then to his hands and knees, stretching and flexing, working his way to a sitting position with the wall for support. "How long was I asleep?"

"Eight hours. Maybe a little more." Claire handed him the mug. "I wanted to move you to the sofa, but Watch said we shouldn't. He thought you needed to be here, near Rain and the dog. He said you'd be fine on the floor."

"Fine." Pierce rotated his ankles again and heard them pop. Had he ever slept on a floor before? He doubted it. Indulgent as his nanny had been, she wouldn't have allowed the namesake son of Pierson Jennings to do that. Not even for a short nap. "Easy for him to say it was fine. He took the chair."

"He played his I'm-an-old-man card." Claire rolled her eyes. "And insisted he had to be here too. After he took time out to put on his slippers."

Pierce sipped coffee, strong, milky, and sugared—not the way he liked it, but the way he guessed Claire thought he needed it. "Did he explain how snoring would help her?"

"Not so far. But if anyone could come up with a reason, it would be him." She lowered herself to the floor beside Pierce. "He's a character. Like someone out of a book about the dysfunctional crusading editor of a newspaper in a town so far out in the woods they get mail only once a month."

"She's family. He loves her." In his voice, Pierce heard conviction he hadn't known he felt. "For all we know, the sound of his snoring may be part of what brings her home."

Pierce swallowed more sweet coffee and studied Rain. She hadn't moved an inch. "I wish we knew how long she'll be, uh, gone."

"And what we should and shouldn't do. When you first fell asleep, I tiptoed around thinking the least little noise might jar her out of it and bring her back before she was ready, or mess something up so she got stuck there. But he," Claire nodded at Watch, "sat in that chair eating the ham sandwich I made for you, complaining because he likes more mayonnaise and cheese and less lettuce. And she didn't stir."

"So she either can't hear us, or isn't concerned by the noise we make." Pierce drained the mug. "After all the charlatans I met, I think I'm a judge of what's not fakery. And I'm 99% positive she's for real."

"I am, too."

"I wonder what time is like there." Pierce turned the mug in his fingers. "If an hour is the same. Or longer. Or shorter."

"And if she falls through a sort of a well to get there, I wonder how she returns." Claire nodded at the huge dog. "I mean, I know he has something to do with it, but what? Does he sprout wings and fly her up the well shaft?"

She groaned and slapped her cheeks. "Listen to me. She and the dog go there as spirits. Of course they can fly. They can fly to the moon if they want to."

Pierce patted her shoulder. "If I'd known you were an expert on spirits when I hired you to take Marlin's place, I would have offered you more money."

"It's not too late for the money." Clutching the windowsill, Claire struggled to her feet. "But I know less about spirits than I do about crocheting potholders."

"I expect we're about to learn more," Watch said in a rumbling voice. "About spirits. Not potholders."

Pierce wondered how long the old man had been awake. Had he pretended to sleep in order to eavesdrop? Pierce wouldn't put that past him.

Taking tiny quiet steps, Claire approached the bed. "Her fingers are moving," she whispered. "And the dog's eyes are open."

"She'll be thirsty," Watch said.

Claire gave him her best interrogator's frown and he raised his hands in surrender. "Well, *I'd* be thirsty. Hungry, too." He sat up straighter and patted his gut. "Heard you banging around in the kitchen. Did you get those pies made?"

"Maybe."

"Crust and all?" Pierce asked.

"I had to keep busy." Claire collected his empty cup. "And the directions were clear and simple."

"Takes more than directions to make a decent crust," Watch said. "You tried a piece yet?"

"I haven't been hungry."

"Guilt does that." He patted his gut again. "My conscience is clear. I'm not the one who pushed her to go to Nightfall Bay. I could eat a buzzard if you stuffed and roasted it. And whipped up enough gravy to float it."

"You better hope I never come across a buzzard carcass or I'll hold you to that." Claire headed for the kitchen, calling over her shoulder. "I'll bring water and make fresh coffee. When she's awake and we know she's okay, we'll all have pie to celebrate. But not before."

"Hard-headed woman," Watch grumbled. "Fortunately, I like 'em that way."

Thinking Claire would be less than thrilled by that piece of information, Pierce followed her example and used the windowsill to lever himself upright. His legs wobbled and for a moment he felt as if he stood on the pitching deck of a ship caught in a storm. He closed his eyes, but decided that made things worse. He opened them again to see the dog staring at him.

195

"Hey, boy," he said, knowing as he did that his tone was too light, too dismissive and condescending. This was no puppy, no spoiled and lazy lapdog. This was a working dog with a mission. This dog was probably smarter than he was. "Is she on her way?"

"On my way where?" Rain murmured.

"Home," Watch boomed. "To the farm. To those pies you were making."

Rain didn't open her eyes, but a smile lifted her pale lips.

Pierce tottered to the footboard and seized one of the decorative wooden spindles for balance. He wanted to shout out questions about her experiences and about Marlin, but held them in. "Claire finished the pies."

Rain's smile broadened. "Even the crust?"

"Claims the recipe was simple," Watch said. "Won't bring me a piece to test, though. Says I have to wait until you're ready so we can all try some."

"Good for her. I feel like I'm sort of putting myself together. I should be ready for pie in a few . . . hours."

Watch groaned but Pierce, registering the way she'd paused for effect, laughed with relief. Whatever happened to her at Nightfall Bay, Rain hadn't lost her knowledge of who she'd been with and what had been happening when she departed. And she hadn't lost her sense of humor.

Claire returned with a tall glass of water with a straw for Rain, and a bowl for the dog. "Chicken and rice. I found the chicken in the freezer and cooked it up for him." She stroked the dog's head, set the bowl on the floor beside him, and came around the bed to place the water on the nightstand. "We'll go out later and get . . . well, whatever kind of dog food Rain thinks we should get for him."

The dog bent to the bowl and emptied it in seconds.

"That was my chicken," Watch groused. "Had plans to make a pot pie tomorrow."

Rain giggled, opened her eyes, and reached for the water. "And I had plans to build a rocket ship in the garage."

Pierce felt another jolt of relief. Not quite a complete reprieve from his self-imposed sentence of guilt and regret and responsibility, but enough for now. "How do you feel?"

She sucked up half the water before she answered. "Thirsty. And hungry."

"I'll get coffee and pie," Claire said.

"Put a slab of sharp cheddar cheese on mine," Watch ordered. "Heat the pie—but not too much. Don't heat the cheese. I like that cold. Maybe put some whipped cream on the side."

Claire paused in the doorway. "If you want something made to order, then you better get your butt out of your cushy chair and help me in the kitchen."

Watch snorted, then hefted himself from the rocker and, slippers slapping the floor, followed her. The dog gave the bowl a final lick, paced slowly to the rug where Pierce had slept, and flopped.

Still gripping the footboard, Pierce sat on the edge of the bed. "Are you sure you're okay?"

"Pretty sure. I mean, I'm weak. Really weak. It's hard to hold this without spilling. Even hard to suck it through the straw." Rain finished the water and set the glass aside. "And like I said, I feel like I'm putting myself together, like I'm hollow or maybe liquid at the core. This water isn't leaking out anywhere, is it?"

"Not that I can see."

"You'd tell me if it was, wouldn't you? You wouldn't lie because you feel bad about what happened?"

Pierce felt a wash of guilt. "If I'd had any idea how hard this would be on you, I never would have come. I wouldn't have let Claire bring you the file."

"But you did. And even though it happened so fast I didn't have time to prepare, now I know what it's like to go to Nightfall Bay. " She stretched out a hand. "And I'm glad."

Pierce recoiled. "I don't think we—"

"Nothing will happen if I touch you. Not now."

"How do you know?"

She considered that for a moment. "It sounds silly, but somehow I just know. I can't go to Nightfall Bay unless I want to. And I can't go until I'm ready to."

"If you drained your energy as much as you drained mine, you won't be ready for weeks." Tentatively, Pierce touched his index finger to hers. Not a spark, not a sizzle. He took her hand. "You're cold."

"I don't feel cold."

"Take my word for it." He slid closer and touched her cheek. "Cold."

"Maybe that's normal."

"Normal?" Pierce laughed. "While your body is here in some kind of trance or coma, your spirit falls through a hole in the ground and lands in limbo where you talk to dead people. Is that normal? And don't get me started on a dog appearing out of nowhere."

The dog opened one eye and thumped his tail on the rug—only once, as if that was all he had the strength for.

"Natty."

"Huh?"

"I'll name him for Natty Bumppo, the Pathfinder from the James Fenimore Cooper novels. Morgan read them to me when I was young."

The dog barked. Again, only once.

"I think he approves."

"He led me to your friend."

Pierce felt a mix of surprise and validation. He squeezed her icy fingers. "Marlin?"

"Yes. Help me sit up and I'll tell you when everyone is here."

"I'll do my best, but when you took off, you drained me like a battery."

He stood, sidestepped to the head of the bed, got his right arm beneath her shoulders and lifted. Too fast. Too far. Rain flopped forward like a cloth doll. "Sorry. I must be getting stronger."

He plumped pillows, leaned them against the headboard, and helped her wiggle into position. "Better?"

"Much."

"You're sure it was Marlin you found?"

"Yes. He's exactly the way Claire described him."

"And you were able to talk with him?"

"Yes." She looked up as Claire set a loaded tray on the bureau. "He told me he knew he was dead and I shouldn't pussyfoot around."

"That's Marlin!" Claire lifted a mug, and handed it to Rain. "Was he—?" She slapped a hand over her mouth and mumbled between her fingers. "I almost asked if he was okay."

"If who was okay?" Watch lumbered in carrying a mug and a bowl mounded high with whipped cream.

"Marlin." Claire unfolded a napkin on Rain's lap and set a plate of pie and cheese upon it. "She found Marlin."

"Never doubted she would." Watch dropped into the rocker, set his mug on the floor, and spooned pie and cheese and cream between his lips, talking as he chewed. "It's in her blood."

199

Pierce accepted a plate of pie from Claire, hearing his stomach rumble as he inhaled the aroma of cinnamon and brown sugar. The crust, he found when he forked off a bit, was perfect—or at least as good as any he'd had at a bakery or restaurant. "The crust is incredible."

"Better than any I ever made," Rain said. "Meadow told me I didn't move fast enough, and the butter got too warm."

"Enough food chatter." Watch tapped his spoon on the rim of his bowl. "Get to what went on down there. Or up there. Or wherever there is."

Between bites of pie and sips of coffee, Rain told them how the dog's prints led her along the beach, through the crowd, and to Marlin. Claire gasped when she described him. Pierce felt his fists clench.

"He didn't see the man who killed him. But it *was* a man, about the same height but a little broader in the shoulders, wearing a ski mask and rain jacket and dark clothing." Rain thrust her chin toward Pierce. "He was also wearing cologne like the brand you used to wear, one Marlin thought was foul."

"I remember the day he told you that." Claire chuckled. "It was—what?—the day we moved into the office. You were unpacking the coffeepot you bought and he blew up and said you were insensitive, uncaring, self-centered, and violating the Clean Air Act."

Pierce grinned, discomfort and irritation far in the past. "Marlin never minced words."

"And he never got the best of you," Claire said in a voice filled with pride. "You were so cool that day. You thanked him for his opinion and for exercising his right to free speech, and you went right on as if nothing happened."

"Just so you know, it took all the guts I had to do that—all the guts and a lot of practice being a punching bag for my father."

200

"But you never wore that cologne again."

Pierce rubbed the stubble on his cheeks. "Ariel bought it for me. I never liked it. I thought it was too . . . aggressive, had too much of a bite."

"But it reminded you of her," Rain said. "Of the good times."

She said that in a way that implied there had been more bad times than good, in a way that made Pierce feel as if she knew how conflicted his feelings for Ariel were. He tried to study her eyes for confirmation, but her gaze was focused on her cheese and pie.

It was Claire who asked the question in his mind. "Did you see Ariel?"

Rain shook her head. "No. I didn't see any of the women the Peddler took."

CHAPTER 27

September
Rain

Rain set plates and silverware on the small table in her cabin. "I'm capable of cooking a meal, you know. You don't have to haul food up here every day. And you don't have to babysit me every night. I have Natty."

Natty barked as if to affirm he was on the job.

Pierce only smiled and continued to unpack cardboard cartons from a huge brown paper bag.

"I'm much stronger than I was last week. I swept the porch and whacked some weeds out front this morning." She'd also driven to the farmhouse to retrieve her revolver, and later hiked to the boltholes to trim blackberry canes so she could squeeze through without sacrificing more than a few square inches of skin. Her other purpose had been to show Natty where they were—although she was certain he already knew. Like the dogs before him, he patrolled the property, slept by the door, and often acted on commands before she gave them. "And I could have done a lot more."

But not much more. She no longer wobbled when she walked or leaned on the banister going upstairs to her bed in the loft, but she wouldn't be taking off on a run anytime soon.

Again, Pierce said nothing. His silence had depth and height and weight. It wasn't pejorative, but neither was it smug or amused. It was simply a wall her words didn't penetrate. Perhaps because they weren't entirely truthful.

She gave up the argument and focused on what he'd brought. "Do I smell shrimp?"

"And chicken. And noodles and other things. I'm afraid Watch relieved me of the Mongolian beef and the pork fried rice." Pierce folded the paper bag and stowed it in the cabinet under the sink. "He seems to think of himself as a tollgate. Won't let me pass until I pay up with conversation or food."

"Preferably vast quantities of both." Rain opened the nearest carton and inhaled the spicy aroma of shrimp and vegetables with walnuts. Pierce always bought more than was necessary. At first, Rain thought that was due to his wealth and a cavalier attitude toward spending money, but lately she chalked it up to a generous heart. If he had only a dollar to his name, Pierce would share it.

"He misses you."

"I saw him just this morning." Rain opened three more cartons. "He could walk up and visit. Or drive Morgan's truck."

"He's nervous about getting the truck up the hill—says he has no idea what four-wheel drive is all about and he'd probably hit a tree trying to turn it around. But one of these days he might walk. He claims he makes it to the mailbox with only two stops."

Pierce pulled four bundles of clothing from his backpack, unrolled shirts and jeans, and revealed bottles of craft beer. "These aren't on his diet, but I doubted medical advice would control him if he heard them clinking, and I wasn't up for a wrestling match."

Rain smiled at the image and tossed a small chunk of chicken to Natty. His teeth snapped together like a trap.

"Wouldn't want to get a piece of my anatomy between his jaws." Pierce folded his clothing into the backpack and carried it to the sofa. "I doubt I'd see it again."

Rain cataloged what he'd brought. Two shirts and two pairs of jeans. He'd definitely stay tonight and tomorrow night. Although she argued that she would be fine on her own at night, she wasn't ready to test that claim. She was weaker than she pretended. And even with Natty on guard, she was jumpy. Besides, she enjoyed Pierce's company, his knowledge of the world, his sense of humor. And she was thrilled by his interest in her life, her editing projects, and what she thought and felt about seemingly everything.

Would she like him as much if he wasn't a wounded creature? Would they have what seemed to be such a strong connection if she didn't have her own scars?

When she edited manuscripts, she often urged writers to add loss and pain to a character's past to explain emotions and actions that might otherwise seem unfounded.

But this wasn't fiction.

Pierce loaded his plate with chicken in an orange sauce, crisp string beans, rice, and noodles with vegetables. "Walking up that hill gives me an appetite."

"You could drive. The car you rented got up here the day before yesterday when you took us to the vet for Natty's shots."

"What a waste of time and money that was. A dog from wherever he's from wouldn't need shots like normal dogs."

Rain smiled. "I gave you the choice of explaining that to the vet and the animal control folks, but you passed."

"Which is why I'm not locked up in a rubber room right now. But back to the hill, the car I swapped for this afternoon might not make it. And there's no place to park it behind the cabin. Better to leave it in the barn. You said your grandfather wanted this place to be close to invisible, and I intend to honor that."

"Then take my little hill climber to the farmhouse and use it to come and go."

"You might need it while I'm away." Pierce set his plate on the table and flexed his biceps. "Besides, a real man walks."

"Is a real man also pigheaded?"

"When it's called for I can oink with the best of them."

Rain filled her plate and joined him at the table. "And it's called for pretty much all the time?"

He raised one eyebrow, but said nothing as he stripped paper wrapping from a set of chopsticks, and put them to work.

Rain decided she liked his silences as much as his comments and conversations. They were comfortable and familiar, even the silence she thought of as a wall. She didn't feel the need to fill the conversational gaps. They were soft and inviting, like comforters or mounds of pillows or puffy chairs. She felt as if she could lie back and relax in them.

How would it feel, she wondered, to lie in his arms?

The day after her journey to Nightfall Bay, when she insisted she return to her home, he'd managed to carry her to Morgan's truck, then into the cabin, and up to bed. Once she'd been able to climb the stairs on her own, he'd offered no more than a big brotherly pat on the shoulder.

That fleeting touch left her hungry for more. Much more.

She reminded herself of Ariel. His life was, at best, on hold. If he hungered, was it for release from pain more than anything else? If they came together, would she come away empty, her longing and need sharper? Would he feel guilt and reject her afterward?

Stop. Enjoy what's here now.

She put thoughts of the future aside, cleaned her plate, and scooped out seconds before she asked about the status of the investigation.

"No promising tips or leads." Pierce chased a sliver of carrot with his chopsticks. "On the other hand, we have no fresh disappearances. Claire's still hunting down people who worked at the insurance agencies where he used the aliases of Mitchum and Reeves. We know height and weight from the driver's licenses he was issued in those names. How he managed to get those and his insurance license we have no idea. Yet. He wasn't in either office much, so memories are hazy, but so far the consensus is that he was muscular but not muscle-bound."

"What about his cologne?" Rain wound a noodle on her fork. She had little experience with chopsticks and most of that hadn't gone well. "If Reeves or Mitchum wore the same kind, it's another brick in the wall, right, another bit of proof that the Peddler used those names?"

"A small brick," Pierce admitted. "And, unfortunately, a brick that investigators with actual experience might scoff at."

"Claire should ask the women who worked with him."

"Do I hear sexism?" Pierce dropped the chopsticks and used his fingers to capture the carrot. "Are you saying women have a better sense of smell? Or are better at remembering details?"

"I don't know. I've never been curious enough to see if there's been scientific research on those questions. But I think he'd flirt with women, get close to them—a lot closer than he would to his male co-workers. If he did, some of them might be able to dredge up impressions and memories."

He carried his plate to the sink. "If I can get a signal, I'll send Claire a text, ask her to dig harder to find women he worked with and take along a sample of that cologne for them to sniff when she interviews them."

As he drew his cellphone from pocket, the landline rang. He glanced at the readout. "It's Watch."

"Probably doesn't like the fortune in his cookie and wants you to bring him another."

"Shall we let him leave a message?"

"He'll only call again." Rain groaned. "And again. And again."

"I get the picture." Pierce slipped his cell into his pocket, lifted the handset, handed it to her, and carried her plate to the sink.

Rain clicked on. "We already ate the last cookie."

"What are the names of those busybody neighbors across the hill on the east side of the orchard? Brother and sister. Noses like dried out red corncobs. IQs not much higher."

"Ethel and Edgar Fitzhugh. And that's not kind. They can't help—"

"No time for being kind. Not now. Man came to their door this afternoon collecting for some bullshit charity. Conned Edgar out of ten bucks and information about their neighbors. Including me and you and our departed relatives. Including speculation—some not that far off base—about the family gift."

"Was it the Peddler?" Rain whispered.

Soapy water dripping from his hands, Pierce reached across the sink and closed the kitchen window. "Put him on speaker."

"Be my guess it was him," Watch's voice crackled into the room.

"How did he—?"

"He followed me!" Pierce slammed his fist on the counter. "He must have."

"But you swapped cars this afternoon."

"Wasn't today he was followed, girl," Watch said. "This guy was up here hoodwinking Edgar before lunchtime while Ethel was out with her knitting group. She checked on the charity when she got home, found it was a scam, and called around to alert the neighbors—after she fixed dinner and tore a strip off Edgar's butt. Edgar isn't the sharpest pencil in the pack. He's more like a nub of a pencil with chipped paint and a worn-down eraser."

"Did he con anyone else?" Pierce asked.

"Far as we can tell, that was his first and only stop."

The only one he needed.

Rain felt weak and dizzy, her mind filled with swirling clouds.

Get it together. You said you were prepared. Now prove it.

She drew in a breath. Held it. Let it out and drew in another, watching Pierce turn off the lamps on her desk and on the table beside the sofa. He moved to the front windows and drew the thick curtains, making sure they overlapped. Natty, who'd been sprawled by the sofa, sat up, sniffing the air.

Rain reminded herself she wasn't alone. And she *was* prepared. Morgan had seen to that.

"I told Ethel to keep her eyes peeled," Watch said. "Made up a story about the guy being the nutjob boyfriend of a woman who wasn't happy with your analysis of her novel. Tried to pry a description from Edgar, but all I got was longish blond hair and beard, sunglasses, squeaky voice, T-shirt with a picture of a dinosaur, and a white car."

"Sounds like a disguise to me." Pierce checked the locks on the front door and the back, and drew the curtains on the kitchen window. Natty paced at his heels.

"Seems to me he won't wait long to make his move. Probably tonight he'll at least get close to check the lay of the land. I've got the lights off and as soon as it's full dark I'll be on the porch standing sentry. He won't come on the road, but maybe I'll spot him crossing a field or making through the orchard. If I see him, I'll call the landline. Two rings."

"That'll work," Pierce said. "Unless he cuts the line."

"Right. Conch shell it is."

Natty whined and paced to the front door.

"Okay," Rain said. "I'll let Natty out to keep watch and we'll get ready."

"But not too ready," Watch cautioned. "Remember what Morgan always said."

"I will. You take care."

"It's not me he wants. Although he doesn't seem the type to be squeamish about collateral damage."

Watch cut the connection.

Natty snuffled along the bottom of the back door.

"This is my fault. I thought I was being so careful, but he must have gotten suspicious that I wasn't using my car or going home." Pierce reached for the phone. "I'll call Claire and get her up here with whatever help she thinks we need."

"No." Rain stood, all indecision gone. She almost felt Morgan beside her. "If he sees Claire, or anyone else, he'll take off. We'll miss our chance to capture him."

She opened the roll top bread box, and took out her handgun. "The next time he comes for us, we might not be prepared." As she threaded the holster on her belt she thrust her chin toward the pantry. "There's a shotgun in there. It's loaded."

CHAPTER 28

September
Pierce

Pierce retrieved the shotgun from behind the broom in the far corner of the pantry. How had he figured things so wrong, so backwards? Why had he felt this woman needed to be sheltered and protected? And why had he thought he was capable of doing that?

"There's a box of shells behind the flour," she told him. "If you don't know how to use a shotgun, speak up now."

"I know how."

His experience came from joining the old man to fire at clay pigeons and trying his best to miss during grouse hunting bloodfests. He wondered how Rain came by her experience. What he didn't wonder was whether he had it in him to shoot the man they called the Peddler. He was certain of that. After what he'd learned since forming the task force, he could shoot him, stab him, or strangle him without a prick of conscience or a moment of hesitation.

Calling Natty to her, Rain knelt by the back door, stroked his ears, and gazed into his eyes. "I want you to find the man who is coming here to try to hurt me. Not hunt. Not bite. Find him. Watch him. Come to me when he's close."

Natty whined and pulled away. The second Rain opened the door, he shot into the dusk.

"He understood that?"

She locked the door. "I hope so. And I really hope I understand what he has to tell me when he returns."

"You're not worried that—?"

"The Peddler will shoot Natty?" Rain smiled. "I'd like to see him try. I'd like to see anyone try."

Pierce laid the shotgun on the coffee table and sat on the sofa. "Natty isn't . . . real?"

"That's a question I can't answer." Rain ran more hot water in the sink and went to work on the plates and silverware. "He sleeps, he eats, he lifts his leg on every tree around the clearing, and I assume when he goes off into the woods he takes care of the rest. But he was there with me at Nightfall Bay—there enough to leave prints in the sand. Could a 'real' dog do that?"

"You're asking me?" Pierce laughed. "I never had a dog, 'real' or not. But I've seen enough to bet Natty can get out of the way of a bullet."

He watched Rain rinse the dishes. She appeared as calm as she had before Watch called. "What did Watch mean when he told you not to be too ready? What did Morgan say?"

Rain told him, drying the dishes as she did, wiping down the counter, stowing leftovers in plastic containers, explaining in a low and calm voice as if the subject was gardening or the best buys on home appliances.

Morgan's philosophy of preparedness, Pierce thought, had a lot in common with the old man's. His father would spend days plotting strategy for some phase of a corporate raid, then shoot from the hip. But the old man had been a predator. Morgan's preparation was about self-defense.

"So, we shouldn't make a plan?"

"Not a set-in-concrete plan." She wiped the table and set out fresh placemats, dark blue with narrow lines of green and yellow intersecting here and there. "We should have ideas. If/then plans to disrupt his plan."

"To kill you."

"And you. And Claire." Rain sat on the sofa and turned toward him, tucking one leg beneath her. Only a lamp in the loft and one above the stove cast light into the room, but her eyes seemed to glow. "Because you won't give up. Because he knows you're getting closer."

"How? How does he know? We've been so careful, moving out of the office, changing our phones, our computers."

"Maybe he was tipped by someone you or Claire spoke with. But I think you were right when you said it was because you stopped using the car in the evenings. And you didn't go home."

It made Pierce's skin crawl to think the Peddler was watching so closely. "I get why he wants me gone, but why you? Wouldn't he think that if you'd learned something we would have acted on it by now?"

"Maybe he wants to stop me before I go to Nightfall Bay again. But also, if he can, um, neutralize us both and get us to a location where he feels secure, he'll hurt me like he hurt the others. And he'll force you to watch."

She spoke with conviction, and Pierce again wondered how he'd missed the signs, gone down the wrong road of assuming Rain was naïve and even fragile.

"Plenty of people know a lot more about my family than Edgar and Ethel—although most value their own privacy too much to gossip. When I was young, it was tempting to break my promise and tell my friends about what Meadow did and what Morgan saw. I never did, but my mother . . ."

Rain sucked in a breath and fell silent. Pierce reached for her hand and threaded his fingers between hers. His parents had been far from adequate when it came to filling his emotional needs, but they hadn't abandoned him like her mother had. On the other hand, as Rain insisted when she told him about her childhood, Morgan and Meadow had never caused her to doubt their love.

"By the time my mother left home, she saw the gift as a curse. I imagine she told a lot of people about it—especially when she was under the influence of the drug or drink of the day."

Although Rain's tone was matter-of-fact, even leaning toward flip, Pierce felt pain radiating from her words.

"And there are others who have—or pretend to have—skills like my grandparents had. Word gets around in their community."

"I met some of them this summer when Claire and I decided to think outside the box. I thought it was a wild-goose chase and wouldn't get us anywhere, so I used my car. If he followed up on where I went and who I saw, he would have realized the approach we were taking. He might have made the connection to you that way."

Pierce released her hand, pushed up his sleeve, and dug his nails into his arm. "Like I said, this is on me."

"No. Stop that." Rain gripped his arm at the elbow. "Morgan saw danger long before we met, long before I read about Marlin's murder, before Claire came out here. That's why I had a shotgun in the pantry. That's why Watch is at the farmhouse."

"But I—"

"You're a catalyst. You speeded things along. But the reaction was inevitable."

For a few seconds Pierce felt insulted, then he forced a laugh. "Only a catalyst? That's a blow to my ego."

"Suck it up. Focus. Tell me what the Peddler knows and what he doesn't know. Tell me what you think he might have planned, and we'll figure out how to use that."

The need to cut subsided and Pierce organized his thoughts. He was good at this, he reminded himself, good at making connections, seeing the forest *and* the trees. "He knows we're both here. But he doesn't know we suspect he's out there, and he doesn't know we're armed. Plus, I doubt he knows about Natty."

"I agree. The neighbors all knew Motley and the dogs before him, but none of them visited since Natty arrived. And he's stuck close to the cabin."

"Except when he patrols at dusk and dawn. But there are shadows noisier and more visible." Pierce rubbed his arm where he'd dug in his nails. "The Peddler likes to be close to his victims, he enjoys watching them suffer and die. But I'm sure he'll have a gun for insurance. And for control."

"Or to kill one of us fast so he can take the other."

"Yes. Look, this is too danger—"

"Don't go there. He has to be stopped." Rain glanced at the front door and then the back. "I think he'll wait until we should be asleep. He'll check to see if there's an alarm and he'll cut the cable to take out the landline. Then he'll pick the lock or break a window. If we're hiding outside, where he doesn't expect us to be, we can stop him before—"

"No. We have to let him get in." Pierce gripped both of her hands. "Maybe even let him get upstairs. So he can't claim he was taking a midnight stroll, got lost, and accidentally trespassed."

Rain stared. "You want him in my house? In my bedroom?"

214

"I don't like it either. But we need enough to arrest him. This guy's been so careful that we don't have a thing to connect him to the murders—at least nothing a jury would consider concrete proof."

"But if he breaks in?"

"Then he goes to jail. We get his prints, his car, his clothing. Maybe a link to the victims. Maybe something to tell us where he's keeping the ones who are still alive."

Rain gasped. "If he's in jail, and they're locked up, who will feed them?"

Pierce recalled the starved bodies on the Anacortes hillside and at the edge of the Oregon landslide. "When he sees evidence against him piling up, there's a chance he'll use the women still alive as a bargaining chip."

Even as he said that, Pierce suspected it wasn't true. The Peddler would hold his secrets close. He'd get off on knowing his victims were dying while he was a prisoner. Imagining their hunger and despair would nourish him.

"All right," Rain said. "If Natty tells us he's here, that's how we'll play it."

CHAPTER 29

September
Rain

An hour passed.

And then another.

The landline didn't ring.

The deep tone of the conch shell didn't echo from the ridges.

Barefooted, stomach roiling, Rain paced the tiny kitchen, moving a canister half an inch, filling the salt shaker, flattening the corner of the doormat that insisted on flipping up. Everything was in place upstairs, the recorder she used to capture her thoughts while editing, lengths of nylon cord, pepper spray, knives, a rope ladder in case they had to escape through a window, and even a rubber club.

She'd discovered that in the pantry behind the scrub bucket and a gallon of white vinegar. Morgan must have slid it there one day when she was out. Beside it she'd found a plastic tub filled with family photo albums and bundles of old letters. Had he wanted to get them out of the farmhouse before Watch took possession? Or was there another reason?

Having turned the television to direct the glow from the screen toward the curtains shrouding the front windows, Pierce flipped through the channels now and then. He'd pointed out the flaw in her suggestion that they mute the TV so they could hear noises from outside—the Peddler might think along the same lines and suspect they knew he was out there. He'd moved the gooseneck lamp from her editing desk, positioning it on a chair and directing the light toward the center of the closed curtains. Now and then he stood and walked between the lamp and the curtains, going to the kitchen or bookshelves, returning with wineglasses, a bottle, a bowl or a book, casting a shadow for the Peddler to see.

If he was out there.

Pierce had called Claire and outlined the situation. She'd agreed that bringing in a strike force might alert the Peddler and abort their opportunity. It would also involve cooperation across state and county lines, a process that meant going through official channels. Unofficially, she said she'd reach out to a few contacts she'd made and stand by at a campground a mile away.

Before she disconnected, she warned them not to use the peepholes in the doors. Obscuring the light from inside, even for a few seconds, might let the Peddler know they were watching for him.

Rain reminded herself of that as she paused near the back door, hoping to hear Natty scratch.

If he was out there.

If he was alive.

She clenched her fists and told herself Natty couldn't die before his time.

But when was his time?

Motley's time came when Meadow died. But the others seemed to have chosen their own moments to move on. If the Peddler somehow managed to kill Natty, would another dog appear?

217

"Stop it," she hissed.

Pierce raised his head. "Stop what?"

"Talking to myself." She crept closer to the back door. "I hate waiting."

"Same here." He raised his left arm and she saw he'd been grinding his fingernails into his skin again. "Especially when—"

"Ssshhh." Rain cocked her head. "Is that Natty scratching?"

"Don't open the door yet." Pierce vaulted from the sofa and hustled to her side, turning off the light over the stove as he came.

They crouched on either side of the door. Rain pressed her ear against the wood below the knob. There it was. A trace of sound. A trace that might have been made by a single claw, or a groping finger.

"Natty?" she whispered. "Is that you?"

The thread of sound came again, followed by a whiffling whine.

"It's him."

Rain reached for the knob.

Pierce gripped her wrist. "Stay behind the door, and open it an inch at a time until you're sure. I'll brace it." He pressed his shoulder against the door and bent one knee.

Rain flipped the toggle to draw the bolt.

"Gun," Pierce said.

She fumbled it from the holster, then paused for a second, reminding herself again of all the hours of practice, visualizing Morgan beside her. Holding her breath, she turned the knob and eased the door open an inch.

Then two inches.

Three.

Four.

A paw appeared in the gap.

Then, above it, a muzzle.

"It's Natty."

She opened the door wider and the big dog squeezed through.

The second he was clear, Pierce leaned on the door. She swung it closed, holding back at the last second so it caught with only a faint click.

Natty bolted to his water dish and lapped up half of it. Rain opened a sack of meaty treats and he wolfed down a handful before trotting to the center of the living area. He swung his head right, then left, then right again, and turned so he faced southwest, tail straight, right paw lifted.

"In the rocks?" Rain asked.

Natty whined.

"Good job." Rain patted his head and offered more treats.

Relieved to find the phone still working, Pierce called Claire to tell her the Peddler was close. Then he glanced at the loft. "Time for our charade."

He returned to the kitchen, got the prop bottle of wine and glasses and took his mark in the beam of light. "We can't let this wine go to waste," he called as he held up the bottle.

"Bring it up to the bedroom." Rain started up the stairs, Natty at her heels.

When she reached the top, she switched on a second gooseneck lamp and aimed it toward the stained-glass window on the west side of the cabin. Now came the hardest part, putting herself—or at least her shadow—on display.

This was the phase of the plan they hadn't discussed except to say they'd act as if they were lovers. Much as she yearned to be close to Pierce, to feel his touch, she had to remain in control, couldn't allow herself to respond. Maybe, when this was all over, when he learned of Ariel's fate . . .

Pierce turned off the downstairs lamp, picked up the shotgun, and followed her upstairs. He leaned the gun against

219

the wall beside the bed and joined Rain in the spotlight, casting their shadows on the stained-glass window.

He tipped her chin and pressed his lips against hers. Not a kiss. Only the fleeting contact of flesh on flesh.

He drew away and stroked her hair. "I wish I'd met you years ago. Before . . ." His voice was thick. Each word seemed to crack and splinter. "When this is over, I'd like us to . . . I mean, I hope we can . . . I hope you might . . ."

"Yes." Rain stood on tiptoe and kissed him.

This time for real.

But only for a second, only until she felt herself wanting to lose control.

Pierce held her close for a few moments, then snapped off the light. They stretched out on the bed, his right hand resting on top of her left. She thought of what Morgan had predicted, that she'd come through this. But she was terrified about what might happen to her before it was over—and what might happen to Pierce.

She hadn't realized she might not go through the ordeal alone.

She'd never asked Morgan if there would be anyone with her. Never asked if that person would also come through.

CHAPTER 30

September
Pierce

In the brief and blissful moment Rain pressed her lips against his, Pierce's mind exploded with dazzling images of experiences they would share. Like fireworks against the night sky, those images blazed and flashed and shimmered. Then they blinked out.

He longed to resurrect each one and elaborate upon it. But that would distract him. While imagining them on a sailboat, on a mountaintop, or beneath a tropical waterfall, he might not hear the click of the lock, the scuff of a shoe.

So he concentrated on the man coming to kill them.

He thought about the Peddler's size compared to his own. He was taller than Marlin had been by a good four inches. And Marlin—or Marlin's shade—had told Rain the Peddler was about his height. That meant Pierce was also taller than the Peddler. And perhaps as broad in the shoulders. His legs were powerful from running, but the weights he'd bought a year ago to improve upper-arm strength were gathering dust. The Peddler had been strong enough to lift Marlin from his chair, strangle him, and haul him to the stairwell. But Marlin had been weakened by at least one stroke.

Summing it up, Pierce called them even.

What about speed and agility? Pierce had taken some martial arts classes as a kid, and had learned the rudiments of boxing and wrestling. But he'd never honed those skills. Odds were that the Peddler had.

Pierce awarded him a point.

Mentally, they would both be determined—one to kill and one to survive and protect. Which drive would be stronger?

Pierce called them even once again.

He considered the element of surprise and gave himself half a point for that.

Then he considered Rain and the gun gripped in her free hand.

Another point for his team.

And then there was Natty.

Pierce felt his jaw muscles relax. He didn't know much about dogs, but he bet the Peddler had never encountered a canine like the one at the foot of the bed.

"How long will he wait?" Rain whispered.

Pierce squinted at the railing of the loft, barely visible in the feeble red light cast by the digital clock on the bureau and the blipping green of the electric toothbrush charger in the bathroom. "I guess that depends on whether our charade convinced him that we're up here—"

"Doing what we want him to think we're doing."

Did her whisper convey wistful teasing? Was she also imagining how it might be?

Pierce smiled at the vaulted ceiling. Then he gave himself a mental kick and got his head in the game.

Natty growled, a rumble pitched so low it was more physical sensation than sound.

A second later Pierce heard the faint scrape of metal on metal, a click, another scrape.

Natty growled again, stood, and padded to the deep shadow beneath the east window.

Pierce squeezed Rain's hand. "When he opens the door, he'll listen to see if we're, uh—"

"I'm the quiet type." She returned the pressure before leaning to click on the voice recorder. "But I've edited a few romance novels. And I've watched some steamy movies. I can fake it."

Cool air eddied around them.

Feeling like the world's worst actor, Pierce groaned and followed up with a series of soft grunts. Then he slid from the bed, gripped the shotgun, and duckwalked to the tiny washroom.

With a couple of breathy moans, Rain slipped beneath the quilt, pulling two pillows along to create the illusion that he was beside her.

Pierce, afraid any sound would give away his new position, kept silent and remained in a crouch.

Rain writhed beneath the quilt, murmuring to the pillow in her arms.

A board creaked.

A shadow rose from the staircase.

"There," Rain whispered. "Oh. Yes. Like that."

The shadow seemed to expand and float into the room. The clock cast a red glow on the gun in its hand.

Pierce raised the shotgun.

"Don't stop," the shadow commanded in a whisper. "Passion excites me."

Rain gasped and was still. "Who are you?"

"Oh, you know who I am, darling." His tone was smug, boastful, with an edge of amusement. It was, in fact, exactly as Pierce had imagined it.

"I don't." Leaving the pillows in place, Rain clutched the quilt beneath her chin and sat up, her voice trembling. "I don't know who you are."

Natty, a shadow himself, peeled away from the far wall and flattened against the floor.

"I'm the man you've been searching for. I came to make you and your lover a deal on a trip. A trip to oblivion."

"Drop your gun. We're not interested." Pierce rose from his crouch and took a step forward, green light playing along the barrel of the shotgun.

"Are you sure? Ariel said you would be."

Ariel!

Pierce's fingers twitched.

The shadow's arm swung toward him.

"Natty," Rain screamed.

The huge dog leaped.

A shot rang out.

A man howled.

CHAPTER 31

September
Rain

"I'm okay," Pierce shouted. "Are you?"

"Yes." Rain snapped on the bedside lamp.

A man lay on the floor between the bed and the railing. His heels hammered the broad planks. His hands, encased in thin rubber gloves and knotted into fists, flailed at the huge dog straddling him.

Keeping the shotgun trained on the man's head, Pierce circled and scooped up a handgun.

"Get him off," the man squealed. "He'll bite me."

"Only if I tell him to," Rain said. "Or if he gets tired of you hitting him."

Natty snarled as if to say he'd already reached that point. But he made no move to clamp his jaws on the man's throat.

Pierce buried the handgun in a nest of socks in the top drawer of the bureau and tried the landline. "Dead." He pulled his cellphone from his pocket. "No signal."

"Try by the opposite window." Rain slid to the end of the bed and leveled her gun at the man on the floor. "I'll back up Natty. Although I doubt he needs it."

Pierce eased along the railing and held the phone aloft by the west window. "Ah." A few seconds later he told Claire, "We got him."

"You got nothing." The man attempted to roll over.

Natty sat, pinning him.

"Get him off. I can't breathe."

"And yet you can talk." Rain opened the nightstand, removed a length of nylon cord, and tossed it to Pierce who went to work wrapping the man's legs.

"Hey! Why are you tying me up? This was all a joke."

"I guess we didn't get it." Pierce pulled at the loops.

"That's too tight," the man whined.

Pierce grinned and gave the knot a yank.

Rain studied the intruder. He bore a faint resemblance to the man in the group photos on the insurance company websites. But he seemed far older. His thinning brown hair was clipped close to his scalp. His clean-shaven cheeks were sunken, his bones jutting, his skin a yellow-gray.

He's sick.

Still, despite his sniveling, there was something deep in his eyes. Something hungry. Something insatiable.

"Okay, it wasn't a joke, it was a dare." The intruder talked fast with a bit of bluster. "I was in a bar down the road and some guys—one of them installs alarms—were talking about this new house and the woman who lives here and—"

A siren throbbed in the distance.

"It was a dare, that's all. The guy who sells alarms wanted me to scare her a little so she'd buy an alarm system."

"Right." Pierce caught the man's left hand and tied it to his belt. "And I bet he gave you the gun and you didn't know it was loaded."

"Yeah. I didn't know. I never touched a gun before."

"And you can't remember the name of the guy with the alarm company."

"That's right." He coughed, a dry rasp of sound. "I can't remember."

Sirens yowled closer.

Rain carried her cellphone to the window and called Watch. "We're okay. We got him."

"Nothing." The man smiled. "You got nothing."

The rising sun silvered the layer of mist hanging in the gorge. A chevron of geese burst through into the pale blue sky, heading south. Sipping coffee, Rain and Pierce followed their flight from chairs on the farmhouse porch beside Watch.

"I keep thinking it was too easy," Pierce said.

"We had a secret weapon." Rain patted Natty's head.

"It still felt too easy. And all wrong. The break-in was rushed, careless. This guy has always been a planner who waited for the right moment."

"He sick," Rain said. "Very sick. He broke his pattern when he killed Marlin and the woman at the hotel. It seems he was half afraid of being caught and half afraid he wouldn't be."

"Still—"

"Stop complaining about easy." Watch reached for the last muffin on the plate. "You got him, that's what matters."

"But can we get him for anything more than breaking and entering and discharging a firearm?"

"You will," Rain assured him.

"Claire and the experts will," Pierce corrected. "I'm the bored rich guy who bought a task force and treats law enforcement like a hobby, remember?"

Rain stroked his wrist. "That deputy didn't mean it. He's young. He was only repeating—"

"What he hears from everyone else."

227

"Screw 'em," Watch growled. "What do they know? You may not have a badge, but you have brains and guts and determination."

Natty thumped his tail.

Watch tossed him the remainder of the muffin. "And you have a hell of a four-legged sidekick."

Rain blocked Pierce as he reached to open his car door. "I know you need to go. I know you have a thousand things to check on." She pressed close against him. "And I know this isn't the right time, or even a good time, but I wish—"

"I wish the same." He bent his head and kissed her. "Soon."

Rain traced the tiny lines at the corners of his eyes and mouth. "When you have answers."

"Yes. When I know whether he was taunting me, whether Ariel is still alive. When she isn't between us."

CHAPTER 32

October
Pierce

Claire ended her call and set her cellphone on the table in the conference room of the original task force office. "Another day of striking out. The gun gets us nowhere. It was reported stolen in Olympia a couple of years ago."

Pierce rubbed his burning eyes. He could count on one hand the number of consecutive hours he'd slept in the past few days. And those had been on the floor in the conference room. "I'm not surprised."

He toyed with the button on his cuff, but resisted the urge to undo it and survey his bruised arm. He hadn't cut, but he also hadn't been able to resist the urge to dig at his flesh with his nails. He thought constantly of the women still unaccounted for—Ariel and two others. He imagined them confined and dying by inches of thirst and starvation. He'd raised the reward fund and spearheaded a media blitz asking the public to be the eyes and ears of the task force, to check their neighborhoods for places where three women could be held captive. Dozens of calls had lit up the tip line but, although police had identified two meth labs and a prostitution ring, not one call led them to the Peddler's prison.

He released the button. "What's the rest of the bad news?"

"They can't get more than a few words off the recording you made—at least not until he started squawking after Natty took him down. The machine wasn't close enough and his whisper is too faint."

"Probably wouldn't have been allowed as evidence anyway," Pierce grumbled. "What else?"

"Our guy still claims his name is Kevin Dunbar and he's homeless which is why he doesn't have a driver's license or other ID. He's sticking to the story that he went to the cabin on a dare from a guy whose name he didn't get and who drove him there from a tavern somewhere in Portland. He insists he would never hurt anyone, especially not a woman. He says he never reads the paper, never watches TV news or listens to the radio, and never heard of the Peddler. And that, with slight variations, is about all he says."

Pierce cursed, a single raw verb. It had been the old man's favorite, but he'd never used it before.

"Oh, and they got a doctor to take a look at him—that's all his attorney would allow, just a look. The doctor's pretty sure our guy has an aggressive form of cancer. But there won't be any tests because 'Kevin' wrote out a document refusing examinations, tests, and medications, including painkillers. The doctor thinks he has a high threshold of pain and doesn't experience it like most of the rest of us."

"Great. So he plans to escape justice by dying." Pierce cursed again. It was an ugly word and only four letters long, but it felt comprehensive. "Any more bad news?"

"So far there's no sign of a vehicle—not a car like the one Rain's neighbor saw or any other model. Not even a bicycle. And if we assume the drivers on duty that day and several days before have reasonable memories, no one remotely resembling 'Kevin' rode a bus out that way."

"So he walked. Or hitched a ride. Or had a friend drop him off."

"Given the shape he's in, that's a hell of a long way to walk," Claire mused, "assuming he holes up in the Portland area. And if he hitched a ride the odds of finding the driver, even with massive help from the media, are in the slim-to-none range."

"That leaves a friend or acquaintance dropping him off." Pierce stood and paced to the window and back. "Hopefully someone who has no idea what his skill set is."

"I know what you mean. I hate to think all the profiling is wrong, that this guy isn't a lone wolf."

Pierce paced to the map and traced the route from Portland to Rain's cabin. "What if his place is on the east side of Portland? It cuts the distance."

"Some," Claire agreed. "But he has to get across the Columbia. And Rain's place is miles from the closest bridge."

"It's a hike. And he's a sick man." Pierce walked the distance with his fingers. "What if he had a boat? Or stole one?"

Claire reached for a notepad. "I'll check to see if anything's been reported stolen, but—"

"I know." Pierce raised his hands. "He could have used a canoe or a kayak or built a raft out of driftwood and put it in the water anywhere. Or his lair could be in Vancouver. Then he wouldn't need a boat."

She pointed at the battered chair she'd dragged up from their bunker office. "Want to kick the chair?"

"Kicking isn't enough. I want to dismantle it with my bare hands and chew the pieces."

"Then you definitely don't want to hear what I've been hearing all day—that this isn't the Peddler."

"It's him." Pierce kicked the chair. "He's a ringer for the guy in those insurance agency photos."

Claire nodded, but didn't remind him they had no proof *that* man was the Peddler.

"And I saw it in his eyes. So did Rain. We know it. And he knows we know it."

He kicked the chair again. "And *you* know it. That's why we tore out the listening devices and moved back up here. Because he's in jail. All we have to do is convince everyone else. And I'll do that if it kills me."

Claire said nothing.

He hadn't expected she would. They'd been down this road a dozen times in the past few days.

"What about his claim that he was attacked by a vicious unlicensed dog?"

"That won't come to anything. He was inside the house and holding a gun when Natty took him down. Natty had his shots and the paperwork was in for his license." Claire tugged at one of her dangling earrings, strings of tiny silver leaves. "And, oddly enough, there wasn't a mark on him to prove his version of events."

Had Natty actually clamped his jaws on the Peddler, or simply threatened? Pierce couldn't remember. But he had a feeling that, even if Natty had torn a chunk out of the intruder, the wound would have healed within seconds, leaving no evidence.

"There's nothing more we can do here today," Claire said. "Get out of the office. Go see how Rain is doing. Take her out to dinner."

Pierce felt a jolt at the mention of her name—part electrical shock to the heart, part punch to the gut, part infusion of heat to the brain, part avalanche of sensory memories. It was a full-body, full-brain experience, far beyond anything he'd ever felt, even in the first days with Ariel. That reaction had been more localized—a tightening in his groin and a sizzling, torturous need eating at his mind.

He'd gone with it.

And gone astray.

Could he trust himself to get it right this time?

"I, uh, talked with her this morning." Twice. And once this afternoon. "She's in the middle of an editing project."

Claire raised her eyebrows. "And she can't take time for dinner?"

Pierce felt himself flush. How much had Claire guessed? "She has a deadline," he muttered. "I'll call her tomorrow."

Claire aimed an index finger at him. "See that you do. Now get out of here while we still have a little daylight. Go for a drive. Go home and do something mundane, wash dishes, do laundry."

Pierce widened his eyes, pretending shock and insult. "You can't mean it! You want me to shame my mother by engaging in such plebeian activities?"

"Exactly." Claire headed for the door. "The more common the better. And spend some money while you're at it. Set that old dude twirling like a pinwheel."

Relishing the image of his father spinning inside a casket that cost more than a mid-sized car, Pierce walked with Claire to the parking lot.

"Go to bed early for once," she advised. "And don't drink. It messes up your sleep patterns."

She was right. He'd stay away from beer and the hard stuff, and try for a straight eight in the sack. He needed new ideas, new angles. Sleep might rewire his brain.

For once, traffic across Portland and out the other side wasn't the usual slow-and-go snarl. His mind drifted to Rain, drifted to all that he imagined in a future with her.

Not yet.

233

Not until he knew what had become of Ariel.

The passage through the trees lay in deep shade. This was the time of day deer grazed along the ditches, leaping at the sight of a car. He flipped on his high beams to shove aside the shadows, gripped the wheel with both hands, and concentrated on the road ahead.

He emerged from the forest, his headlight beams sweeping across the ragged lawn. How long had it been since he mowed? He could almost hear the old man's voice telling him to stop pretending he was competent and hire a yard service.

"Spin, damn you, spin," he muttered.

The beams lit up the long porch and the women waiting on either side of the door.

Emaciated.

Brutalized.

Posed.

Dead.

He braked hard, rear wheels slewing onto the lawn, skidding in a half circle.

Reversing, he let the beams slide across the porch once more, then turned off the headlights and reached for his cellphone.

Either the Peddler hadn't done his grisly work alone.

Or the man they'd captured wasn't the Peddler.

It took half an hour for the first unit to respond. Thirty minutes of straining his eyes for a physical detail that would tell him whether one of those women was Ariel. Thirty minutes of telling himself that even stepping on the paving stones to reach the porch might contaminate the scene. Thirty minutes of chastising himself because he hadn't followed up and installed security cameras when he upgraded the alarm system.

Had that been an act of idiocy? Or denial?

More units arrived, parking behind him along the drive. County. State. Members of the task force. He told the story three times while they set up telescoping light towers, bathing the porch and its occupants in harsh light.

When he was alone, Pierce closed his eyes, rested his head on the steering wheel, and rubbed his left arm. He had a penknife in his pocket. For the past few days, he *always* had the penknife. He was *always* a reach and a flick away from nicking, cutting, slicing. Perhaps if he held the knife for a few minutes, the urge would diminish. Perhaps if he unfolded the blade and ran it along—

Claire opened the passenger door, slid in beside him, and set a paper bag on the console. "Haven't seen this many official cars lined up since the last time a presidential candidate rolled through. Bet I had to walk a quarter of a mile." She opened the bag. "Coffee. And other stuff. It will be a long night and, wrong as it seems, eventually we'll get hungry."

She squeezed his shoulder, slipped out, and closed the door. Using the rearview mirror, he tracked her progress to a knot of men and women gathered around a van. He watched her shaking hands, saw her dig a notebook and pen from her purse and jot a few lines. A man handed her a scope and she peered through it, studying the women on the porch. Then she walked to Pierce's car and slid in beside him once more.

"Collette Chambers and Amelia Austin." She named two of the women missing and presumed taken by the Peddler. "And my educated guess is they haven't been dead for long."

Pierce let out the breath he'd been holding. "Not Ariel?"

"Not Ariel."

Emotions collided in his mind and gut. Hope shattered against despair and both were swallowed by the black hole of all he might never know. Ariel might be alive. Ariel might be a prisoner, tormented and suffering, but clinging to life. Or Ariel

235

might be dead, buried or dumped in a place where she wouldn't be discovered for years. If ever.

"I'm sorry." Claire gripped his hand, slowing the collision of his thoughts. "Crap. Listen to me. That's not the right thing to say."

"It's okay."

"No." Claire pounded the dashboard. "It's a thousand miles from okay."

"I meant you don't need to apologize." He moved the bag to the rear seat, leaned across the console, and put his arm around her shoulders. "You don't need to say anything at all. Not to me."

Claire flexed her fingers. "I thought it was over when you got him. I wanted it to be over. And when you called and I knew it wasn't, I wanted one of them—"

"To be Ariel."

"Yes." She turned to face him, her eyes brimming with tears. "I was certain she'd be here. Because this is a message for you."

Pierce nodded. He'd thought the same thing.

"And, heaven help me, I hoped she'd be here." Claire wiped tears from her cheeks with her fingers. "I want you to . . . to have a life of your own, a life that isn't tied to her. I don't know if it's guilt or loyalty or what, but you're as stuck as those souls waiting on the sand at Nightfall Bay."

She drew in a shuddering breath and faced the window. "I'm sorry. I shouldn't have said that, it's not my—"

"It *is* your business. Where I'm at affects you. We're not robots."

Claire swallowed and blotted her eyes with a tissue she pulled from the pocket of her jeans.

"And . . . I like that you care about me. And that you treat me like a partner, even if I'm not a professional."

"Are you trying to make me bawl like a baby?" Claire blew her nose. "Because you're doing a damn good job if you are."

Pierce hugged her, long and hard. "Get it out of your system. Then get some coffee inside you and get a grip. The game has changed. We can't waste time blubbering."

CHAPTER 33

October
Rain

Rain shook soil from the roots of a frost-blasted tomato plant and tossed it into a wheelbarrow. "If I go to Nightfall Bay, I can find the women the Peddler killed. I know I can."

"You don't know any such thing." Watch shifted on the camp stool he'd carried to the garden, and pointed a gnarled finger at Pierce. "And if you encourage this rash stupidity I'll fry your brains in rancid butter. If you have enough brains in that thick skull of yours to make it worth heating a pan."

"Hey, I'm on your side. So is Claire. When I said I was coming up here to beg Rain not to even think about going, she practically pushed me into my car." Pierce jerked a pepper plant from the ground. "I know what it cost her to find Marlin. I would never suggest she go back. Never."

"And what about me?" Rain slapped the root ball of another plant against the wheelbarrow. It struck with a dull clang, showering them with pebbles and clumps of earth. She didn't apologize. "What about what *I* want to do? You two act like you're running my life, like I have no say, like I'm not standing right in front of you."

Watch brushed at his shirt. Pierce shook dirt from his hair. Whining, Natty abandoned the sunny furrow in which he'd been snoozing and headed for the garden gate and the lawn beyond.

"I'm sick of it." Rain tossed the plant on top of others destined for a growing compost pile on the east side of the orchard. "You're acting like I'm six years old. *And* an invalid." She flexed her arm muscles. "I'm fine. In fact, I'm more than fine. I've been working out here for an hour. That's after the five miles I ran this morning."

"Where?" Watch asked. "When?"

"Along the highway. Early. You weren't up yet."

"What?" Pierce sat back on his heels. "You said you wouldn't run alone along the highway."

"I never said that." Rain put her fists on her hips and thrust her chin out. "*You* said I shouldn't run alone."

"Of course you shouldn't!" Watch bellowed. "There's still a killer out there! That's why I pace you in the truck."

"And when I want to run, you gripe that I'm disturbing you."

"I gripe all the time," Watch blustered. "You never paid attention before."

"Well today I decided I should stop pestering you. Natty came with me." She patted the bulge at her side beneath her T-shirt. "And I had my gun."

"A lot of good either would have done if someone tried to run you down."

"Or shoot you as he drove by," Pierce added.

"He could do that whether I had an escort or not."

She yanked another plant from the ground and swung it against the wheelbarrow. "He might be in the woods with a rifle right now. He might be getting ready to shoot us all!"

Watch craned his neck to glance around, then hunched over as if trying to make himself a smaller target. Pierce, she noted, went on pulling pepper plants without so much as peering over his shoulder. Was he as unaffected by the idea of a sniper as he pretended? Or was he refusing to rise to her bait?

"You know what? You two are making my point for me."

Pierce shook his head, a puzzled frown on his face, but Watch groaned. "Stand by for a dose of convoluted female logic."

Rain tossed the plant on the heap. "It's not convoluted. It's very simple." She crouched so her eyes were level with Pierce's. "The investigation is stalled, right?"

"Well, I don't know if 'stalled' is the right—"

"It's stalled. You have nothing to link the man we caught to the murders. And you got nothing from the bodies left on your porch."

Pierce winced and rubbed his left arm.

Rain laid a hand on his shoulder. She'd felt violated by the break-in at the cabin, but at least she'd had the satisfaction of seeing the man she believed was the Peddler taken down, tied up, and carted off to jail. Pierce had nothing to balance the desecration of his home. He'd rented a suite in a hotel and hadn't returned even to gather his clothing. She doubted he ever would. The house and land were tainted. Someone, some ghoul perhaps, or one of those rare people unfazed by a place marked by horror, would snap it up, contents and all.

"It may be months before you get a lead. It may be never. I have to go to Nightfall Bay."

"No." Watch hunched into a tighter ball. "Get that out of your mind."

"It's almost November." Rain lowered her voice and, ignoring Watch, dropped to her knees in front of Pierce. "This could be the last sunny day. Then it will be rain and mist, long nights and short days. We'll all be looking over our shoulders into the darkness, waking up every time the floor creaks or the wind blows sleet against a window."

"We'll get a break," Pierce insisted. "We'll find something."

"When?"

Pierce glanced away, unable to meet her eyes, recalling again his failure to install security cameras at his home, to get a picture of the Peddler's accomplice.

Rain gripped his shoulders. "I want your help," she whispered. "But I'll do it on my own if I have to."

"How?" Watch straightened on his stool. "How can you go to Nightfall Bay if neither of us will help?"

"Meadow used those letters to make the journey. She drew strength from relatives hundreds of miles away—thousands of miles."

She stood and brushed dirt from her knees. "I have the file Claire gave me. I have the names of friends and relatives of the victims. And I have the letter Claire brought with the file, the letter asking me to help."

"It will never work," Watch said. "You can't use that letter twice."

"We'll see." Rain headed for the gate.

"Stop her," Watch ordered Pierce.

"How? How do you stop someone from leaving their body?"

Grinning at the thought of what they might come up with, Rain whistled for Natty and headed for the track to the cabin.

"I don't know how!" Watch howled. "Think of something. Think!"

Rain heard a series of muffled slaps and glanced behind her to see Pierce whisking dirt from his jeans and gray T-shirt with the edges of his hands.

"Go after her," Watch commanded. "Distract her. Yell. Throw things. I bet she can't travel if she can't concentrate."

Rain accelerated to a trot. She'd lock Pierce out. She'd plug her ears or play music. One way or another she'd get to Nightfall Bay.

"Stop her," Watch shouted.

"Wait," Pierce called.

"No." She looked back and saw him sprinting up the slope. Passing through the gap in the barbed wire fence, she plunged into the forest. "I have to do this. Don't stop me."

"I won't."

"Liar," she panted. "Ten minutes ago you and Watch were ordering me not to go."

"Ten minutes ago I didn't realize how determined you were." Despite the steep trail, his voice grew steadily closer. "Slow down. Don't wear yourself out. I won't try to stop you. I'll help if I can."

Rain halted and turned. "Say that again. Let me look into your eyes when you do."

Red flannel shirt over one shoulder, he jogged closer. "I won't try to stop you. I'll help if I can."

His eyes, rimmed with red, were dark with pain and doubt, but she saw no trace of deceit. Taking his hand, she led him to the cabin, called Natty inside, locked the door behind them, and activated the alarm Pierce had paid to have installed. When she decided she had to go, and go now, she'd considered using Meadow's traveling room upstairs in the farmhouse. But by the time she whistled for Natty, she knew she wanted to be—*had* to be—in a space that was her own.

"I think we need sustenance before we begin." Pierce washed his hands, got two glasses from a cabinet, and pulled a carton of orange juice from the refrigerator. "Natty too."

242

"Right." Rain filled the big dog's bowl with kibble. "I made oatmeal cookies yesterday. With nuts and chocolate chunks. They're in the freezer. Would you nuke a few while I clean up?"

"Right after I call Claire and tell her I won't be back today."

Pierce dialed the task force office, got a recorded message and checked his watch. "Forgot you were out at a meeting. I'm with Rain. She's determined to go to Nightfall Bay whether I help or not. I'm staying here to do what I can."

That accomplished, he thawed six cookies in the microwave and had them on the table along with a sliced apple when she returned wearing a rose-hued turtleneck sweater. "I also think you should be lying down before you begin." He got a slice of turkey from the refrigerator and tossed it on top of Natty's kibble. "Or at least sitting. So you don't fall when you, um, fall."

Rain nodded, took a small bite of cookie, and chewed, forcing herself not to bolt it and rush upstairs to begin the journey. Natty wolfed the turkey slice, then pawed kibble from the bowl, searching for more meat. When the empty bowl was surrounded by an apron of kibble, he sighed, and ate the chunks one by one.

"Okay." Rain finished the cookie and drained her juice. "Let's go. I'll lie down and you read names from the file. Tell me about their friends and families. Tell me about their losses."

In the bedroom, she set her gun on the nightstand and stared for a long moment at the painting she and Morgan had moved from Meadow's traveling room. Then she stretched out, exactly where she'd been the night the Peddler broke in, and called Natty.

"I want to go to Nightfall Bay," she told him. "I want to find the women the Peddler killed. Can you lead me?"

Natty barked once and sat, his chin on her arm, his gaze fixed on her face, his breath warm on her cheek.

Pierce lay beside her, folded a pillow to elevate his head, tuned on the bedside lamp, and paged through the thick file to the section on the grave in the Wenatchee orchard. He held the page so Rain could see the photo of the woman taken from her home in Redding, California. "Mona Bernstein. She was an accountant. I think she'd have an eye for details."

Rain nodded, studied the photo, then closed her eyes. Mona Bernstein had red hair. And freckles. Lots of freckles. She'd know this woman if she saw her at Nightfall Bay.

Pierce read on, describing the evening Mona Bernstein's neighbor dropped by and found the door open, a mirror broken, and Mona gone.

Rain felt the bed tip, felt herself sliding, falling, tumbling.

CHAPTER 34

October
Pierce

Pierce heard Rain's breath catch in her throat and felt a jolt as she drew up her knees, started to sit, and then fell back. "Are you okay?"

When she didn't answer, he turned on his side and touched her cheek. He pushed the sleeve of her sweater up and felt her arm. Her skin was cool, her muscles stiff—like the first time. Natty was also still, but his gaze shifted—from Rain to Pierce, then to the file. "I should keep reading?"

Natty blinked, then closed his eyes.

Pierce read about the four women whose bodies were found on the hillside in Anacortes. So much had happened since then that he felt far removed from those cases, emotionally numb. He read slowly, thinking about the sections to come that he didn't want to read, the pages with the names of the women displayed on his porch, the pages about Ariel.

Was she still alive, chained in a basement or locked in a remote shed? Mentally she was tough, as tough as anyone Pierce had ever known except the old man. And, like the old man, she possessed what Pierce charitably thought of as moral flexibility. She would, he knew, do whatever it took to survive.

But, thin as she'd been when she was taken three years ago, how long, even with a will of iron, could she last on starvation rations?

Afternoon sunlight struck the west window. The stained glass splashed yellow, green, blue, and red patches on the floorboards. Inch by inch, colors washed up and across the bed. Pierce read on, sometimes adding to the clinical details and providing his impressions of the victims. He talked about entering Tanya Harter's home in Medford, about all that her husband had left behind, about holes in lives that would never be filled.

Colors lapped up the east wall as the sun settled into the west. Pierce thought of Rain in that twilight place with its wintry sun and the dark sand marked by Natty's paw prints. He glanced at the big dog, saw his eyes were closed, his nose dry. He glanced at the clock. Less than two hours had passed. How did that translate into time beside the black water of Nightfall Bay?

Flipping through the file, he saw his choices were limited—stop reading, repeat what he'd already read, or move on to the women posed on his porch. And after them, to Ariel.

He felt a paralyzing sense of disgust and dread.

Did Rain require information on all the victims and their loved ones in order to complete the journey? Could his emotional baggage sap her strength?

He gulped air, flexed his shoulders, and tipped the file so it was illuminated by the tinted light through the west window.

Read one word at a time. Read one word and let it go. Don't form mental pictures.

Easier to consider than to do.

For the first time ever, he wished he had more of whatever made the old man so hard and unfeeling. His father would have read this in a bored voice as if it consisted of nothing but numbers and projections and performance comparisons for businesses run by competitors.

Pierce plumped the pillow beneath his head, swallowed again, and cleared his throat.

Natty whined.

Rain sighed.

Pierce tossed the file to the floor, rolled close, and wrapped her in his arms. Her body seemed made of stone, her breath shallow, her cheeks as cold as if she'd been out for hours on a January night.

"Come home," he murmured. "Come home to me. Follow Natty. He knows the way."

Little by little, as sunlight through the west window lapped farther up the east wall, he felt her muscles relax, her skin warm, her breathing deepen.

Natty stood and shook himself as if he'd emerged from a lake. Then he licked Rain's cheek and tugged at her sweater.

"I'm here, Natty," she whispered.

Natty barked and trotted down the stairs.

"I'm here." Rain snuggled against Pierce. "I'm home."

He wanted to ask her a hundred questions, but her voice was so faint he felt she was still half in that other world. He stroked her hair and kissed her forehead, imagining what it would be like to live with her, to wake up in this room and hold her every morning as she shook off her dreams and emerged from sleep.

"How long was I . . . gone?"

"About three hours. In our time."

Rain smiled. "It's different there. Time seems slower. But faster, too. I can't explain it."

"You don't have to." Pierce kissed the soft skin at the hinge of her jaw. "All that matters is that you're home."

"Home to you."

She brought her lips to his. Pierce tasted salt and sleep. He felt the acid sting of sacrifice and sorrow.

"I didn't find Ariel."

"That's okay."

A lie.

He felt the collision of emotions he'd experienced when he learned Ariel wasn't one of the dead women on the porch. "You tried. You did all you could."

"It seemed . . . odd. Natty led me to the others and they were all together, leaning against each other." She closed her eyes and turned her head aside. "It was horrible, what he did to them. I . . . they wanted me to see. They all wanted me to see. They said they had to tell me, and I needed to see, I *had* to see."

Seeing, Pierce knew, was a far cry from reading the summaries of the autopsy reports Claire had included in the file. "You helped them. They have more peace now."

"Maybe, but they don't have what they need to cross the water. They all described the man we caught. Just him. No one else. But they didn't know anything that would lead to evidence, to proof."

"They didn't know where they were held?"

"They were in chains, in cages, in a room without windows with cinder-block walls that were cold and sometimes damp. There were pipes and wires along the ceiling. And a drain."

Rain choked and struggled to speak. "There was a drain in the floor. Where the blood went when he hurt them. And water from the hose when he washed the blood away. Or cleaned their cages."

Pierce held her tight against his chest. A basement, he thought. A basement that could be anywhere. "Did any of them hear anything? While they were there or on the way there. Traffic or sirens? The Peddler talking to someone?"

"When he caught them, he made them drink something." She touched her throat. "Something that made them sleep. For a long time."

Of course he had. He was organized, thorough, careful.

Until the night he came to the cabin.

"Did they say if they felt anything when they were . . . in the prison room? Anything like the vibration when a heavy truck goes by or a plane comes in low?"

"No."

"What about smell? Did they smell anything?"

"Only their own . . . dirt." Rain tucked her head against his neck. "I'm sorry. I tried. I really tried."

"I know you did. I know." He kissed her forehead and smoothed her hair.

"I asked about Ariel. If she'd been in that horrible room. If she was still alive."

Again Pierce felt battered by the avalanche of emotions Ariel's name evoked.

"And they said . . ." Rain frowned. "They said she was with them, but she wasn't of them."

"With them, but not of them," Pierce repeated.

"Yes. Those words, exactly."

"And that's all?"

"Yes. I asked Natty to take me to her, but he led me to the place we started from."

Rain yawned and stretched. "Maybe next time I'll find her. I think I'll be able to go back in a week or so. I'm tired, but not as tired as last time."

"But tired enough. Take a nap. I'll make something for dinner."

Pierce gave her a final kiss, turned off the bedside lamp, and went downstairs, puzzling over what the Peddler's victims had said about Ariel. "With them but not of them."

It was an apt description of the woman he'd known. She'd always prided herself on being different, not "one of society's sheep." Perhaps, even in such a dire situation, she'd scorned other captives and tried to set herself apart for whatever gain might result.

CHAPTER 35

October
Rain

The scent of frying onions brought Rain from a dreamless sleep. She stretched, stood without too much wobbling, and tucked her gun in the holster on her belt. After a few minutes in the washroom, she felt strong enough to tackle the stairs. Then the room below her tilted and it seemed she was stepping off into an abyss. She clutched the banister with both hands and planted each foot before moving the other.

Faced with crossing to the kitchen, she aimed for the edge of the sofa and launched herself on a zigzag course, grateful the cabin was so small. Using the sofa for support, she inched along, then pushed off, bound for the editing desk.

"I was thinking of coming up to get you." Pierce waved a spatula. "My cooking skills are limited, so I was relieved when Natty voted for breakfast instead of dinner. Eggs, biscuits, and fried potatoes and onions—those count as vegetables—with melted cheese and crumbled bacon. A heart attack on a plate."

"Exactly what I was craving." Rain pushed off from her desk and tottered to the table.

Pierce hustled to pull out a chair. "How are you doing?"

She sat, catching her breath while he hovered. "I'm tired. And I'm weak, but nowhere near as weak as last time."

"So, I won't have the pleasure of carrying you?" Pierce flushed and ducked his chin.

"I enjoyed that," Rain whispered. "Although I wouldn't admit it at the time. I kept insisting I could manage on my own. I was the world's worst patient."

"Probably not the worst." With a flourish, he flipped browned potatoes in the heavy skillet. "But in the top ten."

"Does that assessment mean the blinders are off and you see my faults?"

"I see them." Pierce sprinkled shredded cheese on top of the potatoes. "And I adore every one of them. Especially your single-minded determination."

Rain thought of all the terms of endearment she'd received from the lips of boys and men. This was the most backhanded, but also the sweetest, the most honest. If only she'd been able to learn more about the Peddler and the person who hunted with him. If only she'd been able to find Ariel at Nightfall Bay.

"Dinner is served." Pierce set a loaded plate in front of her. "Be sure to put jam on your biscuit. That counts as a serving of fruit."

He shoveled potatoes into a bowl and topped the mound with bacon and a sunny-side-up fried egg. Natty barked and bounced up off his front feet to get a look at it, grunting with the effort.

"Let it cool for a minute," Pierce instructed, "even a dog of your caliber might burn your tongue."

Turning to Rain with a shrug, he said, "He shoved his bowl of kibble into the pantry and tried to tip the frying pan off the stove, so I caved. It won't make him sick, will it?"

"I guess we'll find out."

Pierce fixed his own plate and brought it to the table, then delivered Natty's, scolding when the dog was on it before the bowl touched the floor. "Where are your manners?"

"It's hungry work making the trip to Nightfall Bay." Rain reached for the jar of strawberry jam she'd made in early summer.

"Even though you didn't drain my energy much this time, it was hungry work worrying that you might not return." Pierce jabbed his fork into a mound of potatoes and paused with it halfway to his mouth. "I don't make a contribution like Natty does, but I feel like I have a role—like I'm an anchor. Or maybe a rock you tie a safety string to so your kite doesn't soar off into the sky and be lost forever if you lose your grip."

"Hmmm." Rain watched him devour his eggs and potatoes and considered what he'd said. Meadow had never mentioned the need for an anchor or a rock, but perhaps Morgan, the man she called her willing horse, had filled that role so naturally she'd never understood his purpose. "I have no idea how this works, but I like the idea. I think you're more of a rock than an anchor."

"All right." He set his fork aside. "Then promise you won't go to Nightfall Bay unless this rock is by your side when you depart."

Rain felt her heart swell. This was about more than her journeys to that dark shore. This was a proposal. She finished spreading jam, laid her knife along the rim of her plate, and peered deep into his eyes. "You realize I'll be making that journey for years—maybe for the rest of my life."

"Yes."

"Are you willing to be my rock for that long?"

"Yes. If you want me."

"I do." She stretched a hand across the table to him. "You know I do."

CHAPTER 36

October
Pierce

Later, sitting beside Rain on the porch steps, Pierce tried not to think of all that stood between them, all that might remain unresolved for years, even forever. It seemed she was doing much the same, because she made no mention of the future beyond saying she hoped the dry weather would hold until she gathered enough energy to finish cleaning up the vegetable garden. Otherwise, their conversation centered on the present—the pink and red and gold of the sunset, the first star, the silver-white crescent moon, a fitful breeze rising from the valley, the flitter of a passing bat, the hoot of an owl far off in the trees.

They'd left the porch lamp off, but the soft glow from a lamp beside the sofa streamed through the doorway. It lay across their shoulders and draped the edges of the top step, then melted into the night. Pools of shadow beneath the trees at the edge of the clearing seemed to spread and rise, blue becoming deeper and darker—cobalt, indigo, midnight. Strings of white and red, headlights and taillights, marked the highway on the far side of the Columbia River. But the forest screened the road on this side of the gorge, and blocked light from the farmhouse.

Pierce felt disconnected from the world, floating above it. What would it be like to sit here every evening? To watch the day bow out and the stars appear? And then, to go inside with Rain? Go upstairs?

Natty, who had been pacing the perimeter of the clearing, halted, peered down the slope, and whined.

Pierce squinted into darkness. "Deer?"

"He's usually not interested in deer." Rain shook her head. "Or rabbits or raccoons. Unless they come too close to the cabin. Maybe he's saying he wants to make his rounds."

Natty whined again.

"Go. You don't need my permission. Patrol."

He took off at an easy trot instead of his usual bounding run, crossing the clearing to their right and sliding among the rocks where the Peddler had crouched on the night he came for them.

"Looks like you aren't the only one who needs a rest," Pierce said. "Maybe you should call him back."

"He'll be okay. I've learned enough about Natty to know that he does what I ask him to do only when he intended to do it anyway."

"Much like—"

Rain nudged him with her elbow. "You already covered the 'single-minded determination' part of my character. And, if I remember correctly, you said you adored it."

"Fool that I am." He kissed her forehead, the spot below the V of her hairline. Her widow's peak. Why was it called that? Was there some superstition attached? He expected there must be. A childhood friend had claimed her dimples meant she'd been touched by an angel. And one of his frat brothers had insisted itching palms meant money coming in or being owed, depending on which palm itched.

Pierce studied his hands, turning them to catch the dim light from the lamp inside.

"What are you doing?"

"Thinking about superstitions."

"Ah. Which palm itches?"

"You've heard of that one?"

"Sure. I think the right palm means you'll get money. Left means you'll pay it out."

"And if both itch at once?"

She laughed. "That means you're running a business."

"Or stepping aside and letting Mal run it." He swung his arm around her shoulders and pulled her close. "I'm discovering how few possessions I need, how few I want. But does it bother you that—?"

"You have all the money in the world?" She laughed. "It might if that was important to you, but— Do you smell smoke?"

Pierce jumped to his feet. "Did I leave the oven on?"

"No. I saw you turn it off." Rain reached for his hand. "It's coming from below us."

"A fireplace maybe?" Pierce sniffed the breeze, caught only the faintest whiff of smoke. "Definitely not tobacco. Or exhaust."

"Probably a fireplace," Rain agreed. "Watch said he planned to carry in some wood."

"But you didn't think he'd do more than just talk about it."

She chuckled. "He expends more energy avoiding work than doing it. But I'm glad Morgan had him move up here. He's interesting, he's good company, and he's a link to the past, to my grandparents. I didn't realize how much I needed that."

"I wish I'd known them." Pierce squeezed her hand, thinking that he'd prefer to have no link to his past. Not that he wished his mother harm, but any interaction with her was a strain. It had been that way as long as he could remember.

"I wish they'd known you." Gripping his hand for support, Rain stood.

"The smoke smell is getting stronger." Pierce cocked his head and cupped his ear. "And what's that noise?"

He felt it resonating in his chest as much as he heard it. A deep, droning tone. "It's like a foghorn, but—"

"It's the conch shell. Watch is in trouble." Rain reeled down the steps. "Or he's trying to warn us."

"Like he said he would the night the Peddler came." With a leap and three long strides, Pierce chased her down and gripped her shoulders. "Get in the cabin. Lock the door and call the sheriff."

The deep tone sounded again, fainter, shorter.

"We have to help Watch."

"We will. *I* will." He carried her to the door. "Give me the gun."

Rain pulled it from the holster and pressed it against his right palm. "You have to cock it. All the way."

"Got it."

He opened the screen door.

"It's small, but it has a big kick."

"Got it." He lifted her across the threshold, kissing her as he did. "Lock up and set the alarm."

"Be careful. Come home to me."

"Count on it."

He turned and, without a backward glance, picked his way by memory across the yard to the trail. When he left the clearing, darkness closed around him like a fist. Now it all depended on his feet, on finding a rut and sticking with it.

And not twisting an ankle. Or stumbling and shooting myself.

He ordered himself not to channel the old man's negativity. He told himself he'd arrive at the farmhouse with his body intact. He'd probably find Watch had blown the shell in a bid for attention.

The smell of smoke grew stronger. Maybe Watch had brought in wood that wasn't aged, or had forgotten to check the damper. Or perhaps a careless driver had tossed a cigarette and started a smoldering fire along the highway.

Unable to convince himself of those possibilities, Pierce conjured the memory of Rain beside him on the steps. But the image enlarged until all he saw was the V of her hairline, the widow's peak.

A sign she would lose a husband?

Or someone who hoped to be her husband?

"Not tonight," he whispered. "I'll come back to her tonight. And every night."

The trail twisted a final time, running downhill, steep and fast. The smell of smoke grew stronger, burning his throat. He reached the gap in the barbed wire fence at the top of the orchard and saw smoke swirling in the air, lit by the red glow of flames behind the kitchen window of the farmhouse.

Pierce ran, weaving among the trees, dew-heavy grass whipping at his jeans.

He was only a dozen yards from the house when a woman stepped from the garage.

A woman he knew well.

A woman with a rifle braced against her shoulder.

"I warned him you would never give up," she said.

Pierce raised the revolver.

She fired first.

CHAPTER 37

October
Rain

When Pierce was out of sight, Rain bolted the door, stumbled to the phone, and called for help. Struggling to remain calm, she told the emergency dispatcher about the smoke, gave the address, spelled out Watch's name, and said she had to get off the line in case he called.

When she hung up, she tried to call him. The landline gave her a busy signal. His cellphone went right to voice mail.

Wobbling, she paced to the window, gripped the sill, and peered out into the night.

A futile effort.

She drew the curtains, returned to the phone, and called Claire's cell.

Voice mail again. She left a terse message.

Opening the pantry, she got the shotgun and filled her pockets with shells. Then she turned out the lights, unbolted the door, and crept across the porch.

The smell of smoke was more potent. As her eyes adjusted to the faint light of the splinter moon, she saw a gauzy haze twining among the trees and spreading into the night sky.

This was more than smoke from a fireplace.

259

She sidestepped from the porch and started across the yard, dragging each foot a few inches, placing it with care, and adjusting her balance before moving again. She'd felt stronger after dinner, but what little energy she'd gained was gone now, drained by anxiety. Her feet felt thick and heavy and as if they were rounded on the bottom. Her legs felt like strings. Her heart thudded in her throat.

The owl they'd heard earlier was quiet, or perhaps it had moved off. The tentative breeze didn't rustle the dying leaves. She heard nothing but the scuff of her shoes.

How long had Natty been gone?

Ten minutes? Longer?

She'd never thought to time him as he patrolled the property. He followed the same course at dawn and dusk, heading off to the west, then south down the slope, then along the state road, across the driveway at the mailbox, along the eastern edge of the pasture and orchard, into the trees and up the sharp pitch of the ridge, then west again above the cabin, and back to where he started.

What Natty found along the way would determine how quickly he completed his self-appointed rounds. And if he found the source of the smoke, he—

The crack of a rifle fractured the night.

Two sharp pops followed.

Rain gasped.

Took three quick steps.

Fell hard.

For a few moments she lay there, stunned, her left arm folded beneath her, pain spiking through her shoulder, the coppery taste of blood in her mouth.

Then, sending out a mental apology to Morgan, she used the shotgun as a crutch and pulled herself to her feet.

It was a hundred steps or fewer to the ATV. It would take her to the farmhouse in a few minutes.

But it was noisy.

It would make her a target.

She'd have to get there on foot.

CHAPTER 38

October
Pierce

The bullet punched into Pierce's left leg above the knee, thrusting him backwards, spinning him in a quarter turn.

He fired as he fell, knowing the shots were too high, too wide. Wasted.

Silhouetted against the red glow of the flames, the woman stalked toward him.

Shoving with his right foot, digging with his elbow, Pierce squirmed into the orchard, grateful for low branches still thick with leaves, for knee-high grass left to go to seed, and for the breeze that rippled through it. He angled behind a tree and into the dark oblong of its shadow.

"I told him we should kill you months ago. I told him. But he liked to watch you playing at being a detective."

She raised the rifle.

"If I'd come for you instead of him, you'd be buried by now."

Pierce held still, teeth clamped to hold in a bellow of agony. Had Rain been able to get a call out? How long before anyone would respond?

"I hit you. I'm a good shot. You know I am. Now stand up like a man and take one in the heart."

She sighted just uphill from where he'd fallen.

The kitchen window shattered.

She turned for a moment to watch tongues of flame lick at the eaves. Firelight glinted on her dangling earrings.

Pierce squirmed, making a few more yards, reaching the shadow of another tree.

"You can't help that old man now, Pierce. And he can't help you. He's locked in the cellar." She laughed, a childish crow of joy. "When the fire spreads, the whole house will come down on him."

Pierce tried to focus past his pain and fear, focus on Watch and the inferno inside the farmhouse. Could he, somehow, get around to the front door?

He felt hot breath on the side of his face and the solid slip of teeth along his neck.

Coyote? Wolf? Drawn to his blood?

"This is your last chance to be a man who stands out, Pierce," the woman screamed.

The animal pawed at his head. He raised his right arm, twisted his wrist, aimed the revolver. Then hesitated. If he fired, he'd give away his position. She'd kill him. But if he didn't shoot, this creature would—

"Stop cowering in the shadow of others."

Pierce felt teeth at the nape of his neck, felt his shirt tighten against his throat and armpits, felt a sharp tug. Another. And another.

"Natty?" he whispered.

The big dog whined and tugged again, dragging Pierce at a slant to the eastern edge of the orchard. Pierce dug in his elbows and the heel of his good leg. Yanking up his T-shirt, he wadded it in his mouth and bit down. Then he pushed with all he had.

"Coward," the woman screamed. "You're nothing but a coward. A stupid coward."

Natty released him when they reached the mound of plants pulled from the garden. Pierce wormed his way behind it, sat up, and stripped off his shirt. Thankful that he couldn't see his wound, he ordered himself to ignore the warm stickiness of the blood soaking his jeans. Wrapping the shirt around his leg, he knotted the sleeves.

The pain was ferocious, almost a thing apart from him, a creature gnawing at his wound. He breathed through gritted teeth. Shallow breaths. Holding each one as long as he could.

The breeze carried the pungent smell of smoke, and a feathery, faltering sound. A siren?

"You had your chance."

Pierce flopped onto his good side and peered from behind the compost pile. Still silhouetted against the burning farmhouse, the woman was walking away from it and into the orchard, following the path that led to the cabin.

Even as he aimed the gun, he knew she was too far away, knew all he'd accomplish would be to bring her back for the kill.

"I would have given you a fast trip to oblivion," she shouted. "Now you can lie there and bleed out and think about what I'll do to your precious Rain. She'll curse your name before I'm finished."

Natty growled.

"No, Natty. She'll shoot you if you go for her. And I don't want to bet you'll survive."

Pierce gripped his collar, holding him for a few seconds. "Go to Rain, Natty," he whispered. "Guard Rain. Protect Rain. Help Rain."

Natty whined, jerked free, and hurtled into the night.

Had he understood?

Would he obey a command from anyone except Rain?

He remembered her saying Natty did what he intended to do.

Smoke boiled from the broken kitchen window and flames slid up the side of the house to claim the roof.

Was Watch still alive?

Pierce pounded the ground.

His car was far down the drive near the bottom of the garden. Rain's was in the garage. So was Morgan's old truck. The key was under the seat. The truck was heavy. Maybe he could use it as a battering ram to free Watch. Then get to the cabin and help Rain.

Sparks twisted into the dark sky. Soon heat would scorch the garage wall and set it ablaze.

Wedging the gun beneath his belt at the small of his back, he got his good knee and his hands under him and worked out a lurching, pulling, dragging crawl. It gained him six or eight inches with each effort.

He was halfway to the garage when a second figure stepped from the doorway.

CHAPTER 39

October
Rain

Natty burst from the trees and raced to her side.

"Help me get to the farmhouse." Rain gripped his collar. "We have to find Pierce. And Watch."

Natty whined and nudged her left leg, pushing her away from the trail and toward the jumble of rocks.

"No. The farmhouse. To Watch. And Pierce."

Natty whined once more, lowered his massive head, and bumped her leg.

Off balance, Rain slumped against him, wrapping her left arm around his neck to break her fall.

Natty took her weight without so much as a grunt and plodded toward the rocks, dragging her along. Her feet snagged on hummocks of grass. The shotgun clattered against stones.

The moon, thin but high in the sky, lit the murky air with a silvery glow. Smoke no longer wrapped only the treetops in a gauzy film. It crept along the lowest branches and twined around the trunks. It slithered among the rocks. It prickled Rain's eyes and rubbed like sandpaper in her throat.

"We have to go to the farmhouse," she panted.

Natty growled.

"We have to help Pierce."

She tried to dig in her heels, but she was no match for his power. The only options were to let go, fall, and try to stand again, or to assume Natty had a reason.

She went with the second choice, helping him by leaning forward and lifting her limp feet as much as possible with each step.

If the Peddler's partner was coming, the rocks would provide cover.

And beyond the rocks, along the slope, was the bolthole.

Twenty feet to the rocks.

Maybe forty yards from there to the bolthole.

The bolthole Morgan insisted she stock.

Morgan!

Morgan said she'd come through.

Rain dug in her toes and pushed.

Natty whined and lunged.

"I see you," a woman's voice cried. "No one can help you now. You're mine."

Natty lunged again.

A rifle cracked.

A bullet whanged off the rock ahead.

Natty yipped and bit at his hip.

CHAPTER 40

October
Pierce

The figure took another step away from the garage and cupped its hands around its eyes. "Are you out there?"

The voice was hoarse. The question punctuated by a racking cough.

"Smoke's so thick I can't see a damn thing. Are you out there, son?"

Watch's voice.

"Here," Pierce called. "I'm here." He raised his left arm and waved it.

"Can't see you. Keep talking."

Watch trundled across the lawn and into the orchard.

"Here." Pierce stopped waving. "I'm here. Keep coming."

"Where'd she get you?"

"Left leg. Keep coming. Bear right. She said she locked you in the cellar."

"She did. Thanks to Morgan's foresight, I got out."

Watch loomed over him. "Ah! There you are."

He bent, gripped Pierce beneath the arms, and helped him stand. "Let's get you to the barn so I can see how bad it is. Lean on me and kind of hop along."

"Unnggh." Pierce slung his arm around the old man's neck. "Forget about me. You've got to help Rain."

"Where is she?"

"Up at the cabin. She's got a shotgun and I told her to stay inside, but—"

"Is Natty with her?"

"I think so. He dragged me to safety. I told him to guard Rain and he took off up the hill."

"Then he's with her." Watch paused to cough, then started for the barn. "Odds are she'll be all right. But you won't—not if you try to be a hero and drag yourself up there."

They limped along the slope, Watch leaning uphill. Pierce's left leg dangled, his right turned inward.

"I'd carry you if I could, son, but you know the shape I'm in." Watch paused again to cough and spit. "Wouldn't be much help to Rain, either. She's got the dog. And Morgan saw she'd have a long life."

Teeth gritted, Pierce only grunted in reply. He wanted to be with Rain. No matter what Watch insisted. No matter what Morgan had predicted. He needed to be with her.

They reached the barn, limped through the doorway, and made it to the bales of straw Rain used to mulch strawberry plants. Watch helped Pierce sit and groped along the wall. "Power line to the barn is separate, so we should have—"

A trio of bulbs strung from the rafters flared on.

Pierce glanced at his left leg.

Acid rose in his throat. The walls wavered and shifted.

Put your head down," Watch ordered. "Breathe through your mouth."

Pierce obeyed.

He heard the barn door slide closed. "Keep out some of the smoke," Watch said. "Now let me see that leg."

In a moment Pierce felt Watch's hands loosening the knots in the shirt he'd used to slow the bleeding. "Good job getting this tied. Now don't get your shorts in a bunch when you feel a little pull. I'm taking a box cutter to your jeans."

Cloth tightened across the wound. Tightened more. Ripped. Pierce closed his eyes, dug his fingers into the straw, threw his head back, and howled.

"Well," Watch said after a minute, "you won't be jogging anytime soon, but you did a good job putting pressure on it."

He took off a denim shirt streaked with dirt, turned it inside out, and wrapped it around Pierce's leg. "I'm no expert, but I don't think it's as bad as it looks."

He secured the shirt with a length of rope snatched from a hook near the door.

"There." He wiped his hands on a once-white undershirt with enormous sweat stains under the arms. "That will serve until the cavalry arrives. Which should be damn soon by the sound of those sirens."

Pierce realized he'd been hearing the warbling of emergency vehicles for several minutes. "Get me out to the driveway." He clawed at Watch's arm and heaved himself upright. "We've got to flag them down and get someone to the cabin."

They'd taken three hopping steps when the barn door slid open.

A woman's form appeared against a hellish curtain of fire-lit smoke.

She held a gun at her side.

"Found you," she said.

CHAPTER 41

October
Rain

With another surge, Natty dragged Rain behind the first of the rocks.

Rain released him, dropped to the stony ground, and squirmed to a sitting position.

A woman. The Peddler's partner was a woman.

Natty bit at his hip and whined again.

When he stopped, she heard another whine. Distant. Pulsing.

"Help is coming." Rain stroked Natty's head. "It's too dark to see, and I know this will hurt, but let me feel where you got hit."

The big dog turned and Rain ran her hands along his back and flank. Her fingers settled into a groove. Wet, slippery, but shallow. At one end, beneath the skin, was a triangular lump. Not a bullet. A flake of rock.

"It's not deep. Not bad. When we can get to the bolthole, I'll clean it and put salve on it." She patted his good hip. "And I guess this answers the question of whether you can be hurt."

"You can't escape," the woman shrieked. "You're on your own. That old man is frying in the cellar like a strip of bacon."

Watch!

"I wish I could see him sizzling." Her voice was filled with longing and delight. "Fat as he is, I bet he'll burn for hours."

Rain gagged, choked.

Don't think about it. Not now. Get to the bolthole.

Gripping Natty's collar, she got to her feet. The way through the rocks led downhill. Walking was an act of controlled falling. And she'd already proved she was good at falling.

"Pierce can't help you, either," the woman shrieked. "I shot him."

Rain felt her throat fill with a sob. Swallowed it.

Shot didn't mean dead.

She remembered again that she hadn't asked Morgan whether those with her would come through this ordeal. Perhaps that was for the best. If she knew Pierce wouldn't be with her, what would be the use of fighting for her life, a life of loneliness?

Should she stay in the rocks and hope to get a clear shot, a close shot?

Natty tugged her to the right, making the decision.

Forty yards to the bolthole. But those yards weren't downhill. They were across a slope littered with shifting slabs of rock, and through a tangle of blackberry canes.

Rain bent forward, trying not to put too much weight on Natty.

Loose stones clattered.

We're sitting ducks on this slope, Morgan. If you weren't right, we'll have words.

"I hear you moving. You should have stayed in the rocks," the woman taunted. "I didn't think you'd be so dumb."

Halfway there!

Rain didn't look behind her.

Sirens pulsed in the valley.

"Help is coming," she whispered to Natty.

And then she had a chilling thought. If Watch and Pierce were dead, who would know she was up here and in trouble? How long before someone came?

"All we have is each other, Natty." She thrust her left hand beneath his collar, hooking it in the crook of her elbow, leaning far forward against his neck. "Let's give it all we've got."

Natty whined, lowered his head, and charged for the thicket. Rain fell on the third step. He slowed, but didn't falter, twisting to one side, dragging her. Sharp stones scraped her legs and ankles. Dislodged by her passing, they slid down the slope, grating against each other.

"Could you make any more noise?" the woman jeered. "I expected dumb from Pierce. He's so trusting and simple-minded it didn't occur to him if I bugged his office once, I'd do it again."

They reached the thicket and Natty dropped to his belly. Rain freed her arm from his collar and, pushing the shotgun ahead, wriggled into the tunnel she'd enlarged, following it to her left.

Had she trimmed the canes only a few weeks ago? It seemed like years. Thorns ripped at her hands and snagged in her sweater.

Below, sirens screamed in counterpoint.

"Stay with me, Natty," she urged. "Don't go after her. I need you."

Natty nudged her legs.

She shoved the shotgun to the side. It slowed her down. There were other weapons ahead.

"You can't hide from me in those brambles," the woman sneered. "And they won't stop a bullet."

She fired.

273

The bullet thwacked through the canes and thudded into the earth a few feet to Rain's right.

"Was I close?"

Rain writhed through the crevice between two fallen rocks and into the crude shelter.

"Sorry, Natty, I can't risk a light. Your wound will have to wait."

Natty whined, but she heard his claws click on the stone floor and the explosion of breath that meant he'd flopped on his side. Using jutting rock for handholds, she got to her feet and felt along the wall. She found the mesh bag and the revolver in the plastic box that kept out the damp.

She remembered asking Morgan if he'd seen her cowering in a hole, remembered he said he hadn't. At the time she thought he meant she wouldn't take refuge in a bolthole. Now she wondered if what he'd meant was that he didn't see her cowering.

And she wouldn't. Not as long as she had breath in her body.

A bullet thwacked into the ground at the entrance to the bolthole.

"How about that one? Did it make you flinch?"

The woman's voice was loud, close. She must have crossed the slope, must be on the other side of the brambles.

Only one distant siren still yowled, and now Rain heard shouts and the roar of engines. One engine seemed to be straining. Coming up the hill?

"There's nothing I love more than a cat-and-mouse game, but I need to finish you off before we're interrupted. So, rude as it is to shoot and run, that's my plan."

A beam of light flickered across the narrow opening. Rain worked the box from the mesh bag and pressed herself against the wall.

"I see your hidey hole," the woman chanted in a sing-song voice. "I know where you are."

Rain fumbled the revolver from the box, spilled bullets into the pocket of her jeans.

"You think you're safe in that cave with your shotgun, but you're not."

She likes to talk. Don't listen. Act.

"How fast can you reload?"

Slide into the opening.

"I have an automatic rifle. It's a thing of beauty. Some people don't like them. Can you believe it?"

Aim at her voice.

"They're fools. Sheep, like Pierce."

Fire all six bullets.

"*He* knew right away I was special, not like the others he took. He satisfied my deepest desires. He gave me this rifle right before you took him away from me."

Drop to the ground, roll to the side, reload, and fire again.

"I love every beautiful bullet in the clip. I'll fire them all into your little cave. One of them will get you."

"Not on my watch," Claire shouted. "Drop the rifle, Ariel."

CHAPTER 42

October
Pierce

"Ariel! I should have known." Pierce pounded the gurney with both fists. "I should have seen it. Why didn't I see it?"

"*Nobody* saw it. Nobody." Rain gripped his arm. The flat light from the interior of the ambulance painted her pale face with a greenish tint. "It's not all on you."

"She could have killed you." He brought her hand to his lips and kissed each of her knuckles and the inside of her wrist, then stretched his arm to stroke her cheek. She must be exhausted, he thought. She should be up at the cabin, in bed, asleep. But then she wouldn't be by his side. "Twice I brought danger to your door. She burned the farmhouse. You lost—"

"Things. Material possessions," Rain said in a soothing voice. "But not the family albums Morgan stowed in the cabin. And not my memories of this place. She didn't destroy those."

Watch removed the oxygen mask he'd pressed to his face. "I could have done without losing all those apple pies in the freezer, but Rain's right, and you better listen. If you keep yelling and thrashing around, the emergency team will stop doctoring Natty and strap you down six ways from Sunday.

Then they'll cart you off to the hospital before Claire gets finished talking to the brass."

"He has a point," Rain whispered. "And I hate to say it, but Natty's a much better patient."

Pierce craned his neck. Natty, illuminated by the glow of the burning farmhouse and the lights of emergency vehicles, stood with his back to the man and woman cleaning his wound. Only the twitching of his ears signaled pain or, more likely, annoyance.

"Or maybe I'll hit you with this tank and save them the trouble." Watch clapped the mask to his face again, then tipped it. "Right after I suck it dry. This is good stuff. Could have used a mess of it down in that cold cellar."

"That's where you were?" Pierce asked.

"Yep." Watch set the mask on his knee and leaned forward in the rickety lawn chair, one of several he'd hauled from the barn and dragged along the driveway to the ambulance. "If she was half as smart as she thought she was, I woulda been tied to the refrigerator or something. But she fell for the old Br'er Rabbit manipulation."

He grinned and pitched his voice higher. "At least I'll go fast tied up in the kitchen. I was afraid you'd lock me in the cellar and I wouldn't die until the house fell in on me."

"There's a tunnel from the cold cellar up to the garage," Rain explained to Pierce. "Morgan dug it years ago as an escape hatch in case a tornado leveled the house."

"Morgan was always preparing for one catastrophe or another. Dug it to his size, not mine." Watch coughed and took another hit of oxygen. "If I hadn't been sweating the state of my future, I might not have made it through."

Rain frowned. "If you were in the cellar, how did you blow the conch shell?"

277

"I did that before. See, I had this exercise program going where I walked to the mailbox most evenings. She musta come across the pasture, let herself in somehow, and started a fire in the recycling bin."

He set the mask on his knee again. "I smelled smoke when I got to the porch. Knew I hadn't left a burner on when I heard her tossing things around. I grabbed the shell I set out on the railing the night you took the Peddler. Got in two pretty decent honks before she poked me with that machine gun of hers."

"An automatic rifle." Pierce reached out for Rain. "If Claire had been a few seconds slow—"

"But she wasn't." Rain rocked forward in the wobbling chair and wove her fingers with his. "Thanks to finding the bug in the task force office, she got here in time."

"In time for the gunfight of the year," Watch cackled. "It musta sounded like Fourth of July up there."

"Fourth of July on steroids." Claire exchanged a fist bump with Watch, leaned over the gurney to kiss Pierce on the cheek, hugged Rain, and dropped into an empty chair.

"Not that I'm questioning your marksmanship," Watch said, "but she had a hell of a lot of ammunition to throw at you. How did—?"

"Two words: muzzle rise."

"Don't be modest." Rain smiled at her. "Pierce says you're a great shot."

"Not great, but as good as practicing every week can make me. And I have sense enough not to rely on a weapon I don't have much practice with."

"I never doubted you," Rain said. "But she seemed so sure of herself."

"That was her way. And she was a good shot. The one thing she and the old man had in common was the ability to make slaughtering birds look easy." Pierce winced. "Sad to say, her confidence was one of the things that attracted me to her."

"In another lifetime," Watch said.

"Yes," Rain agreed. "Think of it like that."

"I'll try. But . . . I wish this had ended another way."

"She had a choice," Claire said.

"I know."

"She was sick," Watch said. "Wearing those dead women's rings in her ears. Doesn't come much sicker than that."

Claire stood and put a hand on Pierce's chest. "Keep the good things about Ariel here. Clear your mind of all the rest. And remember this. Rain never fired a shot. *I* killed her. I can carry that weight."

Pierce could almost feel a burden shift from his shoulders to Claire's. No matter that Ariel had teamed up with a serial killer, *loved* a serial killer. No matter that Rain would have fired in self-defense. Ariel's death would have been between them.

"By the way, there's a car behind the grocery store a mile down the road. They think it's hers. They hope they'll find evidence to lead them to—"

"I don't want to know," Pierce said. "Except for paying the bills, I'm no longer part of the task force. It's all yours."

"Got it." Claire made a check mark in the air. "But it may take months to wrap everything up."

"Months. Years. Whatever." Pierce waved a hand. "If you get bored, find other killers to hunt. Keep my chair around in case I decide to drop in for a visit."

"Done." Claire made another check. "Well, we'll all have statements to make and questions to answer tomorrow, but they're finished patching up Natty so I'll take Rain to the cabin before she collapses." She pointed at Pierce. "And you, get to the hospital and get stitched up."

"What about me?" Watch asked. "My bed's burned to a cinder. Where am I supposed to sleep?"

"Anywhere you want." Pierce turned on his side, dug his wallet from his hip pocket, and handed over a gold credit card. "On me."

Watch turned the card with grimy fingers. "Room service included?"

Claire groaned.

Rain chuckled.

"Room service, bathrobe and slippers, massage, new wardrobe," Pierce said. "Whatever you need. Whatever you want."

Watch got to his feet and slid the credit card in the front pocket of his soot-stained corduroy slacks. "New threads would be good. But what I could really use is a new computer."

"Get one. Get the best one around." Pierce thrust his chin toward the farmhouse, now a blackened skeleton scavenged by flames. "It won't make up for what she torched—your manuscript and all your research."

"Outsmarted her there, too. Morgan wasn't the only one with a bent for taking precautions." Watch plucked a flash drive from his pocket. "Got almost everything right here."

CHAPTER 43

December
Rain

"I don't think I ever sat and watched it snow before," Pierce said. "At least not for this long."

Rain snuggled closer beneath the comforter they'd carried out to the porch steps just before sunset. Since he moved in the morning he was released from the hospital, they sat here every evening. He said it was exactly as he'd imagined it would be on that night of terror.

The Peddler was dead now, killed in weeks by a wasting disease, refusing to the end to share his secrets, taunting those who sought to learn his real name or comprehend his twisted mind. He and Ariel were buried in unmarked graves a continent apart. Pierce had seen to that. And, in her dreams, Rain had seen their victims, Marlin included, board a white ship with tall masts, and set sail from Nightfall Bay.

"I never realized snow made noise." Pierce cocked his head. "It's kind of a hiss and a whisk."

"Because it's fine snow with tiny ice pellets. Big flakes are softer and wetter and quieter."

"Hmmm. Speaking of big flakes, has Watch decided where he wants to have his farewell dinner?"

"Probably the most expensive place around. He loves spending your money."

"He earned it."

"Still, I'm glad you didn't feel obligated to give him the okay to write Ariel's story." Rain squeezed his hand. "I just wish we could stop all the others who are slapping something together to make a quick buck."

"Hey, making a quick buck is the American way," Pierce protested. "At least that's what the old man always said. But the quick-buck writers won't get any help from me. Or Claire. At least for now. Maybe someday, if I thought it would help us understand what happened, and if Watch gives us the right to review and approve what he writes . . ."

Rain squeezed his hand again and they sat in silence for a few moments. Then Pierce cleared his throat. "Since Watch announced we didn't need him and started making plans to move back to Las Vegas, I've been thinking of setting up a kind of trust fund. Something to pay him a chunk every month. Do you think he'd be offended?"

"Would Natty be offended if you grilled him a steak?"

At the mention of his name, Natty strutted from the forest, shoveling snow with his muzzle and tossing it in the air.

"You're acting like a puppy," Pierce called.

"I don't think he's ever seen snow before. I doubt it snows at Nightfall Bay. Or wherever he's from."

Pierce kissed the soft skin beneath her earlobe. "We may never know where that is."

"I can live with that. Correction—I have to live with that."

"*We* have to live with that."

"Yes. We." She laughed. "I'll get the hang of this being a couple stuff."

"Good, because I'm not going away."

"Except to an occasional board meeting for your corporate empire," she teased.

"Yes, but only until my mother agrees on her share and I get out from under it all."

"And then what will you do?"

"Easy. You have the gift and you need to carry on Meadow's work, right?"

"It's more an obligation than a need." She leaned to face him, careful to keep her tone free of defensiveness or defiance. They were still feeling their way with each other, still exploring boundaries. "But, yes, that's what I hope to do."

"Okay, then when I'm not raising money for programs for crime victims, and taking you on long vacations, I'll see to rebuilding the farmhouse, pruning the apple trees, plowing and planting the garden, and helping you travel to Nightfall Bay. I don't have his long sight, but I'll do my best to be what Morgan was for Meadow."

He smiled and pulled her in for a long kiss. "I'll do my best to be your rock."

Also by Carolyn J. Rose

The Catskill Mountains Mysteries
  Hemlock Lake
  Through a Yellow Wood
  The Devil's Tombstone

Subbing isn't for Sissies
  No Substitute for Murder
  No Substitute for Money
  No Substitute for Maturity
  No Substitute for Myth
  No Substitute for Mistakes
  No Substitute for Motives

And others
  An Uncertain Refuge
  Sea of Regret
  A Place of Forgetting

With Michael A. Nettleton
  Death at Devil's Harbor
  Deception at Devil's Harbor
  The Hard Karma Shuffle
  The Crushed Velvet Miasma
  Drum Warrior
  Sucker Punches

Carolyn J. grew up in New York's Catskill Mountains, graduated from the University of Arizona, logged two years in Arkansas with Volunteers in Service to America, and spent 25 years as a television news researcher, writer, producer, and assignment editor in Arkansas, New Mexico, Oregon, and Washington. She's now a substitute teacher in Vancouver, Washington, and her interests are reading, swimming, walking, gardening, and NOT cooking.